"One of the most effective tools for conservation has been the documentary film. Among the pioneers and best exemplars of this genre is Chris Palmer, who knows how to tell a story that reaches both heart and mind. His book is a major contribution to our understanding of the role mass media plays in protecting our planet."

   —Ted Danson

"Chris Palmer's compellingly readable account of the wildlife film business reminds me of everything I love about nature films, while serving as a call to action to correct its abuses. It will change the way we look at wildlife films."

   —Richard Leakey

"The ideal wildlife film should enlighten, entertain, alert us to problems, and stimulate us to conservation action, urges Chris Palmer. Anyone who watches wildlife films—and millions do so—must read this perceptive and enlightening book."

   **—George B. Schaller, Wildlife Conservation Society,
   author of *A Naturalist and Other Beasts***

"Who *hasn't* wished they could make films about wild animals? Yet how many have any idea what's involved? This is a rare insider's look at the pitfalls and the pinnacles of filming in the wild. And it points the way toward taking the genre to the next level. A terrific view into a hidden realm and an exacting profession."

   **—Carl Safina, author of *Song for the Blue Ocean*
   and *The View from Lazy Point***

"*Shooting in the Wild* is a fascinating, insightful, and comprehensive story of the thrill and challenge of capturing nature on film . . . a thoroughly inspiring look at what can be accomplished and why we should continue to try. It is also a who's who of filmmakers who have profoundly affected our view of wildlife. A must read for filmmakers and for anyone in the audience."

   —Jean-Michel Cousteau, president, Ocean Futures Society

"Capturing wild animals on film can be a wild and woolly adventure! Readers will experience the myriad trials and tribulations faced by wildlife filmmakers in Chris Palmer's fantastic new book."

   **—Jack Hanna, director emeritus of the Columbus Zoo
   and host of TV's *Jack Hanna's Into the Wild***

"Chris Palmer's riveting account of the wildlife film business will change the way we look at wildlife films."
— **Larry J. Schweiger, president and CEO, National Wildlife Federation**

"In this pioneering book, Palmer chronicles the history, the personalities, and the business side of wildlife filmmaking, while confronting urgent questions of ethics, morality, and the filmmaker's obligation to the natural world."
— **Adam Ravetch, codirector of the National Geographic film** *Arctic Tale*

"As fascinating as it is educational, *Shooting in the Wild* communicates on every page a calm respect for the ethics of craft and, even more important, for the responsibility of dignity and honesty in the relationship between artist and subject: in this case, the wildlife film industry. It is a responsibility that is incumbent upon not just the filmmakers but upon viewers. It's unlikely we'll ever look at nature films the same way after reading this book."
— **Rick Bass, author of** *Winter: Notes from Montana*

"A passionate, entertaining, and moving account of what it takes to produce a film set in the natural world. Chris Palmer's lifework has been to communicate his environmental vision by beautifully and respectfully documenting the wild world, which we too often forget is the foundation of our own."
— **Jonathan Lash, president, World Resources Institute**

"Informative, revelatory, and entertaining, Chris Palmer's book takes us on safari into the darkest heart of wildlife filmmaking. This is a top insider's account of a media world that increasingly defines how we view our natural world. Reading *Shooting in the Wild* is like watching a great wildlife documentary. It will leave you enthralled."
— **David Helvarg, author of** *Rescue Warriors*

"Chris Palmer has an encyclopedic knowledge of the wildlife filmmaking business, and he tells an exciting tale of what goes on out there in the natural history jungle."
— **Alastair Fothergill, series producer,** *Planet Earth*

"This is an important book, revealing the inner Oz-like working of nature documentaries in all their glory and gore. The investigation is long overdue, and Chris Palmer tackles it with insight, humor, and the highest purpose: to save the wild heart of our living planet."
— **Julia Whitty, author of** *The Fragile Edge* **(John Burroughs Medal, Pen-USA Literary Award)**

"As filmmakers, we struggle to stay true to our art form and our ethics on a minute-by-minute basis, just to bring back one ecstatic moment of pure nature on screen. *Shooting in the Wild* should open a discussion about topics that have been taboo outside the industry."

  —Dereck Joubert, Emmy Award–winning filmmaker
  and National Geographic Society explorer-in-residence

"The wildlife film industry has devolved from high-quality natural history presentations to TV shows about croc wrestlers and crab catchers. In his insightful and fascinating book, Palmer analyzes and documents the dramatic rise and tragic demise of wildlife programming on television."

  —Marty Stouffer, creator and producer
  of the *Wild America* series for PBS

"A sharp and searching assessment of the contemporary wildlife media universe from someone who loves the field and wants to see it live up to its greatest promise."

  —Wayne Pacelle, president and CEO,
  Humane Society of the United States

"Few people are as qualified as Chris Palmer is to explore the often inspiring and sometimes sordid nature-film world, where the balance between conservation messages and commercial pressure can deceive audiences and pose direct threats to the wildlife itself. Filled with anecdotes galore and riveting, behind-the-scenes detail, *Shooting in the Wild* allows readers to experience these films in a whole new light."

  —David Seideman, editor, *Audubon* magazine

"It's often hard to step back from the smoke and thunder of day-to-day work— especially in a hectic fast-changing world like television production—and gauge the wider implications of what you're doing. Chris has managed to combine a real sense of the hurly-burly of wildlife filmmaking with some deep insights into where we're all going, and what we're in danger of missing along the way."

  —Brian Leith, BBC producer

"For every time I've oohed and aahed at an incredible scene in a wildlife film, I've also wondered, 'How in the world did they get that shot?' Thanks to this captivating new book, now I know. This is a 'don't miss' book that will forever change the way you watch animals on screen."

  —Diane MacEachern, author of *Big Green Purse: Use Your*
  Spending Power to Create a Cleaner, Greener World

"A fascinating, behind-the-scenes look at the challenges and ethical questions Palmer and others have faced in portraying the natural world accurately on screen."

—**Mark Wexler, editorial director, *National Wildlife* magazine**

"Palmer's expertise in filmmaking and wildlife makes him the perfect guide for this journey through the world of wildlife films. This is a fun and lively read for those who love wildlife, filmmaking, or just a great adventure."

—**Charles Knowles, cofounder and executive director, Wildlife Conservation Network**

"At last! An insightful and engaging exposé of the wildlife filmmaking industry. There is no other book like this—a really great and thought-provoking read."

—**Harriet Nimmo, CEO, Wildscreen film festival**

"I've admired Chris Palmer's films for years, but I had no idea of the moral, political, and financial conflicts that lay behind them. Palmer recounts his war stories, and the reader quickly learns that the weirdest animals in his wildlife films are the humans behind them. A terrific book—once I started reading, I couldn't put it down."

—**Denis Hayes, cofounder of Earth Day**

"The definitive insider's book on the world of wildlife filmmaking, celebrating its extraordinary achievements at the nexus of conservation and art, and exposing in a sobering manner the less than honorable manner in which certain practitioners exploit the craft, thus trivializing the wonder of the wild."

—**Wade Davis, National Geographic Society explorer-in-residence and author of *Light at the Edge of the World***

"Countless people depend on films to learn about the wonderful creatures with whom we share our planet. *Shooting In the Wild* explains the ins and outs and ups and downs of wildlife filmmaking, so that readers will appreciate what is real and what is not, and what is ethically acceptable as we intrude into the worlds of animals to record their lives. I hope this important book enjoys the wide readership it deserves."

—**Marc Bekoff, author of *The Emotional Lives of Animals***

"A really thought-provoking analysis of wildlife filmmaking—sure to stimulate great debate."

—**Neil Nightingale, creative director, BBC *Earth***

SHOOTING IN THE WILD

SHOOTING IN
THE WILD

AN INSIDER'S ACCOUNT OF
MAKING MOVIES IN THE ANIMAL KINGDOM

CHRIS PALMER

Foreword by Jane Goodall

SIERRA CLUB BOOKS
SAN FRANCISCO

The Sierra Club, founded in 1892 by author and conservationist John Muir, is the oldest, largest, and most influential grassroots environmental organization in the United States. With more than a million members and supporters—and some sixty chapters across the country—we are working hard to protect our local communities, ensure an enduring legacy for America's wild places, and find smart energy solutions to stop global warming. To learn how you can participate in the Sierra Club's programs to explore, enjoy, and protect the planet, please address inquiries to Sierra Club, 85 Second Street, San Francisco, California 94105, or visit our Web site at www.sierraclub.org.

The Sierra Club's book publishing division, Sierra Club Books, has been a leading publisher of titles on the natural world and environmental issues for nearly half a century. We offer books to the general public as a nonprofit educational service in the hope that they may enlarge the public's understanding of the Sierra Club's concerns and priorities. The point of view expressed in each book, however, does not necessarily represent that of the Sierra Club. For more information on Sierra Club Books and a complete list of our titles and authors, please visit www.sierraclubbooks.org.

Published by Sierra Club Books,
85 Second Street, San Francisco, CA 94105

Sierra Club Books are published in association
with Counterpoint (www.counterpointpress.com).

Sierra Club, Sierra Club Books, and the Sierra Club design logos
are registered trademarks of the Sierra Club.

Book and cover design by Blue Design (www.bluedes.com)
Photo inserts designed by Elizabeth Watson

Library of Congress Cataloging-in-Publication Data

Palmer, Chris, 1947–
  Shooting in the wild : an insider's account of making movies in the animal kingdom / Chris Palmer.
     p. cm.
  Includes bibliographical references and index.
  ISBN 978-1-57805-148-9 (alk. paper)
1. Wildlife films. 2. Wildlife photography. 3. Cinematography. I. Title.
  TR729.W54P35 2010
  778.9'32—dc22   2009046993

Printed in the United States of America on Heritage (for text) and Productolith (for photo inserts) acid-free paper, both of which are Forest Stewardship Council certified

Distributed by Publishers Group West
14 13 12 11 10
10 9 8 7 6 5 4 3 2 1

To Gail, Kimberly, Sujay, Kareena, Christina, and Jenny

And to all the wildlife filmmakers who are
dedicated to making films that matter

CONTENTS

FOREWORD
by Jane Goodall

hooting in the Wild is a very important and much-needed book. Without doubt, wildlife documentaries have played a major role in raising awareness in the general public about the wonders of the natural world and the need to conserve it. But just how are these films made? Can we always believe everything the narrator tells us? For example, was a stunning sequence of a female polar bear giving birth really filmed in the arctic wilderness, as claimed? If (as was the case) the event actually took place in a European zoo, should viewers be told, or will this make them less engaged, less willing to help a conservation cause? Is it acceptable to contrive a sequence—placing a freshly shot antelope in the territory of a leopard, for example, in order to get close-up shots? To what extent are wild animals disturbed by the activities of the film team during the making of a film? How concerned should we be about decisions made in the editing of the film: Is it permissible to illustrate an interaction between two animals by the clever juxtaposition of separate shots of each of them, when in fact they were not filmed at the same time? And how much artistic freedom should the scriptwriter be granted? Can we tolerate anthropomorphic interpretations of behavior to gain the viewers' sympathy, or to get a laugh?

In this book, Chris Palmer examines in detail, and from a wealth of personal experience, the ethics—or lack of them—shown by producers, directors, and the crews of nature films of all sorts.

When I was a child, growing up during and just after World War II, there was no television and we could seldom afford to go to a cinema. I learned about nature in part from books about fabulous animals in far-off places—but mostly from spending hours and hours outside, observing birds and insects, drawing and painting wildflowers, keeping caterpillars until they became chrysalises from which emerged butterflies, and watching tadpoles slowly turn into frogs. Children today more often learn about these and other wonders by watching documentary films on television or on the Internet.

Chris sets the stage by outlining the history of wildlife filmmaking. He describes some of the first people to bring nature into the cinemas and, subsequently, into the living room through TV. When I got to Kenya in 1957, I met two of the pioneers of wildlife film, Armand and Michaela Dennis. I had no access to TV at that time, and I don't remember watching any of their films. But my first husband, Hugo van Lawick, worked for them—they sent him out with an old Bolex 16mm cine camera and a dilapidated Land Rover to film animals in Nairobi National Park. As a boy in the Netherlands, Hugo had been a passionate photographer of animals, creeping as close to them as he could in the fields and woods. Although he could scarcely "creep" in his noisy car, he used similar techniques to get film of giraffes and wildebeests and lions.

In 1962, when I had been studying the chimpanzees of Gombe National Park in Tanzania for just over a year, the National Geographic Society decided to send someone to document my work—and they sent Hugo. I was delighted because when I arrived at Gombe I had no scientific training of any sort, and some tended to discount my observations as merely those of a *National Geographic* cover girl." But with Hugo's film I hoped I would be able to prove that the chimpanzees really did use tools; hunt and kill animals; kiss, embrace, and hold hands; and so on.

Prior to Hugo's arrival, I built simple blinds of grass near fruiting trees and stuck empty bottles out of holes to mimic camera lenses, to condition the animals to such activity. I don't think they helped—the chimpanzees ignored them for the most part. And they were at first quite spooked by the real thing: Hugo crouched in a small space with his camera aimed hopefully at a bunch of ripe fruit. But gradually the chimpanzees accepted Hugo and his cameras, just as they had already accepted me. We were harmless. They were not fooled by the blinds in which Hugo sat, and they often approached and peered inside. Soon we decided he might just as well sit out in the open.

The film *Miss Goodall and the Wild Chimpanzees* was a big success, as Chris notes. It was the first of three major National Geographic films about the chimps of Gombe. And there have been scores of others—over the years Gombe has been featured in documentaries shot for companies such as Animal Planet, HBO, and IMAX in the United States, and the BBC and Partridge Films in the United Kingdom. Other teams have come from South Africa, France, Germany, Hungary, Spain, and Japan. All this has meant that the chimpanzees and baboons of Gombe have become completely habituated to cameras, tripods, microphones, reflectors, and all the rest. So blasé indeed that the first time the young male named Galahad saw the huge and noisy IMAX camera, he approached upright, fascinated by his reflection in the big lens, and reached out to touch the glass.

I have been impressed by the determination and endurance of some of these film teams, who must carry their heavy equipment up steep slopes and sometimes through thick undergrowth. The crews also must watch out for their belongings at all times, for the chimpanzees are quick to make off with any equipment left unattended. They love to chew on cloth of any sort and to suck materials impregnated with sweat. I well remember the anguish of one cameraman as he watched Figan take his camera bag up a tall tree. After sucking on the material for thirty minutes or so, Figan dropped the bag; fortunately the precious long lens, worth thousands of dollars, was unharmed. Sometimes, too, Frodo (one of the largest males we have ever known, and a real bully) delights in charging members of a film team and knocking them over. When Gil Domb and John Waters were filming for the BBC, this happened so often that they were able to take shots of each other flying through the air as part of documenting the making of the film.

One of my first pre-Gombe jobs happened to be with a documentary film studio in London. There I learned all about the importance of cutaways, different angles, and simply getting additional footage for insurance. Hugo and the other filmmakers who followed were lucky to work with such a cinema-savvy researcher—sometimes scientists whose work is being filmed simply cannot understand why a scene, already documented successfully, needs to be repeated.

I understand too the desperation felt when filming does not go well. It is difficult to get funding in the first place, and when it begins to seem that the hard-won money will be wasted because good footage cannot be obtained in the allotted time, a sense of despondency pervades the shoot. When Berndt Dost and his team were filming for Bavarian Television at Gombe, they saw only a couple of female chimpanzees and their infants for five whole days. And it rained hard for almost all of every day. Even when we found locations that seemed suitable for recording interviews—away from the huge waves that battered the beach and the noisy, rain-swollen streams—the cicadas would start their shrilling chorus. Things became so dire that I provided extra bananas for Fifi and her family when they did show up, so as to give the film team every opportunity to get at least some good footage.

Sometimes, in their efforts to get good footage in the prescribed time frame, filmmakers get too close to their animal subjects, upsetting both them and those who are studying their behavior. When must ethics intervene? At what point must we insist that the ends (excellent footage, a film that will generate high ratings and educate people about chimpanzees and the threats they face in the wild) do not justify the means? This is a question that is raised by Chris and asked again and again by those concerned with the ethics of filming wild animals.

One topic Chris discusses concerns the use of captive animals in "wildlife" films. When Hugo was taking still photographs on the Serengeti, we frequently met Alan and Joan Root, who in many of their films used tame animals that Joan had raised or rehabilitated. Hugo was incensed by this "cheating," yet the Roots were able in this way to get behavior sequences they never could have filmed otherwise—and without disturbing the wild animals, the real subjects of the film.

Of course, the ethics of using captive animals depend very much on the conditions in which they are kept. Too often, as Chris points out, these leave much to be desired. And, surely, using captive animals as bait to induce hunting behavior can never be justified. A prizewinning sequence of still photographs showing a leopard "hunting" a baboon was later shown to depict a slightly overweight captive leopard and three or four different baboons—all in the one sequence. The last photo—of the leopard leaping at its victim—depicts an old, nearly toothless baboon wearing an expression of absolute terror. Such manipulation is surely unethical in three ways: animals are abused, viewers are deceived, and the photographer competes unfairly with those who wait patiently for days, weeks, months—even years—to get a similar but real shot.

Very often the vehicle of a film team disturbs the animals being filmed. Hugo and I spent weeks getting the lions, hyenas, jackals, and bat-eared foxes of the Serengeti used to our Land Rover, so that eventually they behaved in the same way when we were close as when we were far away. But before reaching this level of habituation, many of the animals, while seeming to ignore our presence, actually responded by remaining completely inactive. Bat-eared foxes, for example, would curl up with their eyes closed—possibly a form of "stress sleeping" commonly seen in newly captured wild animals. Apparently our presence disturbed them for longer than we believed. Was this ethically acceptable?

Once, at Gombe, a highly venomous bush viper was captured near the tourist facilities so that it could be released in another location. An IMAX film team decided to keep it overnight in a container, then filmed it as it glided to freedom in the morning. One of our researchers was incensed, feeling that the snake was being unduly inconvenienced and that people who watched the film would be misled. I personally had no concerns about this.

So where should we draw the line? How should we feel about Hugo attracting fruit flies to land on a twig by smearing it with ripe banana, so they could be hunted for his camera by a captive, hand-fed jumping spider? Strictly speaking, we were misleading the viewers, but was our spider treated in an unethical way?

Chris also talks about films that focus on extreme behaviors, such as sex and violence, that fascinate many viewers. One documentary about chimpanzees, made in various African locations, showed them hunting prey of various kinds. Often the killing of prey animals is brutal to our eyes, and many people responded to this film with shock, even horror. "I never realized chimpanzees were so bloodthirsty," some told me. Yet a study at Gombe showed that, in fact, meat makes up only about 2 percent of these chimpanzees' diet during a given year; mostly they feed on fruits, leaves, and other plant material. By serving up a series of hunts all in one course, so to speak, the film drew a far more violent picture of chimpanzee nature than is actually the case. Are such films unethical? Perhaps not, but I find them disturbing because they show aspects of behavior isolated from the whole picture and give a wrong impression.

From my perspective, the time for real concern is often after the filming has been completed—when the final version of a documentary lies in the hands of the director, scriptwriter, and editor. *Miss Goodall and the Wild Chimpanzees* (a title I loathed, incidentally, as it underscored my lack of scientific training) was filmed by Hugo, but neither he nor I was consulted during post-production. Only after the cutting was finalized and the narration (by Orson Welles) added did we have a chance to see the film and read the script. We were appalled by its blatant anthropomorphizing and by many statements that were simply untrue. I made such a fuss that, though the film was "locked," we were allowed to make changes to the script. By this time Welles was in hospital in Switzerland, having broken his leg skiing, so that was where the final recording took place!

Another topic Chris introduces is the importance of including information about the conservation issues surrounding the animals being filmed. How necessary is it to include this message? Is it enough to sensitize people to the wonders of the natural world, so that when they learn of the threats to so many wild places and amazing animals they will be more highly motivated to help conserve them?

All these important and often controversial subjects are discussed in detail in this book. Chris is scrupulously fair, describing not only what is clearly unethical behavior on the part of filmmakers—at least insofar as animals are disturbed or viewers deceived—but also any positive impact of the finished film in stimulating interest in wildlife. As Chris says, some of the ethical issues may never be resolved to the satisfaction of all concerned. But it is high time they are faced squarely and discussed openly. We owe this to the animals themselves, to the filmmakers who practice truly ethical behavior, and to the viewing public.

PREFACE

"Russ, we strongly recommend that Chris Palmer be fired."

That directive from a senior vice president of the National Audubon Society to Russ Peterson, president of the organization, nearly spelled the end of my career in filmmaking—before it had even begun. It was 1982, and I had just persuaded media magnate Ted Turner to partner with the National Audubon Society to produce wildlife documentaries for television. I'd barely entered the field of wildlife filmmaking, and already I was fighting for survival.

The saga began when a colleague told me that Barbara Pyle, a former *Time* magazine photographer, had recently joined Ted Turner's staff to bring conservation-related programming to his cable network, SuperStation WTBS. I knew nothing about the entertainment industry, yet I sensed an opportunity. So I sent Pyle a detailed proposal for a celebrity-hosted show focused on persuading viewers to get actively involved in conservation issues.

One morning shortly thereafter, I was surprised and delighted to receive a call from Bob Wussler, the head of SuperStation WTBS. "Mr. Turner wants to see you and Mr. Peterson. How soon can you come to Atlanta?" I put down the phone, pumped my fist in the air, and let out a whoop. I had a feeling that Wussler's call would change my life.

The world of documentary film production was a far cry from my previous jobs. Starting in 1976, I'd been chief energy adviser to Senator Charles H. Percy of Illinois, worked for President Jimmy Carter's Environmental Protection Agency, and was now lobbying Congress on energy and environmental issues for the National Audubon Society. In the Audubon job it was not unusual to spend days preparing testimony for a congressional hearing on a critical environmental bill, only to arrive in a Capitol Hill conference room to find one lone senator. The old quip about talking to a brick wall was, in my case, too often true.

I credit my career shift to one of the great statesmen of our time, the leather-jacketed, heavy-booted scholar and gentleman known as "the Fonz," played by actor Henry Winkler. On ABC's *Happy Days*, not only was the Fonz charismatic and funny, but he also changed lives. After an episode in which he signed up for a library card, millions of kids swarmed the nation's libraries and applied for their first cards.

When I heard about that episode, I couldn't help wondering how the power of television could be used to promote conservation. At the time, TV wildlife documentaries were most often about straightforward natural history (for example, the life cycle of the wildebeest). But I soon became convinced that the way people viewed nature and wildlife could be revolutionized by television documentaries that combined celebrities and good storytelling with an in-depth exploration of the political and social problems that threaten animals' habitats and our environment in general.

Well-meaning friends ignored my naïveté and spurred me on. I asked Dennis Kane, who had headed National Geographic's film and television department for twenty years, what television had done for his organization. He replied, "Chris, in 1964 we weren't on television and we had two million members. Then we got on prime-time television and now, twenty years later, we have eleven million members." His comment inspired me to press on, even as a tiny skeptical voice inside my head whispered, *But how do you know that TV was really the cause of this happy outcome?*

When Ted Turner, Russ Peterson, and I first met, Turner was reading the latest volume of the Worldwatch Institute's *State of the World* series, which calls for a reassessment of economic and environmental priorities. "This book is incredibly important," the founder of the country's largest cable network told us. "I make it required reading for all CNN reporters."

Over the next ten years, I would learn just how ardent a conservationist Turner is. In the living room of his Montana ranch house hangs a nineteenth-century landscape painting by Albert Bierstadt that portrays the High Plains before Columbus—a landscape teeming with wolves, bald eagles, grizzly bears, bison, prairie dogs, black-footed ferrets, and songbirds. Turner yearns to bring that Bierstadt painting back to life. When he bought the 114,000-acre ranch for $22 million in 1989, he immediately announced his intention to sell the four thousand head of cattle that grazed there and return the land to its natural state. The work involved reintroducing bison and removing fences, cattle pens, outbuildings, and overhead power lines. All told, Turner currently owns nearly two million acres in the United States, making him the country's largest individual landowner. His goal is to revitalize and reintroduce vanished native species on as much of this land as possible.

I learned in our first meeting that Turner's plans for TBS involved saving the world while making money. He wanted to create not only a commercially successful network but also a forum for conservation and world peace. My ideas about revolutionary television fit right in. Convincing the National Audubon Society to jump at this opportunity was another story.

Russ Peterson was supportive, but senior staff and volunteer leaders at the organization were dubious, believing that television was financially risky and untested as a conservation tool. At the time, the idea of environmental television was still somewhat radical. Greenpeace would occasionally be featured on the news for putting its volunteers between harpoons and a whale, but no environmental organization had an ongoing television show. Nature-oriented cable channels such as Animal Planet and Discovery Channel, movies such as *March of the Penguins* and *An Inconvenient Truth,* and concerts such as Live Earth didn't exist yet.

Barbara Pyle and I spent days pitching our proposal to Audubon leaders and explaining how the organization (and the world!) would benefit from communicating its goals and mission via television. But hostility to the proposed partnership persisted. Donal O'Brien, then chairman of the Audubon board, pulled Peterson aside and told him that I was a "Pepsodent boy"—someone with a bright smile and not much else—and suggested that I was inexperienced and naïve. Three senior vice presidents, representing more than fifty years of collective experience with the organization, warned that my ideas for television programs were distracting the organization from its historic mission, which focused on *Audubon* magazine as the flagship for advancing the society's cause. The best thing Peterson could do, they said, was to fire me.

Russ listened to them carefully, then bluntly told them that we would be crazy to give up this opportunity to produce prime-time TV specials. Rather than fire me, he promoted me to a newly created position of vice president of television, reporting directly to him. Our collaboration with TBS became a reality.

Russ Peterson took a big risk. As O'Brien had warned him, I *was* inexperienced. My knowledge of documentary filmmaking and of television in general was limited to my ability to turn on a TV set. Yet that same year I charged ahead with *The World of Audubon,* covering everything from black-footed ferrets to California condors. My spirits soared when Oscar-winning actor Cliff Robertson agreed to host our first five one-hour episodes.

But even the backing of a celebrity host, a major environmental organization, and a billionaire power player in television did not guarantee smooth sailing. As we began producing shows with strong political content, they immediately resulted in boycotts against TBS. Now Turner had to choose between his commitment to conservation and his network's interest in revenue. Although I was in television to promote conservation, I was forcefully reminded that advertisers and sponsors had different motives.

Today, twenty-five years later, I've worked as a film producer for several different institutions and traveled all over the world producing hundreds of hours of environmental and wildlife television programs and IMAX movies on topics ranging from rainforests to the Galápagos Islands, and whales to wolves. During that time, wildlife filmmaking has grown and prospered, proving itself a useful tool for informing, entertaining, and inspiring a broad segment of the public. I've learned a great deal about the art, science, and business of bringing powerful stories about wild animals to the screen. And I've learned that animals face not only the huge and obvious threats of habitat destruction, poaching, and pollution, but also threats from filmmakers themselves. Over these twenty-five years, this unexpected discovery would come to haunt me and in large part prompt me to write this book.

I have provided source citations (beginning on page 202) for the numerous books, articles, and Web sites I consulted in the research and writing of this book. Many of the quotations are taken directly from e-mail messages I received from my colleagues in the wildlife filmmaking industry or are reproduced to the best of my memory from face-to-face conversations. I have done my utmost to recount my own adventures and to retell others' anecdotes faithfully; any misstatements or errors of fact in these accounts are inadvertent and my own.

INTRODUCTION
Movies That Can Change Your Life

When Bruce Weide was growing up, he considered wolves a menace. "I remember being told stories about how a wolf once tried to kill Grandpa," he says. "In the fourth grade I wrote a report about wolves, in which I listed the things wolves ate: elk, deer, cattle, sheep, and *people*." For a long time, it seemed only natural to Weide that his home state of Alaska offered a fifty-dollar bounty for dead wolves. In his eyes—and in those of his friends and family—anyone who collected that bounty was performing a service to the community.

One fall in his teenage years, Weide, his best friend, Derek, and their fathers boarded a train heading north out of Anchorage to hunt moose. They disembarked at an abandoned train station, set up camp, and began to hunt. On the third day, as Weide and Derek searched for moose, Weide noticed a wolf hugging a low ridge about a hundred yards away. He motioned Derek to stop, put a finger to his lips, and pointed.

Derek's eyes grew large, and he whispered, "He's yours." Weide raised his rifle to his shoulder and sighted the animal through the scope. The wolf stood with its narrow chest fully exposed. A slight breeze stirred the gray fur around its neck. Weide slowly exhaled and released the rifle's safety, holding a finger over the mechanism to muffle the sound. The wolf cocked its head to the side and perked up its ears.

Weide curled his finger around the cold metal of the trigger and began to squeeze.

"Through the scope," Weide recalls, "the wolf's amber-green eyes stared at me. I know this will sound far-fetched coming from the memory of a boy, but I felt as if the wolf's eyes peered into my soul. I felt exposed and naked before a primal and enduring force."

"Take him," Derek pressed, his voice tense and urgent. "Shoot!"

Weide looked again; he had a clean shot straight to the animal's heart.

But the wolf was still staring. "The eyes reflected an intelligence that I couldn't come close to comprehending at the time," Weide says. "My finger around the trigger relaxed. Then tightened. Then relaxed."

A couple of weeks earlier, Weide had watched a Canadian film about wolves, *Death of a Legend*. This 1971 documentary broke new ground by refusing to paint wolves as evil killers. As the film depicted them, they were superb predators, but they rarely attacked livestock and almost never harmed humans. They were also loyal and affectionate caregivers and good communicators that could use a wide variety of facial and body expressions. The perceptions of people who saw them differently had been poisoned by fairy tales, folklore, and legends.

As Weide stood with his rifle aimed at the wolf, a particular scene from *Death of a Legend* replayed in his mind: A wolf is running across the snow while a group of men, lined up like a firing squad, open fire. Patches of snow explode around the desperately fleeing animal, and then a bullet slams into it. As the wolf falls, rifles continue to blast away. The wolf struggles to stand and is hit repeatedly. It slumps to the snow. The men keep firing even though the animal doesn't move—except when bullets cause the body to jerk in epileptic-like spasms. Tufts of fur burst into the air. Finally the rifles cease and the men run to the wolf. One lifts its head for the camera. The wolf's tongue hangs from its mouth, and its eyes glaze as the men smile and congratulate each other.

Lost in this memory, Weide slid his finger off the trigger and lowered the rifle.

"What are you doing?" Derek hissed.

"Nothing," Bruce replied.

"You just threw away fifty bucks," Derek said with disbelief.

Years would pass before Weide found the words to tell people he'd been stared down by "a supreme predator honed by millions of years of evolution." In fact, for a while, Weide never spoke of the incident. On one level, he felt foolish for not pulling the trigger. But on that autumn afternoon, he felt he had no other choice. He didn't want to be like the men in the film.

Soon Weide's life took off in new directions. He attended college, bought land in Montana, and married wildlife biologist Pat Tucker. He worked as a logger for a while, climbed El Capitan in Yosemite National Park, and taught at the wilderness-based school Outward Bound. All the while, his curiosity about and respect for nature were growing. Later, from the earth-sheltered home that he and his wife built in Hamilton, Montana, the couple began to research the predator-prey relationship between wolves and white-tailed deer in Glacier National Park. The National Wildlife Federation recruited Tucker to work on reintroducing the long-absent predators in Yellowstone National Park, and Weide, who had dabbled in filmmaking for years, made a PBS documentary, *The Wolf: Real or Imagined?*

In 1991, Weide and Tucker founded Wild Sentry: The Northern Rockies Ambassador Wolf Program, an educational organization aimed at correcting misperceptions about wolves. Wild Sentry toured the country, especially in areas where anti-wolf sentiment was strong, to present its program at schools and community groups. Inspired by a wildlife film he had seen as a teenager, Weide had gone from wolf hater to wolf protector.

A whole generation of wildlife lovers was shaped by films they saw decades ago. Whether it was *Death of a Legend,* Jacques Cousteau's *The Silent World,* Marlin Perkins's *Wild Kingdom,* or a movie in the Disney *True-Life Adventures* series, images on a screen sparked a fascination with nature. In some cases, as with Bruce Weide, that fascination turned into a lifelong dedication to wildlife conservation.

Today, venues for wildlife films abound. On TV, half a dozen channel choices have become hundreds, creating a greater need for specialized programming. Wildlife shows have filled some of these niches, especially on the Discovery Channel, PBS, National Geographic Channel, and Animal Planet. The Discovery Channel offers high-quality series such as *The Blue Planet* (2001) and *Planet Earth* (2006). PBS's *Nature* airs prime-time specials on such topics as harpy eagles, dolphins, and wolves. National Geographic features painstakingly researched films such as *Eye of the Leopard* (2006). And Animal Planet, an offshoot of the Discovery Channel, is all about animals, all the time.

Mainstream movie producers have gotten in on the action, too, with blockbusters such as *March of the Penguins* (2005) and *Winged Migration* (2003). Then there's the stunning world of 2D and 3D giant-screen nature films produced for the global network of IMAX theaters. At the other end of the spectrum are the burgeoning low- to no-budget amateur efforts posted on Internet sites such as YouTube.

This boom in wildlife filmmaking has been fueled partly by new technologies. Cameras are smaller and lighter, lights are more efficient, and editing tools are more compact, which makes it easier for filmmakers to work in remote, wild places. Filmmaker Danny Ledonne manages to fit all his production equipment in a single backpack: a broadcast-quality high-definition camera, a lightweight tripod, a shotgun mic, a lavalier mic, batteries, charger, headphones, lens filters, lens wipes, a waterproof camera housing, and a binder with contact information and releases.

New technology has also boosted film quality. In 2006, BBC's *Planet Earth* series was shot in high definition, nearly doubling the video resolution. The use of high definition in conjunction with the Heligimbal—a motion-stabilized camera housing mounted under a helicopter—allowed for undreamt-of wildlife action footage to be obtained from the air, free from wobbles and of unprecedented clarity. At the lower end, small, inexpensive cameras and convenient desktop editing systems have allowed aspiring filmmakers to enter the field more easily. Almost anyone with a mobile phone or digital camera has video capability these days, which means that much more footage is being captured.

But perhaps the biggest factor fueling the wildlife film industry's growth is the expanding number of people interested in what the genre has to offer. We live in a highly visual culture. Children in the United States spend an average of three hours every day watching television (not to mention the time they spend staring at computer and movie screens) and increasingly less time outdoors. Wildlife films offer a visual, dynamic way for them to connect to the natural world.

At the same time, the urgency of threats to wildlife arising from climate change, pollution, habitat loss, and human population growth has boosted interest in environmental issues. Membership in the Sierra Club, for example, has boomed from 16,000 fifty years ago to 750,000 today. And who could have imagined that former vice president Al Gore's no-nonsense 2006 film about global warming, *An Inconvenient Truth*, would win an Oscar and gross nearly $50 million?

The educational aspects of wildlife films are a big draw for audiences eager to find enriching entertainment in a TV universe full of empty calories. Parents in particular want their families to watch programs that are meaningful and educational. For city dwellers who yearn for an intimate connection to the natural world, wildlife films can be the next best thing to a two-week wilderness vacation.

But not every wildlife-film enthusiast is a tree hugger or a student of nature. Some people are attracted to these films simply because they have become more entertaining in recent years. On-air presenters such as National Geographic's Brady Barr and Animal Planet's Jeff Corwin and the late Steve Irwin, while sometimes lacking good judgment (an issue we'll explore in later chapters), have brought a new intensity to wildlife shows—and become household names at the same time.

The industry's latest statistics are impressive. Natural history and wildlife programs on the National Geographic Channel often draw twice as many viewers as the average audience for an entire evening of non-nature programming. During prime time in September 2008, more than 30 million viewers tuned in to Animal Planet, which is now seen in 94 million households in the United States and more than 220 million internationally. When "crocodile hunter" Steve Irwin was killed by a stingray in September 2006, *People* magazine featured him on its front cover, and the story topped the headlines at FoxNews.com for four days after his death.

On the big screen, *March of the Penguins,* a 2005 film that cost $3 million to make, sold $127 million in tickets worldwide. The world's largest producer and distributor of IMAX films, MacGillivray Freeman Films, has brought in more than a billion dollars in gross box-office receipts over the last thirty-two years, and its films often have wildlife and conservation themes. (Full disclosure: I work for MacGillivray Freeman Films.)

The Walt Disney Company sees rededicating itself to wildlife film-making as a wise business move. In 2008, the company launched the Disneynature label, with plans to produce two nature films a year. According to an article in the *New York Times,* "Disney hopes that nature's broad appeal will help the studio expand overseas." Disneynature's first feature, *Earth,* repackaged material from the BBC's *Planet Earth* series and was a mainstream hit in early 2009.

The expanded markets, increasingly receptive audiences, and technological advances that characterize modern wildlife films have also brought to light certain ethical issues that have always shadowed the enterprise. Specifically, how do you truthfully depict the complex processes of nature and the lives of wild animals—without endangering them or the filmmakers—in a way that will capture viewers, draw sponsors and funding, and succeed in terms of ratings and profits? Addressing this question is the task of everyone involved in the business, but in my experience, it starts with the individual creator at the center of every project.

In the mid-1980s, I recruited cameraman Ray Paunovich to film one of the rarest mammals in North America, the black-footed ferret, for one of our Audubon productions. Paunovich was in his late thirties when I first met him—six and a half feet tall and 250 pounds. He looked like a former linebacker and worked out every day—a self-discipline that extended to his filmmaking. He always insisted on shooting only authentic footage, with animals that were unmanipulated and unstaged. As *TV Guide* once remarked, "Paunovich abides by a strict code of ethics that is as scrupulous and demanding as any in his profession."

At the time, I was such a novice in wildlife filmmaking that I didn't fully grasp what he meant by "authentic films," but I liked him and the sound of his philosophy. For the next two years, Paunovich got up early morning after morning to document the natural behavior of black-footed ferrets. Because of bad weather or uncooperative animals, entire days would often go by when nothing would happen. He could have sped up the process and greatly eased his effort by filming captive animals as if they were wild and free, but he did not. He simply didn't believe in passing off captive animals as the real thing.

Not all filmmakers are so scrupulous. The industry has its share of producers, directors, and camera operators who value getting a great shot over the welfare of the animals they are filming. Some filmmakers bother animals by getting too close; others stage phony scenes to make animals seem more dangerous than they really are.

What should viewers make of Animal Planet host Jeff Corwin, who regularly manhandles frightened animals, or MTV's *Wildboyz* hosts, who grab crocodiles, stick their tongues in a giraffe's mouth, and chase cheetahs? The proliferation of wildlife shows in recent years has created a species of wildlife paparazzi—filmmakers who harass and even endanger animals in their zeal to get that "money shot." The aggressive tactics they use to draw animals to the film site and capture unnatural scenes, such as man-made feeding frenzies, can produce "wildlife pornography" in which animals are exploited for viewers' pleasure—and funders' return on investment.

This book will take you on a journey into the strange, exciting, and sometimes ethically challenged world of wildlife filmmaking. Drawing on my own experience as a wildlife film producer for the past twenty-five years, as well as the perspectives of many other respected professionals in the field, I'll pull back the curtain on how wildlife films are made. My aim is to provide a lively look at current practices in the industry and an unflinching examination of its problems and challenges.

You'll meet filmmakers whose lives are as captivating as those of their subjects and learn about their crushing defeats and euphoric successes.

You'll hear about bitterly contested ethical battles and depictions of nature that range from the horrific to the sublime. You'll get an inside look at films that have the power to promote conservation and inspire wildlife protection, as well as some that undermine those values.

The first three chapters define the art of wildlife filmmaking. Chapter 1 explores the extraordinary diversity of this entertainment genre on television, in movie theaters, and on the Internet. Chapter 2 examines the industry's twentieth-century roots, looking at the history of wildlife filmmaking from Osa and Martin Johnson to Frank Buck, Walt Disney, Marlin Perkins, David Attenborough, Jacques Cousteau, and Steve Irwin. Chapter 3 focuses on how wildlife films are made. It's an insider's view of the process, starting with the germ of an idea and tracking step-by-step what happens in scouting, pitching, principal photography, and post-production.

Chapter 4 delves into the wildlife filmmaker's biggest challenge: finding financing. No money? No film. But I'll also talk about sponsors who expect to have editorial control and about factors that can cause sponsors to cut and run. Two controversial films I made, on clear-cutting and overgrazing, were subject to aggressive—and successful—boycotts by the logging and ranching industries, whose constituents felt they were unfairly criticized in the films.

The next four chapters focus on ethical issues. In Chapter 5, which takes a close look at presenter-led shows and the cult of celebrity, I examine the phenomenon of popular TV presenter Steve Irwin as well as the case of celebrity host Diana Tilden-Davis, who was attacked and severely injured by a hippo during a shoot for Animal Planet's *Wild Kingdom*. Chapter 6 exposes the myriad ways in which audiences can be deceived—chiefly by filmmakers who stage phony wildlife action scenes—and describes some regrettable mistakes I've made along these lines. Chapter 7 discusses why some filmmakers and presenters feel compelled to go after "money shots" and get too close to their subjects, harassing the animals and putting their own lives in danger. In this chapter, I tell some harrowing stories about "Grizzly Man" Timothy Treadwell, reptile scientist Brady Barr, and other up-close-and-personal filmmakers.

Getting too close is controversial. Cruelty toward animals, on the other hand, is just plain wrong. Chapter 8 investigates cases of such abuse and explores what can be done to stop them.

Another challenge that relates to animal welfare is the role of films in wildlife conservation. Chapter 9 looks at what's necessary for wildlife films to make an impact on public policy and motivate their audiences to support conservation. This chapter also examines "blue-chip" films such as *Planet Earth*—are they just pretty pictures designed to distract and entertain us, or can they really make a difference?

The book's final chapters discuss how filmmakers can meet these challenges and become a powerful force for good. Chapter 10 offers portraits of people who have moved wildlife filmmaking to new heights by bringing us authentic footage of animal behavior we'd never seen before, by boldly and effectively dramatizing conservation issues, or by demonstrating innovative ways to protect their animal subjects and involve local communities in doing likewise. And, finally, Chapter 11 examines what's needed to ensure that wildlife filmmaking survives and thrives.

I wrote *Shooting in the Wild* partly to share my experiences and explain why I love environmental and wildlife filmmaking, with all its excitement, adventures, and risks. But I also wanted to search for solutions to the ethical problems filmmakers wrestle with on a daily basis. In this image-driven age, wildlife filmmakers carry a heavy responsibility. They can influence how we think and behave when we're in nature. They can even influence how we raise our kids, how we vote and volunteer in our communities, and how we decide the future of our wildlands and wildlife. If the stories they create are misleading or false in some way, viewers will misunderstand the issues and react in inappropriate ways. People who consume a heavy diet of wildlife films filled with staged violence and aggression, for example, are likely to think about nature as a circus or a freak show. They certainly won't form the same positive connections to the natural world as people who watch more thoughtful, authentic, and conservation-oriented films.

After reading this book you'll be better able to judge which kind of wildlife programs to support and which to ignore. You'll be equipped to ask tough questions about the animal exploitation, harassment, and cruelty that go on behind the scenes in some films, and you'll know what it feels like to be a filmmaker faced with difficult choices. Do budget and time pressures, as well as the relentless search for larger audiences, sometimes justify putting animals at risk? If so, how much risk and for what larger goals? Is there a different way to operate?

Whether you're an aspiring filmmaker, an animal lover, or someone who is simply captivated by the spectacle of nature's beauty, this book will help you tell the difference between the heroes and the charlatans of this industry, and discern real art from cheap tricks. It will provide you with an insider's appreciation for the work that goes into the best wildlife films—and maybe even an intriguing new list of must-see movies, TV shows, and Web sites. But, be careful: as Bruce Weide can tell you, wildlife films can change your life.

1

STATE OF THE ART
The Many Faces of Wildlife Filmmaking

In 1986, the International Whaling Commission imposed a moratorium on whaling. It was a great victory for the forces working to protect whales, but one of several loopholes allowed hunters to kill whales, take a few measurements of the bodies in the name of scientific research, and then sell the meat. The practice was nothing more than commercial whaling disguised as science.

Enter Hardy Jones. He appeared in my National Audubon Society office one day in 1986 to pitch a film on whales. "What separates the films we do here at Audubon from other nature shows is that they are about conservation, not just pretty pictures," I told him. But I was preaching to the choir. Jones and his then wife, Julia Whitty, wanted to swim with sperm whales, not only to capture the creatures' lives on film but also to prove that they could study them without killing them. Jones had already spent nine years with dolphins in the wild, so swimming with sperm whales was a natural next step. I greenlighted the project, and Jones and Whitty were off to the Galápagos Islands.

Sperm whales are the species made famous by *Moby-Dick*. These magnificent creatures have the largest brains on Earth. The biggest of the toothed whales, they sometimes exceed forty-five feet in length and weigh more than fifty tons. But that does not necessarily make them easy to find—even in the Galápagos, where hundreds of them gather. Jones and Whitty sailed for two weeks without seeing a single whale. With only four days remaining in the expedition, if they didn't find some soon, the trip would be an expensive failure. There would be no film.

Dehydrated and fatigued from long days in the sun, Jones wrapped his arm over the boom of the forward mast. His head kept nodding onto his chest as, half asleep, he shook off fitful hallucinations. Then he thought perhaps he saw something—a small puff of white in the distance. Another followed, and Jones bolted upright. Was it a whitecap? He scrunched his eyes. No, it was a sperm whale blowing! He snatched up his camera gear along with mask, fins, and snorkel. Adrenaline surged through his body, vanquishing all fatigue. He and Whitty leapt into a small inflatable motorboat and headed toward a small cluster of whales undulating at the surface.

"We pulled ahead of four whales," recalls Jones, "and I slipped into the water. Coming from the whales was a faint *click, click, click* sound. I began to make sounds that I thought would project through the water—anything to raise their curiosity. I began a long series of whoops and howls into my snorkel. Lying on the surface with my head in the water, peering toward where I thought the whales were, I could see nothing but thirty feet of cloudy, green water. I turned to Julia in the boat to get her read on the situation. She yelled down to me, 'They're turning toward us!'

"The sound of the clicks intensified. I hoped the whales would be friendly rather than aggressive, but I had no way of knowing what they were about to do. One whale had her calf and might be protective, especially after hearing my bizarre vocalizations." As Jones continued treading water, four blunt gray heads cut through the wave crests, light reflecting off their oily skin as they bore down on him. He checked the light readings and set the aperture on his lens. His mind wandered to thoughts of the many whales that had died at human hands in these same waters. Were these whales just curious? Or were they out for revenge?

"And then they were there," says Jones. "At first there was a change in the bright green color of the sea, and then individual shapes formed, moving slowly, effortlessly, relentlessly toward me—a female with a calf on her left side, another female just behind them. The largest female approached so as to pass me on her left. Her course brought her so close that the calf was forced to split off from her to avoid running straight into me."

Jones knew that a sperm whale could annihilate him with a simple swat of its tail—after all, the species has been known to sink small ships. But the closer the whales came, the more his fear turned to wonder. "This whale looked at me with an eye as large as a grapefruit. As she moved past, her eyeball rotated in its socket to focus on me. A sense of tremendous calm descended upon me, and I felt intensely alive."

A few seconds later, the whales were gone. Jones swam back to the inflatable. "I was ecstatic. We had met the whales, and they were friendly. This was a moment when the ordinary disappeared and the world became magical."

Amid such revelations, Jones and Whitty managed to capture re-markable footage for what became a groundbreaking film called *Whales,* which Jones produced for our National Audubon Society program in 1987. It allows the viewer to relive the excitement of Jones's quest: traveling all over the world, investigating the current state of whales, and making new discoveries about their behavior and the threats to their well-being. The film offers exciting action as well as serious analysis. In one scene, a beached sperm whale is rescued on Long Island. In another, experts analyze Japan's strenuous efforts to keep commercial whaling legal. By the end of the film, the mighty sperm whale looks less like a fearsome threat and more like a gentle and curious giant. Jones even set up an organization, BlueVoice.org, for viewers who wanted to take action to protect whales and dolphins.

Conservation films such as *Whales* generally alert us to a problem, examine it, point to a solution, and call us to action. But conservation films represent only a small portion of the multitude of films about wild animals today. In search of big audiences, some wildlife filmmakers studiously avoid controversy and advocacy. They emphasize the beauty and drama of nature but exclude material that might be interpreted as a call to action—or, worse, just produce crude entertainment, full of lies and misimpressions. The motivations for making these films differ, too. Some wildlife filmmakers care deeply about the welfare and survival of their subjects; others are interested mostly in profits or are simply risk junkies.

In this chapter, I'll survey the world of wildlife filmmaking. We start with television, where wildlife shows offer tremendous variety, ranging from high-quality scientific programming to crude, exploitative sensationalism. Then we move on to the well-funded and awe-inspiring, but sometimes cautious, films that make it to mainstream theaters and giant IMAX screens. Finally, I discuss the quirky, often innovative kinds of films available only on DVDs and the Web.

Anything Goes on Television

At one end of the spectrum of television offerings are the blue-chip wildlife programs that brim with information about animal behavior and natural history while steering clear of politics and policy, which their producers believe will date the film or taint it with controversy. Rarely featuring any people, these programs instead tend to focus on charismatic species such as bears and sharks, filmed in a magnificent, pristine landscape without any visible power lines or fences. Their spending is grand, too: about $1 million per hour of finished film.

Take *The Blue Planet,* for example. Narrated by David Attenborough and coproduced by the BBC Natural History Unit and the Discovery Channel, this series hit television screens in 2001. Each of its eight one-hour episodes examined a different aspect of marine life and featured amazing, never-before-seen footage of life in the world's oceans. Its filmmakers traveled to two hundred locations on all seven continents, logging three thousand days in the field. Topics included coastal sea mammals, tidal and climatic influences, and sea creatures ranging from bioluminescent squid to a fangtooth fish whose teeth are so big that it can't close its mouth. It also featured the deep-sea "Dumbo" octopus, which uses its earlike fins to move about, and the blue whale, the largest animal ever to have lived on Earth.

The series included dramatic footage of a pod of fifteen killer whales attacking a gray whale calf. During a six-hour chase, the pod separated the calf from its mother and harassed and killed it, eating only its lower jaw and tongue. At the time, this type of predatory behavior had been seen by only a handful of scientists. *The Blue Planet* was also the first to record bottlenose dolphins working in teams. They were observed to circle a large school of sardines from below and release walls of bubbles to corral the fish into a confined area, making it easier to feed. In another scene, *The Blue Planet* featured beluga whales trapped by twenty miles of solid ice and confined to a small breathing hole during the entire winter season. Polar bears attacked the whales as they surfaced, scarring them savagely. One hungry bear managed to drag a fourteen-foot beluga from the water, providing a month's worth of food for herself and her cub.

For all its amazing footage, though, *The Blue Planet* doesn't mention climate change, pollution, or endangered species. Had the producers felt so inclined, they could have added conservation messages—for example, about the warming Arctic. ("Polar bears need to take advantage of this opportunity to feed on belugas because climate change has deprived the bears of seals, their usual prey.") But they chose not to. The film's purpose was not to proselytize—or even to inform people about these problems—but rather to show viewers creatures and wild places they've never seen before. It's meant to be educational entertainment rather than advocacy.

The National Geographic Channel also features high-end wildlife films. One of these, *Eye of the Leopard* (2006), produced in Africa by filmmakers Dereck and Beverly Joubert, is an enthralling journey of birth, life, and death as a mother leopard and her cubs fight off marauding baboons and elude scavenging hyenas. The Jouberts, both dedicated conservationists, spent three years in the wilds of Africa unobtrusively capturing footage of the life of a leopard they called Legadema, or "Light from the Sky." In one particularly poignant moment, Legadema kills a female baboon only to find a baby still clinging to its mother for protection. To the Jouberts' amazement, instead of killing the young baboon, Legadema lies down protectively around it and, at the approach of a hyena, gently lifts it to safety.

Closer to the blood-and-guts end of the TV spectrum is Animal Planet's *The Grizzly Man Diaries*. This eight-part series, which first aired in the summer of 2008, documents the life of grizzly-bear enthusiast Timothy Treadwell, who spent thirteen summers filming the grizzlies of Alaska's Katmai National Park. *The Grizzly Man Diaries* draws upon hundreds of hours of Treadwell's own footage, private pages from his journals, and more than 10,000 still photographs in an attempt to tell the story that Treadwell himself might have told had he not been killed by the bears he loved so passionately.

Each episode reminds the viewers of how savagely Treadwell died, while also showing him touching grizzlies, singing to them, and tracking them across the years. He gives the bears endearing names such as Aunt Melissa and Rainbow. In one episode, an unusually high number of large male bears congregate around a creek near his campsite in late summer. Competition for fish and space is intense. Treadwell witnesses fierce fights between alpha males as they struggle for supremacy, while mothers and cubs are relegated to scavenging on the sidelines. This behavior begins to worry Treadwell, as many desperate bears have been visiting his campsite at night. His last diary entry before he died reveals that he didn't sleep well. He had a terrible nightmare of being eaten alive by a bear. (Although *The Grizzly Man Diaries* was produced by the same team as the 2005 feature film *Grizzly Man,* directed by Werner Herzog, the results are dramatically different. Herzog's film digs deeper, by exploring Treadwell's mind and behavior and showing that he was foolhardy as well as passionate about his "bear friends.")

Bigger and more ambitious than *The Grizzly Man Diaries*—but just as sensational—is the annual week-long series of programs that the Discovery Channel calls *Shark Week,* which first aired in the summer of 1987. Some of the episodes' names signal the emphasis on violence: "The Worst Shark Attack Ever," "Shark Feeding Frenzy," "Teeth of Death." During the week, shark shows are broadcast every evening in a two- or three-hour block. On the channel's Web site, visitors can watch videos and podcasts, read stories, play games, and generally gorge themselves on shark lore.

It's a popular series; some twenty million people tune in to at least part of *Shark Week* every year, hoping to be scared senseless by watching a massive array of very large, sharp teeth bite down savagely into a critical part of a person's anatomy. Sensationalism flows through every moment, and undoubtedly some learning seeps in too. The programs deal sensibly with questions such as these: Do the vibrations caused by a flapping injured fish attract sharks? Does chili powder repel sharks? Does kicking and splashing attract them? If you're stranded in the ocean, is it safer to stay in a group or tread water alone? What are the best strategies for staying safe when in the water? But the series' heart is really in making hearts pound.

Even farther along television's sensation-and-violence spectrum are the filmmakers who act like wildlife paparazzi, harassing animals and endangering human lives to boost their ratings. For example, *Jackass,* shown on MTV from 2000 to 2002, once showed two men dressed up in zebra outfits, running around wildly (in an undisclosed location, which could have been a game farm or the Serengeti) until they were attacked by a lion. Another time, the two—their names were Johnny Knoxville and Bam Margera—swam with sharks, recklessly goading them for the sake of entertainment. Although it was popular, *Jackass* went off the air after three seasons—partly because of a campaign led by Senator Joe Lieberman, who in early 2001 rightly blamed *Jackass* for helping to cause injuries and even death among teens who were inspired to attempt similar stunts.

Although *Jackass* was gone, its concept lived on in a spin-off, *Wildboyz,* that aired on MTV from 2003 to 2006. The *Wildboyz* hosts, Chris Pontius and Steve-O, performed stunts with animals, often putting themselves in life-threatening situations. Steve-O deliberately subjected himself to the sting of a scorpion, and Pontius was attacked by a wild jaguar and nearly bitten by a black bear. Disguised as seals, the pair also attracted a great white shark but escaped unhurt. Their fearlessness was matched by their lack of training and education. This series was axed after the death of Animal Planet host Steve Irwin, who was far better trained in handling wild animals than the *Wildboyz* hosts. If a professional like Irwin could die, the hosts said, then "we've got to look out for our own safety."

Shows such as *Wildboyz* and *Jackass* are part of the larger phenomenon of reality television that has blossomed all over the medium like a ferociously growing weed. Wildlife documentaries, like all documentaries, are reality television but in a good sense: they feed a hunger we have for a direct experience that isn't always available to us. But more recently we've seen that devolve into an appetite for watching human beings do stupid, humiliating, and even dangerous things. I'm particularly distressed when this sometimes ugly programming extends to wild animals, who have no say in the matter.

Fact and Fiction at the Multiplex

Wildlife-related movies can be found on mainstream movie screens throughout the world. Offerings that feature fictional stories have included *Jaws, Never Cry Wolf, FernGully: The Last Rainforest, Arctic Tale,* and *Happy Feet*. Fictional films such as these are characterized by compelling stories and dramatic situations that play powerfully on people's emotions. Some feature animals and humans interacting (*Jaws, Never Cry Wolf*), while others focus solely on animals (*Happy Feet, Arctic Tale*). With *Happy Feet* and many other animated movies with "wild animal" characters, the explicit and pronounced anthropomorphism makes the animals seem like virtual stand-ins for people, more or less in the tradition of children's literature.

Marine mammals have figured in some of the best-known feature film stories. The movie *Flipper* (1963) became a long-running TV series in the 1960s and was subsequently revived as a series in 1995 and another feature-length film in 1996. *Flipper* could be seen as merely the seagoing version of the classic boy-and-dog friendship saga, but it did bring dolphins into the lives of millions of boomer-generation kids and surely contributed to winning hearts and minds for their protection. A real orca named Keiko was the star of *Free Willy* (1993), which pushed lots of politically correct buttons in relating the efforts of a white boy, a black social worker, and a Native American shaman to liberate Willy from a performance tank, and which spawned two sequels.

Two of the ten highest-grossing animal films of all time (not counting dog stories) were the unusual movies made by French director Jean-Jacques Annaud in which animals were truly the protagonists. In *The Bear* (1988), an orphan cub survives hunters and the harsh wilderness of late nineteenth-century British Columbia with the aid of an older male grizzly. This daring film contained no dialogue at all, the director believing that the animals' behavior and good visual storytelling communicated all that viewers needed to follow the plot. Annaud used the same principles in his 2004 film *Two Brothers*, about sibling tiger cubs in French Indochina—though in this case the human characters did speak some dialogue.

It's noteworthy that most action-adventure movies about wild animals center on the bonds those creatures form with children, as seen again in two examples that feature primates: *Monkey Trouble* (1994) and *Buddy*, a 1997 offering about a girl and her pet gorilla.

On the documentary side, some well-known films are *Winged Migration, March of the Penguins, Gorillas in the Mist: The Story of Dian Fossey,* and *The Wild Parrots of Telegraph Hill.* By definition, nonfiction movies such as these are rooted in reality and facts, which doesn't mean the truth isn't sometimes stretched and distorted. The filmmaker's key challenge in a documentary is to build a compelling story around the slices of real life the camera can capture. We'll explore many of these films in more detail in upcoming pages.

Whether fact or fiction, big-screen films tend to have high production values and gripping storytelling—and they often cost far more to produce than their television counterparts. Those that become box-office successes can reach much larger audiences than TV fare. Most aim primarily to entertain, though some surreptitiously sprinkle in some education and even advocacy.

The National Geographic film *Arctic Tale* (2007) is among the few recent big-screen offerings to combine star power, entertainment, and a strong conservation message. Narrated by actor-singer-rapper Queen Latifah, the film depicts the lives of Nanu, a polar bear cub, and Seela, a walrus calf, in a melting Arctic threatened by global warming. Polar bears like to eat seals, which they seize and devour when the seals come up for air in holes in the ice. But global warming means less ice, so the polar bears go hungry. In the film, both bears and walruses take refuge on a rock island, where the bears launch predatory attacks on the much bigger walruses.

The film is an intriguing cross between a documentary and pure fiction. Close-up shots help the audience get to know Seela and Nanu and identify with their fight for survival. Codirector Adam Ravetch explains, "We wanted to show the spirit, intelligence, and adaptability of these two animals. We also used the camera angle known as 'point-of-view' (in which the audience sees the same things that the animal sees) to create an intimate experience of what Seela and Nanu were experiencing as they battled the harsh consequences of global warming." (Jean-Jacques Annaud also notably used the animals' point of view in his fictional films.)

The two characters are composites of animals filmed in the Arctic over ten years. According to Ravetch and codirector Sarah Robertson, it would have been impossible to follow an individual animal for the eight-year cycle of the film. Other than that, though, all the scenes are authentic, with no staging or manipulation. Ravetch gets close to the animals but never tries to touch them or do anything that would make them behave in an unnatural way. In terms of the gear and crew he brings to the wild, he describes himself as a "minimalist" filmmaker. His goal is to move in slowly, so that the animals become comfortable with his presence and behave as if he or his cameras weren't there.

Ravetch and Robertson want their film to be a message of hope and inspiration that will change the way we live. "*Arctic Tale* is really a metaphor for humans," asserts Ravetch. "It says to our audience that if polar bears and walruses in the Arctic can figure out how to overcome the difficult circumstances of their lives during a changing, warming world, then we should be able to as well." The film was used in elementary schools all across North America and in twenty other countries to help teach young people about climate change.

For all its virtues, however, *Arctic Tale* failed to do well at the box office, generating only $2 million worldwide. The Oscar-winning animated comedy *Finding Nemo* (2003, Pixar and Disney), on the other hand, grossed $900 million—perhaps because it had better marketing and distribution, perhaps because of its greater intrinsic mass appeal. In animated films, the creators are free to make their characters as appealingly human as they wish, and tell stories that could never transpire in nature. *Finding Nemo* centers on a young clownfish that escapes from an aquarium in a dentist's office and reunites with his father in the ocean. The film had an inspiring message about freedom and respect for animals, but it also led to a frenzied demand at pet stores for clownfish, many of which ended up dying because kids didn't take care of them properly.

The 1975 Steven Spielberg film *Jaws*, a fictional tale in which a wild animal is the villain rather than the hero, also had unintended consequences. Based on a novel by Peter Benchley, it famously depicts a summer resort town visited by a great white shark. The police chief decides to close the local beach when he hears that a shark is lurking, but the town council overrules him to keep the tourist dollars flowing. After several people are attacked, the police chief recruits a scientist and a shark hunter to eliminate the menace, and the chase is on.

As a result of *Jaws*, sharks became a terrifying, man-eating nightmare for many people contemplating swimming in the sea. To Benchley's profound regret, this made them targets for mindless violence by people whose ignorance of sharks was exceeded only by their enthusiasm for slaughtering them—especially great whites. On the other hand, *Jaws* encouraged young people to become interested in sharks. The knowledge and wisdom of fictional marine biologist Matt Hooper inspired a new generation of shark scientists who have done much to encourage shark conservation. Like many influential wildlife films we'll discuss, *Jaws* had multiple outcomes, some bad and some good.

In the realm of nonfiction, one of the most celebrated films to emerge yet is *Winged Migration*, a beautiful documentary from Sony Pictures about bird migration. Nominated for an Oscar in 2003, this film didn't offer much of a plot, but it riveted audiences with intimate shots of birds flying vast distances over continents and oceans. Seventeen pilots and fourteen cinematographers spent four years in forty countries on all seven continents to make the film.

The film's French producer, director, writer, and narrator, Jacques Perrin, claims that no special effects were used. This may be true, but many of the birds were trained from birth to tolerate the presence of cameras and noise, so that when the migrations were eventually shot, the birds accepted the cameras as part of their world.

Early in *Winged Migration,* the camera captures a sparrow perched in a tree. As we back away from the bird, it follows the camera, hopping from branch to branch. This is wonderful to watch, but it could have been done only with a trained bird. Perrin may not have used cinematic special effects, but he tried numerous other devices—balloons, helicopters, gliders, airplanes—to get close to storks, cranes, condors, puffins, pelicans, eagles, ducks, and scores of other species.

Directed by yet another Frenchman, Luc Jacquet, and narrated by actor Morgan Freeman, *March of the Penguins* won the 2005 Oscar for Best Documentary Feature. Like *Winged Migration, March of the Penguins* took immense fortitude to film. A dedicated two-person crew spent fourteen months on the ice recording the yearly journey of Antarctica's four-foot-tall emperor penguins as they survived horrendous temperatures of 100 degrees below zero and ferocious winds of more than 100 miles per hour. In the fall, the penguins leave the ocean to waddle and slide inland to their ancestral breeding grounds, a trip of seventy miles. Courtship ensues, followed by the birth of a chick, but for the chick to survive the next few months, both parents must make harrowing journeys between the breeding grounds and the ocean to feed themselves and their baby. Though death beckons in every direction, the penguins' will to survive is extraordinary. The familial ties the film traces are so strong that Freeman calls it a love story.

Like most mass-market films, *March of the Penguins* contains no mention of climate change or threats to the penguins' habitat. Is that a lost opportunity? Perhaps, but the filmmakers brilliantly meet another goal: that of drawing the audience's attention to the stark conditions these birds have to endure. That can't help but increase public appreciation of the natural world.

IMAX Films on the Giant Screen

The past forty years have seen the birth and growth of the giant-screen film industry, which has thrilled and educated more than a billion people. Invented by the Canadian IMAX ("Image MAXimum") Corporation, giant-screen cameras use film that is ten times larger than the 35mm frame size shown in regular theaters, providing images that are significantly sharper. Brad Ohlund, director of photography at MacGillivray Freeman Films, says, "The format provides the sharpest, clearest, richest, most colorful, and near lifelike images of any visual medium." In the theater, these giant screens can be eight stories tall, offering a powerful, total-immersion experience. Extraordinarily clear pictures fill a viewer's entire field of vision, complemented by state-of-the-art multispeaker sound. What other entertainment medium could show a whale life-size on screen or put viewers so squarely in the center of the action?

One giant-screen conservation classic is *The Living Sea* (1995). Narrated by A-list actress Meryl Streep and directed by Greg MacGillivray, this film offers scientific hope for the recovery of endangered underwater ecosystems. *Amazon*, a 1997 IMAX film directed by Kieth Merrill, examines a collaboration between American ethnobotanist Mark Plotkin and a tribal shaman on a mission to find rare medicinal plants. *Island of the Sharks* (1999), produced and directed by Michele and Howard Hall (profiled in Chapter 10), explores an underwater mountain that boasts the world's highest concentration of large marine predators, including whitetip, hammerhead, blacktip, and silky sharks.

Films shown in giant-screen theaters, especially those in institutional settings such as the Smithsonian, are designed to educate as much as to entertain, offering teachers an exciting tool. But they present special challenges for wildlife filmmakers. Filmmaking costs grow with the size of the camera, and these are some of the biggest and heaviest around.

Big cranes, beefy dollies, and rugged winches are also needed to move the cameras smoothly and to withstand the increased vibrations from the larger-than-usual camera motors. Setups take more time, more people, and greater care. Lighting costs are higher for giant-screen films, too—wider fields of view require more lights and larger lamps—as are the costs of film editing, sound editing, and mixing. Moreover, the environmental impacts of film equipment become an issue. What an irony it becomes if films designed to promote conservation are themselves heavy polluters and energy pigs. We'll revisit that issue in the last chapter.

Creating giant-screen films underwater is particularly challenging. When used in the ocean, IMAX cameras must be encased in special housings, which can triple or quadruple their weight. The IMAX 2D (two-dimensional) camera with its underwater housing weighs 250 pounds; the underwater IMAX 3D weighs 1,500 pounds and is almost as big as a Volkswagen. With that much weight, pursuing fast-moving marine creatures such as whales, sharks, and manta rays becomes almost laughable. Moreover, the camera makes a noise like a chainsaw, which scares animals away, and it can shoot for only three minutes before it must be hoisted to the surface for film reloading. "If someone were to hold a competition to create the most impractical motion picture format for capturing underwater wildlife behavior," observes Howard Hall, "it is hard to imagine a more creative entry than IMAX."

Al Giddings directed the photography on the first giant-screen film I ever worked on: *Whales,* which came out in 1996 (no relation to the earlier film with the same title I made with Hardy Jones). Giddings once held the *Guinness Book* world record for holding his breath longer than anyone else—more than eleven minutes. When we filmed humpback whales off Hawaii, he didn't want to use scuba tanks because the bubbles sometimes spook the whales. So he would take a huge breath and sink down to a depth of seventy feet with the heavy giant-screen camera. He'd shoot whatever he could and then race to the surface to get a breath, abandoning the camera. We anxiously watched as the slightly buoyant million-dollar camera would slowly float to the surface. First we'd retrieve the camera and then we'd retrieve Al.

Giant-screen films have their own distribution network and theaters. As of January 2010, around 36 percent of the world's 569 giant-screen theaters are in prestigious museums and science centers in metropolitan areas. So once a film is made, it's likely to find a large, education-oriented audience. More than eighteen million people have seen MacGillivray's Oscar-nominated *The Living Sea* since it opened in 1995. (That's five times more than saw Al Gore's popular global-warming documentary, *An Inconvenient Truth,* in theaters.) Some eighty million people see a giant-screen film every year, and the format is becoming a prominent force in the entertainment industry.

These films have traditionally provided a fascinating, family-friendly blend of entertaining thrills and valuable learning, often related to the natural world. Adding to their educational value, many of these films are augmented by supplementary lectures, Web sites, study guides, and related books. Giant-screen films' reputation for educational content is waning, however, as Hollywood action films such as *300, Transformers,* and *Eagle Eye* take to the giant screen. These violence-filled spectacles often cost twenty times as much to make as traditional giant-screen films and offer far higher star power and marketing oomph.

At a conference in Los Angeles in 2001, I warned that the reputation of the giant-screen experience was being damaged by violent commercial films, and argued that giant-screen films should remain education-oriented or risk losing their core audience—families. The producer of the giant-screen horror film *Haunted Castle,* Belgian-born Ben Stassen, argued passionately against me, contending that no subject should be taboo, including horror, sex, and violence. He considered my speech a direct attack on his film (which it was) and angrily denounced me for encouraging censorship. What right did I have to tell filmmakers what films they should or should not make? Tension rose in the jam-packed conference room. I said that I didn't support censorship but that each of us had to make a choice about the kind of films we would make. I thought we should make that choice based on our own conscience and what was best for the industry and the public. IMAX film producer Bayley Silleck described my public clash with Stassen as one of the "few occasions in the history of IMAX conferences when candor excitingly superseded civility."

Today's realities make that incident seem rather quaint. In 2002, IMAX developed a method of digitally converting 35-millimeter Hollywood features to big-screen format. This brought to big-screen theaters the R-rated violence of the *Matrix* films and *300,* which made the scary torture scenes in *Haunted Castle* seem tame by comparison. But it's not just the violent action genre that has moved to IMAX; it's family fare like the Harry Potter franchise as well. In this evolutionary process, I believe it's important that some giant-screen space be reserved for documentaries, especially in institutional settings.

The Wild Web and Beyond

In the past five years, there's been an explosion of films that are never broadcast on television or shown at movie theaters but instead are posted on the Web and distributed as DVDs. With more computers connected to the Internet and faster connections, such films can have a big influence—for example, on conservation—if the organization that makes them can stir up interest in the film. Marketing guru Steve Michelson, founder of Lobitos Creek Ranch (a film production and distribution company outside San Francisco), recommends "piggyback marketing," which might include holding events for legislators and for the media, hosting viewing parties in members' homes, and selling DVDs on the organization's Web site.

One of Michelson's films is *Oil on Ice,* produced by Dale Djerassi and Bo Boudart in 2005. Michelson partnered with fourteen nonprofits to promote and market this film. The Sierra Club and some of its 750,000 members hosted 2,500 house parties to screen the film and distribute posters, educational guides, DVDs, and a "grassroots action" tool kit aimed at preventing oil drilling in Alaska's Arctic National Wildlife Refuge.

TERRA, a nonprofit organization at Montana State University in Bozeman, produces environmental programming for the Web and in the form of a podcast, which can be automatically sent to subscribers' computers. Created by Ronald Tobias and Eric Bendick in 2005,

TERRA is part of the graduate program in science and natural history filmmaking at MSU. Its mission, says producer Eric Bendick, is to "develop an environmentally literate community that can mobilize and influence public policy." Bendick talks passionately about creating a "more choice-driven media system in which passive 'viewers' are replaced by active 'users.'"

TERRA's programs have included *A Cat Called Elvis,* about a snow leopard in Mongolia whose territory is shrinking as human populations increase, and *Pablo's Hippos,* a film about a group of hippos imported to South America by a drug lord, which raises interesting questions about politics, farming, and biodiversity. As of September 2008, TERRA films had been downloaded more than eight million times since they debuted three years earlier.

The films coming from Lobitos Creek Ranch and TERRA are professionally made, but communications innovations now allow amateurs to enter the field as well. Popular sites such as YouTube enable almost any moderately savvy computer user to post and view digital video clips in mere seconds. Viewers can play a major role in the publicity and promotion of programming they like, as they e-mail links to video clips, add video clips to their Facebook or other social-networking pages, and download podcasts via iTunes or other software that manages digital sound and video content.

Not surprisingly, Web-based videos are usually produced on a shoestring budget and thus aren't as polished as their television and feature film counterparts. But differences in quality don't matter if there's an audience hungry for the information and images. Brief, even blurry, footage can sway elections, reach millions of people, and change society.

In 2004, a Texan named David Budzinski was on safari in South Africa's Kruger National Park when he saw six lions and a crocodile attacking and trying to kill a water buffalo calf. It looked as if the calf was doomed, but then a herd of angry buffalo appeared to fight off the attacking predators. Although he wasn't a professional, Budzinski videotaped the entire eight-minute life-and-death drama. When he got home, Budzinski tried to sell his footage to television networks, including National Geographic Channel, but was rebuffed because the quality was too amateurish.

In the spring of 2007, a friend posted Budzinski's fuzzy but riveting video on YouTube. It took off like a cheetah after a gazelle. Within the first few weeks, several hundred thousand people had watched it, and by the fall of 2009 that number had climbed to forty-six million, bigger than the audience that watched Barack Obama's acceptance speech at the 2008 Democratic National Convention. After hearing about the sensational popularity of Budzinski's clip, National Geographic changed its mind. The result was a one-hour special that investigated the story behind the footage, explored the biology and behavior of the animals involved, and reunited Budzinski with his safari companions at the watering hole where the drama unfolded.

For some advocacy organizations, a video camera and a Web site can be powerful weapons. People for the Ethical Treatment of Animals (PETA) scored points in June 2006 after they shot an unauthorized video of American singer-songwriter and actress Beyoncé. Members of the group had won a dinner with the celebrity in an eBay auction. Beyoncé was not aware that the winners were associated with PETA, however, or that there was a hidden camera rolling as the group dined. Had she known, she might have been wary, since she uses fur in her fashion line, and PETA considers wearing fur to be a serious offense.

After the diners had placed their orders, the PETA members took out a portable DVD player and began to play a video about fur. Starring actress Pamela Anderson, it highlighted the horrors of the fur industry with gruesome and graphic images of animals that are gassed, strangled, and skinned alive for fur coats. They also quizzed Beyoncé about her use of fur. Even though the PETA members were quickly escorted out of the restaurant (and the stunt seems to have had no effect on Beyoncé's business decisions), the media buzz it generated made the public aware of the group's concerns. The video of Beyoncé's reaction had been viewed by more than 35,000 people on YouTube alone by October 2009, and coverage by the celebrity news and online gossip outlets widened its impact. In the past, the event might have been a blip on one evening's entertainment news, but now the video can be played countless times as word spreads among Beyoncé fans and ordinary citizens.

Whether used for advocacy, entertainment, or education, the Web-based film revolution will continue. And it will continue to diversify and decentralize as millions more people carry phones and other devices that can capture video and "generate content."

The Truth about *An Inconvenient Truth*

If you look at the choices made by the best-funded wildlife filmmakers, you'd have to conclude that controversy and serious advocacy are bad for business. *Arctic Tale,* an expensive conservation-oriented effort, bombed at the box office, while the gorgeously neutral *Winged Migration* earned big bucks. But one powerful example runs counter to that trend: Al Gore's Oscar-winning 2006 film, *An Inconvenient Truth.* Although the film doesn't feature wildlife, it's relevant to this discussion as evidence that films with an environmental message can be popular and compelling. While some filmmakers scoffed at the film for being little more than a sophisticated slide show, it grossed nearly $50 million worldwide, won an Oscar for Best Documentary Feature, and played a large role in earning a Nobel Peace Prize for Gore in October 2007.

It also changed minds. According to a *Washington Post*–ABC News survey, the film's impact doubled the number of respondents who rated climate change their top environmental concern. "There was widespread denial and indifference to the facts until Al Gore jolted the world with *An Inconvenient Truth*," remarked renowned field biologist George Schaller.

Since Gore's film was released, Discovery, National Geographic, BBC, and the History Channel, among others, have all earned surprisingly high ratings for serious documentaries on the state of the planet. The difficulties for those who try to make these kinds of films have by no means disappeared—as stories in Chapter 9 demonstrate. But environmental topics are no longer instantly dismissed as "eat your vegetables" television, says National Geographic Society senior vice president Michael Cascio.

State of the Art

When you add up all the offerings on television, in theaters, and on DVDs and the Web, the wildlife filmmaking industry appears to be thriving. But a closer look reveals an industry shooting off in different directions without much apparent purpose beyond making money.

Many honorable filmmakers today spend countless uncomfortable hours, days, months, and even years out in the elements to bring us rare and amazing wildlife footage. They shiver in the deep ocean or breathe in minus-twenty-degree air to capture footage of whales, polar bears, or penguins. Some filmmakers also work hard to conserve wildlife. But the part of the wildlife filmmaking community that is dedicated to conservation is relatively small.

Many other filmmakers, producers, and broadcasters have given in to the temptation to exploit animals for profit. At the 2008 Wildscreen Festival in Bristol, England, Bethan Corney, a commissioning editor at the British commercial Channel Five, said she would rather have shows about "exploding snakes" than about conservation. Programs that are "extreme, strange, and shocking" are what audiences want, she said. "We are tabloidy and we're not ashamed of it."

"Extreme, strange, and shocking" is not so different from what the industry's pioneers were seeking almost a century ago. In the next chapter we'll look at the daring characters who planted the seeds for this show-business style of wildlife filmmaking, as well as the talented people who pioneered the industry's most artistic, informative, and influential work.

2

HOW DID WE GET HERE?
A Brief History of the Business

In 1958, I was eleven years old, growing up in the south of England. My family didn't have a lot of money, so going to the movies was a rare and exciting treat. One Saturday afternoon, we went to see a new movie from Walt Disney called *White Wilderness*. Advertised as a "true-life adventure," it was the first wildlife documentary I'd ever seen. The stirring orchestral music, the "ferocious" polar bear and its cuddly cubs, the bloody combat of wolves and caribou, the lemmings racing off a cliff—I was thrilled by the whole wondrous Arctic world.

Half a century later, *White Wilderness* remains a touchstone in wildlife filmmaking circles for both its high-impact storytelling and its breakthrough production values. Part of Disney's celebrated *True-Life Adventures* series (released between 1948 and 1960), *White Wilderness* took three years to make. A dozen daring cinematographers were given time to get the shots they wanted, many depicting animal behavior never documented before. Promoted as an "animal-packed adventure for the whole family," the film won an Oscar for Best Documentary Feature in 1958. While working on this book, I decided it was worth taking another look at the film to see how well it holds up against modern standards of wildlife filmmaking. This viewing left me both newly impressed and uncomfortable.

At the beginning of *White Wilderness,* an authoritative male voice declares that "this is the bleakest environment on earth." On the screen is a dramatic vista of snow, ice, and ocean. "Winter's grip is loosened," intones the narrator, as glaciers calve and rivers surge with the spring melt.

A massive herd of walruses sun themselves on the rocks. The calm is suddenly disrupted by the arrival of a hungry polar bear, which the narrator calls an "ever-present menace" and a "ferocious carnivore, king of the Arctic." The frightened walruses pile into the sea in seething turmoil and escape. This time the polar bear will go hungry, the narrator says, but next time perhaps he'll be lucky.

As winter turns to spring, two adorable polar bear cubs snuggle with their mother to nurse. Later these bundles of white fluff explore their snowy surroundings. The cubs have an "innate sense of play," says the narrator, and they are "intelligent and have a sense of humor." For a while they push snowballs at each other, and then one ascends a snow-covered mountain. Up and up the little bear climbs until it loses its footing and starts slipping down. "The long toboggan ride begins," says the narrator lightheartedly, as the screen shows the cub gathering speed and tumbling head over heels down the mountain. The cub eventually falls to the bottom, where it bangs against rocks before coming to a dazed stop.

Next the cubs chase some ring seals, the bears' main food source, but fail to catch them. Then they scare off a herd of walruses, even intimidating a walrus bull. The narrator tells us this intimidation is known as "trading on your father's reputation."

As spring turns to summer, we visit the Arctic Ocean and meet "friendly" beluga whales, as well as "vicious" killer whales, "lazy" ptarmigans, and "bloodthirsty" ermines.

We see lemmings, described as "nasty little rodents," underground in their burrows and nests, and then follow their migration. "A compulsion seizes each one and they move in formation," the narrator informs us. Despite predation by jaegers, Arctic ravens, and ermines, the lemming migration continues. They are victims of an "obsession," pushing on blindly to new feeding grounds. They fall down rock faces as they relentlessly pursue their "fatal journey." Finally we watch them throw themselves off a cliff, their small bodies plunging into the sea hundreds of feet below; they survive the dive, but exhaustion soon claims them and they drown. The sea is dotted with bodies. Here begins the "legend of lemmings' mass suicide," says the narrator, "a final rendezvous with death."

The spring thaw also brings waterfowl, including the colorful king eider duck, "nature's dandy—sartorial splendor personified." The polar bear cubs have captured a loon in their claws and are trying to subdue it; a heart-wrenching struggle ensues, with the battered loon finally escaping. Next we meet the musk ox, with its formidable horns, a "living legend surviving from the Ice Age." When threatened by wolves, musk oxen group in a defensive circle with their horns pointing outward, "an unassailable position." After a bit, the attacking wolves leave, "pretending indifference." The wolf, we learn, is a "much maligned species and a symbol of all things villainous," but the film notes that wolves mate for life and shows them affectionately caring for their pups.

Soon we meet the wolverine, described by the narrator as "cunning and bloodthirsty" and "a demon as a fighter with a voracious appetite." Weighing only thirty pounds, it's able to drive wolves from their kills using its prodigious strength and ferocity. Wolverines are "accomplished tree climbers," and we see one in a tall tree. At the top is an osprey's nest with a chick not yet able to fly, but the mother osprey has "murderous talons," the narrator advises. As the wolverine climbs, a bloody confrontation ensues. The mother osprey dive-bombs the wolverine again and again but fails to knock it out of the tree. The wolverine climbs into the nest and kills the baby bird, leaving a "grieving mother."

We see polar bears again. A blizzard strikes. The voice-of-God narrator tells us that, with winter's approach, "bitter cold returns to this land of long black shadows."

When I saw this seventy-two-minute film as a kid, it went by in a flash of pure enjoyment. Today my thoughts are more complicated. I'm filled with admiration for what the film accomplished in introducing viewers to the Arctic world yet dismayed by its blind spots and blunders: the heavy-handed anthropomorphizing, the obvious (to an informed eye) staging of scenes, and the misrepresentation of animal behavior or outright cruelty in some cases. We'll come back to this film and the issues it raises, which are still being debated by wildlife filmmakers today. The industry has made progress, but it has taken a winding path.

When people first started filming wild animals at the beginning of the twentieth century, most were simply pursuing fame and fortune. The work of these pioneers led to the more education-oriented *True-Life Adventures* series in midcentury and then to films that adopted the ethical, do-no-harm approach that represents one school of wildlife filmmaking today. It also led into some dark corners.

Martin and Osa Johnson Take the Stage

Originally from Kansas, husband-and-wife team Martin and Osa Johnson became celebrities through their bold adventures in faraway lands. Born in 1884, Martin was a crew member and cameraman on Jack London's Pacific voyages aboard the *Snark* from 1907 to 1909. Later, he made a living giving lectures, capitalizing on London's name and showing movies of their trip. Martin met Osa Leighty in 1909, when she was sixteen. They instantly fell in love and married the following year. They began an exciting life together pursuing what became a cross between filmmaking and show business. They mounted safaris, captured dramatic footage of hunting, and, for the first time in filmmaking history, brought audiences images of exotic wild animals. Their primary goal was to astonish and entertain the American public.

According to journalist Patricia Eliot Tobias, the Johnsons' films were often structured as quests. First they went to find and film cannibals in the South Seas, the Solomon Islands, and the New Hebrides. In the process, they were captured by Chief Nagapate and his warlike Big Nambas. It's impossible to know how much danger the Johnsons were actually in—perhaps not much, because they were released unharmed—but the escapade provided a compelling title for their first film, *Among the Cannibal Isles of the South Pacific* (1918). After that adventure, the Johnsons moved on to look for lions in *Simba* (1928), for gorillas in *Congorilla* (1932), and for orangutans in their last film together, *Borneo* (1937).

One of Osa Johnson's contributions to the partnership was her expert marksmanship. When filming in Africa, she used this skill not only to protect her husband and herself from stampeding elephants, charging rhinos, and attacking lions but also to create dramatic film sequences. Unbeknownst to audiences, their hunts were often staged, with the Johnsons goading a dangerous animal into charging the camera so they could then shoot it in "self-defense."

Reprehensible as this may seem, we need to consider the world in which the Johnsons worked. In the 1920s it was acceptable to hunt exotic species, which either were or seemed to be plentiful. In the early part of the century, President Teddy Roosevelt was a renowned conservationist as well as an ardent hunter. Animal welfare and conservation groups were not yet focused on African wildlife. "Ultimately," writes communications professor and wildlife film analyst Derek Bousé, "although their filmmaking practices could be questionable, their skills limited, their scruples dubious, and their self-indulgence undeniable, the Johnsons themselves were popular and so were their films. They brought more popular acceptance to wildlife films than anyone prior to Disney."

In the end, the Johnsons influenced several generations of filmmakers by showing that educational films (or what passed for educational films in the 1920s) could attract a large and passionate following. The prototype they created by making entertaining films that focus as much on the hosts as on the wildlife has been mimicked relentlessly.

Flamboyant Frank Buck

Born in 1884, the same year as Martin Johnson, Frank Buck was a hunter, film producer, director, writer, and actor, and a heroic figure to many growing up in the 1930s and 1940s. Like the Johnsons, he traveled extensively to film and capture animals. The titles of his films—*Fang and Claw* (1935), *Jungle Menace* (1937), and *Tiger Fangs* (1943)—suggest his approach; many featured fights to the death between aggressive animals. The daring Buck was even the inspiration for Carl Denham, the fictional hunter and filmmaker in the *King Kong* movies, who, with intense energy and self-promotion, launches the voyage to Skull Island.

As a child, Buck had collected small animals. In his late twenties, he won $3,500 in a poker game and set out for Brazil. When he found he could make money in the United States selling exotic birds, he began to travel the world, bagging wildlife in faraway places for profit and filming as he went. He brought back thousands of animals for zoos and circuses, including elephants, tigers, leopards, hyenas, orangutans, pythons, and king cobras.

Like the Johnsons, Buck staged confrontations to capture audiences' attention. He would put different species of animals together in small enclosures and provoke them to fight. Using this technique, he captured sensational contests between a spotted leopard and a python, a black leopard and a crocodile, a tiger and a buffalo, and more. But Buck's films gave the viewer the impression that the animals had accidentally come across each other in the wild jungle. As Bousé puts it, "These staged confrontations call to mind the bread-and-circus spectacles of a decaying Rome—except that Buck's animals fought it out in enclosures somewhat less glorious than the Coliseum."

The films made by the Johnsons, Buck, and a few others were part of the hugely diverse movie programming people could experience in theaters in the days before television: full-length features (often double features) in proliferating genres, feature shorts, newsreels, and cartoons. Buck's success with films, as well as with books such as his 1932 best-seller, *Bring 'Em Back Alive*, did much to whet the public's appetite for images of the natural world—but mostly its bloody, violent side. In Buck's films, wild animals were invariably depicted as menacing and dangerous. Nevertheless, his lifestyle inspired many young people to follow animal-related careers and may have even helped lay the groundwork for the far more polished films produced by Walt Disney in the 1950s.

Disney Animal Films and the 1950s Zeitgeist

In contrast to the Johnsons' and Buck's productions, which crudely shocked audiences, Disney's films used emotion-filled stories and rich symphonic scores to enthrall them. According to the Disney Company, Walt himself once exclaimed, "The habits of real animals are often funnier and more surprising than the antics we dream up for our cartoon characters." Innovative and influential, Disney's *True-Life Adventures* woke people up to the beauty and enchantment of the natural world.

Disney portrayed nature within a middle-class moral code, which was the prime reason the *True-Life Adventures* series became a cultural force. In the 1930s and 1940s, many Americans worried about the way movies seemed to encourage immoral behavior. Hollywood was widely perceived to glamorize sex, drugs, and violence. Further, after the volcanic upheavals of World War II and the Korean War, and the looming threats of Cold War nuclear armament and communism, audiences yearned for entertainment that offered the comfort of traditional values. Disney realized that he could tap into a profitable market by producing nature films that not only entertained but also championed moral behavior and traditional values. Films such as *White Wilderness* were positioned by Disney as improving popular culture. Good behavior by animals was celebrated, while bad behavior was condemned and punished—"good" and "bad" being measured in human terms, of course.

Audiences bought into Disney's premise that there is great value in observing and learning about the natural world. People saw the behavior of wild animals as representing how human society was organized, or should be; we could learn from "good" animals about what constitutes "good" behavior and a well-organized society. In a film such as *White Wilderness,* viewers could identify with the animals and the challenges they faced, and see their own struggles in the animals' efforts to survive, stay safe, and raise a family. Disney used nature to promote the values of hard work, faithfulness, and frugality—partly because he believed in those things but also because he could tap into a cultural mood and sell millions of movie tickets.

At the same time, Disney took advantage of advances in film technology, including Technicolor, to make his nature films shine. The *True-Life Adventures* series used nature footage from some of the best cinematographers in the world, edited it to make a good story, and added music. An earlier animated film, *Bambi* (1942), was the prototype for this kind of entertainment package. Its story focused on the challenges animals faced in nature rather than the goofiness that animated films had emphasized before: animals singing songs or piloting steamboats. In addition to *White Wilderness,* Walt Disney's *True-Life Adventures* series also included films such as *Seal Island, The Living Desert,* and *The Vanishing Prairie.*

Although these films lacked people, their anthropomorphized animals were portrayed in situations that expressed drama, conflict, and humor—and the creators sometimes crossed the line between fact and fantasy. In *The Living Desert* (1953), Disney took film footage of two scorpions, printed it backward and forward, added music, and thus cleverly made it look as though the scorpions were square-dancing with each other. Some criticized the production for attributing human characteristics to animals in this unscientific and misleading way.

The most infamous example of misleading information in a Disney film involves that scene from *White Wilderness* in which the lemmings jump off a cliff en masse—or so it appears. In fairness to the film, the narrator states that the lemmings are likely not attempting suicide, but the visuals overwhelm the narration. So memorable were these images that even today many people believe that lemmings engage in blindly self-destructive behavior. But the whole scene was fabricated. A 1982 investigation by reporter Brian Vallée of the Canadian Broadcasting Corporation revealed that Disney filmmakers had forced a few dozen lemmings to run on a snow-covered turntable and even threw some into the sea to create the dramatic scene. Yet they had the audacity to state at the beginning of the film that "the hand of man had no influence in what you are about to see."

Two wrongs were committed here: the false depiction of animal behavior and the mistreatment of lemmings. Some species of lemmings do become overpopulated, do migrate in swarms, and sometimes do drown crossing streams, but they never jump off cliffs suicidally. Disney defended the staging of the sequence by claiming that the filmmakers were trying to depict lemming migration, a fascinating natural phenomenon.

White Wilderness deceived audiences in other ways as well. The avalanche was almost certainly triggered by the film crew with explosives after the cameras were carefully placed to capture the snowy onslaught.

The polar bears and walruses never appear in the same frame, which suggests that the polar bear scenes were probably filmed in a zoo and then combined with footage of walruses to make it look as though the bear was wild rather than captive.

The panicked walruses careening off the iceberg to escape the predatory polar bear were almost certainly scared into action by a gunshot or other loud noise. The mother polar bear and two small cubs were probably filmed on a set, perhaps at a zoo. The *awww*-inspiring footage of one cub pushing a snowball onto the head of the cub beneath it was staged, as was the scene of the cub sliding down the mountain and banging into rocks—which was also an example of what we would consider gross animal abuse today. I shudder to imagine how many takes were shot of the cub crashing down the hill until the director was satisfied.

The two polar bears attempting to subdue a loon with their claws and jaws, the wolf-wolverine interactions—all were staged with captive animals. And consider the wolverine climbing the tree to kill and feast on the osprey chick while its mother dive-bombs the predator to protect its young. When the narrator says, "tragedy strikes," the audience isn't watching a wild wolverine that happened to come upon an osprey nest. Rather, a captive wolverine was almost certainly deprived of food so it would perform deadly deeds for the cameras. For the filmmakers, it would have been a tragedy if the wolverine *hadn't* killed the chick, because a "money shot" would have been lost. Tactics such as those described here (based on my educated speculation) became standard for many wildlife films, as we'll see in chapters to come.

I once asked Roy Disney, Walt's nephew, who worked on the series as a young man, if his company was embarrassed by what it had done to animals in the 1940s and 1950s. His answer was, "Apologies are needed, but the awareness raised by the films far outweighed anything bad that was done during production." He claims, "We were decades ahead of the ecology movement. I can't tell you how many times I've run into park rangers who told me they found their careers after growing up on *True-Life Adventures*."

It would be wrong to dismiss the *True-Life Adventures* series as no more than popular escapism. The series encouraged many viewers to befriend and protect the natural world. But did the ends justify the means? That's a question that was raised again and again by the best and brightest wildlife filmmakers who followed, and it remains pertinent today.

Marlin Perkins's Journey

Even as the Disney *True-Life Adventures* series was entertaining and educating millions of viewers in movie theaters, the new medium of television was becoming a factor in how people received images of the wild world. In the mid-1940s, Marlin Perkins was beginning his assignment as the director of the Lincoln Park Zoo in Chicago. Understanding the importance of promotion and publicity to the zoo's financial success, he jumped at the opportunity to host a Sunday afternoon television program called *Zoo Parade,* in which he would show audiences the animals and talk about their biology and behavior. *Zoo Parade* went on the air locally in 1945, went national in 1949, and stayed on until 1955. Fast-forward to 1968, when Perkins, then director of the Saint Louis Zoological Park, was selected to host the famed nature show *Wild Kingdom.* That show had launched in 1963, but with affable and knowledgeable Perkins at the helm, its ratings would grow. At its peak, it reached an audience of more than thirty million people each week.

The sponsor of the series was rewarded by having the program named after it: *Mutual of Omaha's Wild Kingdom.* In addition, Perkins worked his sponsor's name into the content of the show by making comments such as "Just as the mother lion protects her cubs, you can protect your children with an insurance policy from Mutual of Omaha."

In its first ten years, the series won four Emmy Awards and more than a dozen honors for children's programming and outstanding contributions in the service of wildlife conservation. Perkins proudly reports in his autobiography that 61 percent of the respondents in a Yale University study said that *Wild Kingdom* had had "a very strong or at least moderate influence" on their views of wild animals.

The first few shows were set in the studio with zoo animals. Then *Wild Kingdom* moved outdoors. To make the shows more interesting, strong young assistants Jim Fowler and Stan Brock lassoed, wrestled, and captured terrified wild animals on camera. Perkins and his team took their audiences to exotic locales such as West Africa, for its gorillas; the Kalahari Desert, for its hyenas and lions; South America, for its snakes and pink dolphins; and the Great Barrier Reef, for its sharks. At various times Perkins himself was bitten by venomous snakes, tossed by an elephant, and abandoned at sea while filming a pod of whales.

A 1966 *San Francisco Chronicle* review naïvely notes, "One of *Wild Kingdom's* admirable features is its honesty about its subject. This is nature as it is. . . . Perkins and Fowler are active participants in each episode, not merely narrators of wildlife films. They are *there*." Yet *Wild Kingdom* used extensive staging, with many of the animals filmed in enclosures and many of the "adventures" set up by the film crew. *Cruel Camera,* a 1983 documentary produced by the Canada-based Fifth Estate, accused the show not only of deceiving audiences with staging but also of animal cruelty. According to the documentary, *Wild Kingdom* producers placed a dead deer in an open area and then separately introduced captive wolves and cougars to the deer to make each animal think it owned the deer. Next the producers released the wolves and the cougars simultaneously to create a manufactured—and bloody—conflict.

In another *Wild Kingdom* episode, the audience was told that Perkins and his team had accidentally come across a wild black bear floundering in a Florida swamp. Actually, a captive bear had been dropped off by the team. Then Perkins and Fowler attempt to "save" this highly agitated bear to manufacture entertainment for the viewers. Another time, cougars were set upon a pig and an armadillo—all staged but dressed up for television to look natural. Indeed, *Wild Kingdom* animal handler Ted Gorsline says in *Cruel Camera* that faking wildlife footage is a "fundamental tool of the wildlife film industry."

At one point, the Emmy-winning host of *Cruel Camera,* Bob McKeown, boldly interviews Perkins on camera. At first, the questions are fairly innocuous. McKeown asks about the philosophy behind the show. "Well, the thing that I'm trying to do is to tell the animal's story," Perkins says. "The philosophy behind this is educational, primarily, as far as I'm concerned. We know that if you don't entertain a bit, and have something that people enjoy seeing, perhaps with a bit of action, the animals doing something special that holds their attention, then you wouldn't have the opportunity to tell their story."

McKeown then asks how it is possible to get such good footage. Perkins avoids any mention of staging. "Sometimes it takes weeks of photography in order to acquire the film that you see on the air," he says. On the unpredictability of wildlife, he adds, "That's a thing you cannot predetermine, and as a result we do not predetermine the exact script of any of our programs. We work exactly opposite from Hollywood."

McKeown gets tougher, noting that Roy Disney has told him that Disney, and most wildlife filmmakers, had to stage or fake scenes to get good footage. Perkins responds, "We try not to do that. Most of the footage that you see on *Wild Kingdom* is taken exactly where it was filmed, in the wild kingdom itself."

McKeown grows more insistent and skeptical: "With due respect, virtually everyone with whom we have spoken, from Roy Disney . . . on down, say fakery, even fraud, sometimes cruelty are everywhere in this business—and they said even in *Wild Kingdom*. Can I give you an example of what they say?"

An agitated Perkins snaps, "No, I would like not to have this on the air, and I would like to have you stop your camera right now, please." He then thrusts his hand into the camera lens. McKeown later told me that, after the camera was turned off, Perkins, then eighty-one, punched him angrily in the shoulder.

According to a 1986 *New York Times* article, WNYC-TV in New York City showed *Cruel Camera* once and then withdrew the show even though a second airing had been planned. Allegedly, someone connected with *Wild Kingdom* complained that *Cruel Camera* producers did not have the right to use footage from the series. The documentary never again aired in the United States.

Despite critics such as McKeown, Perkins always saw himself as ethical. He remained convinced that anything he did that someone else might construe as unethical was more than offset by the educational benefits of his shows. Undoubtedly he nurtured the public's interest in the natural world, and the fame he gained enabled him to become an advocate for the protection of endangered species. He writes, "The more I learned about animals, and the better I understood ecology . . . the more I realized the imbalance of habitats caused by man when he plowed the prairie, felled the forest, or drained the marsh." Like many in the filmmaking industry at the time—and even today—Perkins was full of contradictions.

Cousteau Brings Conservation to the Screen

By the 1960s, new faces were appearing in the world of wildlife television. One whose name became a household word was Jacques-Yves Cousteau. A world-renowned scientist, explorer, and ecologist who had worked as a spy for the French Navy during World War II, Cousteau co-invented the Aqua-Lung, a self-contained underwater breathing apparatus, today known as scuba. In 1950, Cousteau bought the *Calypso*, a former Royal Navy minesweeper, and converted it into an oceanographic vessel equipped for diving, filming, and research. To fund his trips and teach the public about the world's oceans and their inhabitants, Captain Cousteau produced films and television shows and wrote numerous books.

Cousteau's television series, *The Undersea World of Jacques Cousteau*, premiered on ABC television in 1967 and remained on the air for eight years. Earlier in the 1960s, the TV-watching public had been entranced by a couple of fictional series about undersea adventure: *Sea Hunt* and *Flipper*, so the time was ripe for Cousteau's deeper documentary approach. In any case, all these programs fed the public's hunger for more information about the sea—at that time still one of the last unexplored frontiers.

The *Undersea World* series was so highly regarded for both its educational merits and its entertainment value that Cousteau's formula of travelogue-cum–scientific documentary soon became the industry norm. Moreover, as he warned audiences that humans were poisoning the planet, the charismatic Cousteau himself became the first global environmental star. "Cousteau consecrated his life to teaching the world about marvels that are at once exotic to us and yet ordinary in the abyss of the ocean," said former vice president Al Gore. "Through his lyrical writings and his films that took your breath away, he placed the underwater world at the door of an audience as extensive as the oceans themselves."

As a passionate advocate, Cousteau did something that other leading wildlife filmmakers often neglected to do: he provided context. Viewers not only saw amazing footage of sea creatures but also learned about the sea itself and the threats to its inhabitants. In this way, his films were more real, and more rooted in a bigger picture of what was happening to the ecosystems on which we depend, than those of many of his contemporaries.

Stories occasionally circulated about Cousteau and his team harassing and killing sharks and other animals, but the only footage that depicts such activities is found in his early theatrical film *Silent World* (1956). According to Cousteau biographer Richard Munson, the filmmaker did this only when he was pressed for time and "couldn't wait for unprovoked drama." Cousteau's grandson, Philippe, vigorously defends his grandfather, declaring, "We cannot view past events through a modern lens. It was a different time then and in many respects they created the ethical standards as they went along. What they did in the 1950s was not something they would ever have dreamed of doing in later years as their understanding evolved."

I first met Cousteau in the mid-1970s when he came to Capitol Hill to lobby Senator Charles H. Percy about the perils of nuclear power. I was struck by his contagious enthusiasm, his wonderful sense of humor, and his passionate attacks on nuclear power, all delivered in his distinctive French accent. Whatever his ethical lapses may have been (and I think they were minor), he was a tireless and outspoken environmentalist who brought his passionate concerns for wildlife and wilderness not only into living rooms but also to world leaders.

BBC and the Blue-Chip Wildlife Film

Wildlife filmmaking got a fresh start in 1957 when the British Broadcasting Corporation (BBC) established its Natural History Unit. The unit has produced a great many innovative and popular natural history shows, including *Life on Earth* (1979), *The Living Planet* (1984), and *The Trials of Life* (1990), which came to define the highest-quality wildlife films. In these series, cinematographers often spent months, even years, tracking and filming animals. David Attenborough, a charming and enthusiastic zoologist and natural history expert, became the on-camera host.

Coauthored by Attenborough, *The Living Planet's* twelve episodes covered deserts, jungles, oceans, islands, grasslands, forests, and other ecological systems in an effort to depict animals in a broader context. The filming fell into three categories. The first featured Attenborough in front of the camera in an extraordinary variety of locations, including the Himalayas, the Amazon, Antarctica, and the Sahara. He swam with sharks, stuck his head into the nest of a great gray owl, and stood within a paw-stretch of a hibernating black bear. He also walked through Death Valley at noon, stood next to an active volcano, and hauled himself two hundred feet up into a giant kapok tree.

The second and most difficult type of filming took place with the animals themselves. Attenborough took little active part in these shoots, which were usually done without sound recording and dubbed during editing. For this work, the film crew was cut to a minimum, sometimes just a single cameraman.

The third type of filming involved "laboratory work," in which the subjects to be filmed, such as leaf-cutter ants or termites, were brought into a studio to be filmed under controlled conditions in specially created sets and tanks. "Reptiles, fish, and insects can be flown thousands of miles from their native habitat and encouraged to go about their normal business in the seclusion of a laboratory," writes journalist Andrew Langley.

In his 1985 book, *The Making of The Living Planet,* Langley states that the BBC developed more expertise in blue-chip natural history films than any other production entity in the world, citing its "high standards of production, the integrity of its attitudes, and the adventurous spirit of its projects." Those attributes, along with Attenborough's superb hosting skill, have won BBC wildlife documentaries every possible award, including many prestigious "Pandas" from the preeminent wildlife film festival, Wildscreen. The BBC's grand tradition of producing highly regarded and widely watched landmark wildlife television programming continued with *Life in the Underground* (2005), about terrestrial invertebrates; the stunning *Planet Earth* (2006), which we'll explore later; and *Life in Cold Blood* (2008), about reptiles and amphibians.

National Geographic Television: Education That Entertains

In 1963, the National Geographic Society started its first television production unit. Today National Geographic Television is renowned for its emphasis on education and its ability to combine interesting information with riveting storytelling, thus contributing to the positive wildlife filmmaking trend begun by the BBC's Natural History Unit. Typical of National Geographic's outstanding early work is a 1965 special about Jane Goodall's scientific research, *Miss Goodall and the Wild Chimpanzees*. Part of a larger series dealing with animal behavior, the film showcased the intelligence and deep emotional and social bonds of chimpanzees, which came across a lot like human beings. It didn't hurt that Goodall herself was so engaging and telegenic.

It was a time when a good program could easily draw a huge audience. There was no cable television and only a fledgling network for public broadcasting. Much of the country had only three commercial stations to choose from. On one evening in December 1965, fully one-third of American television viewers had their "consciousness raised about the nature and plight of wild chimpanzees, helped by the film's focus on its slender, young, blond protagonist," says communications professor and filmmaker Tom Veltre.

The BBC Natural History Unit and National Geographic Television became the first major players in the history of wildlife filmmaking to achieve a successful combination of entertainment and education without deliberately abusing or exploiting animals. By the end of the 1960s, the fabricated fights and other transgressions that were so prevalent in earlier decades of wildlife filmmaking seemed to be a thing of the past—or at least were far less visible. Filmmakers began to focus on nature's exquisite beauty, diversity, and fragility, and some even explicitly espoused conservation of the natural world. Producers and networks came to realize that, with the environmental movement blossoming, the public would no longer tolerate phony, staged wildlife films or those that involved abusing the creatures being filmed.

Marty Stouffer's *Wild America*

A couple of decades later, one influential filmmaker decided that all the beauty and sensitivity these high-end films were offering was a bit too precious. A handsome and muscular man with a bright smile and an obvious passion for nature, Marty Stouffer created a half-hour outdoor series, *Wild America,* that aired on PBS from 1982 to 1996. He claimed it was unlike any wildlife series ever seen before, thanks to its focus on the "sometimes shocking reality of life in the wild—including birth, death, mating, and predation." Stouffer's winning personality and great storytelling helped make *Wild America* an almost instant hit. But what set it apart from the other programs at the time was its engaging use of photography, employing slow-motion, time-lapse, telephoto, and close-up shots, as well as what Stouffer chose to point his cameras at, including animal sex and predation.

In its first years, each episode drew audiences of 3.5 million, and in some seasons, the show's high Nielsen ratings made it the number-one regularly scheduled series on public television. According to Stouffer, *TV Guide* called *Wild America* "the next best thing to being there," and the *Los Angeles Times* described it as "literally breathtaking." In 1997 Stouffer's early life story was featured in *Wild America: The Movie,* an action-adventure film starring teen idol Jonathan Taylor Thomas and produced by Steve Tisch of *Forrest Gump* fame.

Growing up in Fort Smith, Arkansas, Stouffer could experience wild America right outside (or, in some cases, inside) his front door.

His mother encouraged him and his siblings to know and understand not just their pets but also the nearby wildlife. The Stouffer family took orphaned birds and mammals into their home, including Leona the Owl, Foxy the Fox, and Stanley, a baby beaver who for months lived in the Stouffer bathtub. Stouffer's father taught him to hunt and track. Along with his two brothers, Stouffer created self-described "corny" home movies about their adventures and the animals they encountered.

When Stouffer was eighteen, he set out on a trip to Alaska with some friends, and when his friends went home, Stouffer stayed on for more adventure. Like many young men, Stouffer felt invincible and eager to explore the world. He writes in his memoir, "I had no idea that I would come close to not making it back."

Filming a colony of sea lions at Cape Chiniak, Stouffer was almost swept off a small island by a thirteen-foot-high tidal wave. Luckily, just before the powerful wave threw him into icy waters, a Coast Guard helicopter came to his rescue. Resolving to be more careful, he moved on to the remote valleys of Brooks Range to work as a carpenter for a hunting guide. But when an early snowstorm moved in, there was no room for Stouffer in the evacuation plane's first load. He spent the next fourteen freezing days in an unheated cabin waiting for the weather to improve enough so that the plane could come back for him. He survived by eating part of a Dall sheep ram he had hunted before the storm. Whatever people say about Stouffer, one thing is certain: he's a tough guy who feels at home in the wilderness.

When he got back home, Stouffer turned his crude Super-8mm footage into a film called *Alaska*. He got a microphone, set up movie screenings, and narrated at each showing. To his amazement, each show sold out completely, with about 1,800 people per showing. Surprised by the positive response to his amateur film, he decided to get back out in the wilderness with his camera.

He flew to Botswana to produce a film for a safari company—this time with a 16mm camera. While the lions, Cape buffalo, and elephants captivated him, he found their mass slaughter for camp meat and for trophies horrifying and sad. It was on this trip that Stouffer dedicated his career to creating films that would promote wildlife conservation. He also decided to focus his energies on American wildlife, which his Arkansas and Oklahoma audiences found more interesting. "In Africa I filmed death," he said. "I returned to America to film life."

Financial success is hard to come by in this business, and Stouffer struggled early in his career. He produced and marketed his films *Bighorn* and *At the Crossroads* to schools, libraries, and parks. He also sold photographs to magazines such as *National History, Audubon,* and *Reader's Digest.* In the mid-1970s, Stouffer and his brother, Mark, financed and coproduced the feature film *The Man Who Loved Bears,* narrated by Will Geer, and the NBC prime-time special *The Predators,* narrated by Robert Redford. Although they featured well-known actors and were warmly received by audiences, these films still did not make much money.

They did, however, make for some interesting experiences. While following a bighorn ewe, Stouffer found himself trapped on a narrow, icy ledge where a fall of a thousand feet seemed inevitable. He made it down after several hours, but his peril was for naught: the film he shot that day and hoped would reveal the life-and-death cycle among bighorns came back from the lab blank. In Alaska, Stouffer intruded on an ill-tempered sow grizzly as she fished for salmon along the McNeil River. As the bear eyed him with flattened ears, he reached for the pistol he was wearing, bandolier-style, in a holster slung over his shoulder. "She charged, and I slowly stepped backward while I wrestled with the pistol and holster tangled in the straps of my backpack," he recalls. "When I finally stopped, she stopped, too. Bears often charge for bluff, or to get a better look at what they're charging at. She sure got an eyeful of me."

Stouffer's big break came in 1981 when PBS accepted his proposal for *Wild America.* After months of last-minute filming and frantic editing, the show began airing in autumn 1982. "I try to do things that haven't been done before," says Stouffer. "Until we started breaking the rule many years ago, sex was literally taboo. Then we went in for close-ups." Stouffer broke the rules with gusto. In the *Wild America* episode

"Hog Wild!" viewers saw that a wild boar's penis is corkscrew-shaped, and in "All-American Animals" they learned that a male opossum's genital is forked.

Several years ago, Stouffer proudly displayed "Hog Wild!" at a British wildlife film symposium. The program showed a boar ripping apart a hunting dog with its razor-sharp tusks. The audience was not amused. "Not only do British commoners not hunt, they dearly love their dogs," says Stouffer. "They were booing, yelling, and shaking their fists. They said it was too bloody, too confrontational. I'm sorry, but that's the story of wild hogs down in Georgia. Their lives are violent, they are bloody. When a hunter chases a hog with a dog you get a confrontation, and we were blamed for filming it as documentation of reality."

Close-up looks at predation, sometimes in slow motion, were another hallmark of *Wild America*. "I've always related to wildlife in practical and even brutal terms," says Stouffer. "They're out there killing and dying; 85 percent of rabbits die in their first year. It's not hearts and flowers. It's not Walt Disney." Stouffer's methods came under highly critical scrutiny later in his career (see Chapter 6), but there's no doubt that he set the stage for today's "in your face" school of wildlife filmmakers.

PBS, Discovery, and Animal Planet

Stouffer was at the leading edge of a boom in wildlife television. A year after *Wild America* debuted in 1982, the hour-long Sunday night program *Nature* was launched on PBS to great public acclaim. In 1985, the Discovery Channel came along, and in 1996 Discovery's sister network, Animal Planet, was born. Never before had so much prime-time TV been devoted to wildlife. The rise of the miniseries had accustomed audiences to multi-episode programming, so that in the case of nature shows, filmmakers could delve more deeply into a subject than would be possible in a single program or even a feature film. The proliferation of environmental and animal rights groups had boosted interest in the genre and, at least for a time, raised the industry's ethical standards.

As standards rose, though, pressures to use unethical tactics actually increased. Marty Stouffer's troubles in the mid-1990s were symptomatic of struggles throughout the industry to produce films that attracted big audiences without selling out to sensationalism.

And those pressures have only increased. Wildlife film producers seek not only dedicated nature enthusiasts but also the restless reality TV crowd. The former might still be satisfied with watching a humpback whale breach or lions relax on the African savannah, but not the latter. As many producers see it, the public has seen so much that well-behaved wildlife films no longer cut it.

So the industry has come full circle in at least one sense. The personality-driven work of the Johnsons, Buck, and Perkins, which led to ethical lapses, was supplanted by people like Cousteau and Attenborough, who moved the industry forward and showed that even the most charismatic hosts could let wildlife take center stage. But today's celebrities seem to be pushing the real stars aside again. In the next few chapters, I'll examine the modern money game and the worst of the current ethical lapses.

But first let's go behind the camera to learn more about how contemporary wildlife films are made. From pitch meeting to distribution, the business has much in common with other kinds of moviemaking and also poses challenges all its own.

3

BEHIND THE CAMERA
How Wildlife Films Are Made

In 1996, I commissioned film producer Larry Engel to make a National Wildlife Federation film called *Wildlife Vets*. Engel was to follow wildlife veterinarian David Jessup as he globe-trotted the world as a wildlife biologist for the state of California. One assignment sent Jessup to Africa to look into the causes of a horrible disease that was afflicting female elephants along the shores of Lake Zimbabwe. These elephants slowly lost their ability to hold things with their trunks, hence the name "floppy-trunk syndrome." As the disease progressed, the suffering elephants could no longer forage and eventually starved to death, the process of decline sometimes taking a year or more. African vets would shoot the debilitated animals well before the end to stop the suffering. Jessup helped mount an international effort to examine the animals in order to gain a better understanding of the disease.

"We all worked fast and efficiently," Engel recalls. "Part of our concern was that when filmmakers are around, the work tends to slow down. Elephants are really big creatures. They do not naturally spend much time lying on the ground, for a good reason—if they spend too much time on their sides, the weight of their bodies will start to kill internal organs. As adults, elephants stay on their feet even when they rest or sleep. An animal on its side is an animal in jeopardy. With the first patient, everything went fine. They tranquilized the elephant to perform a biopsy and fit it with a radio collar. The film's host, actor Alicia Silverstone, participated; the vets and helpers worked as quickly as possible. When an antidote to the tranquilizer was injected into a vein in the elephant's ear, she quickly rose. "We ran from her as she awakened and rolled awkwardly to her feet," says Engel. "Shaking her head a few times, staggering on all four legs until she regained her balance—and looking ominously in our direction—she finally trotted off to rejoin her herd, bellowing along the way."

Near sunset, however, a second ailing elephant had been down for more than half an hour while the vets and Silverstone worked on her. She was given a dose of the antidote and responded by shaking her head and trying to roll but couldn't regain her footing. Instead, she just lay there with her eyes open.

The vets waited patiently for the antidote to take effect fully, but nothing happened. Then they yelled at her until they were hoarse and slapped her on the rump until their hands hurt, but the elephant did not respond. She remained in a stupor. Silverstone retreated to the Land Rover, staring at the unfolding scene with one hand over her mouth in disbelief. Engel kept filming.

The vets decided to take more drastic action. They tried to drag the elephant into an upright position by looping ropes around her tusks and tying them to one of the trucks. But, even in four-wheel drive, the truck did not have the horsepower to lift an elephant. She had been down now for almost an hour, and hope was rapidly slipping away.

"Toward the end, I was thinking that we, or I, had become responsible for this sick animal and that we had killed it," Engel recounts. "In our zeal to film another darting and exam, perhaps our decision-making had become clouded. If the camera were not there, perhaps the vets would not have chosen to do the procedure, realizing that the disease had weakened the elephant too much. I kept saying to myself, 'I have never killed an animal before; this is not what we're supposed to be filming.'"

Jessup decided to administer one final dose of antidote and enlist everyone to push the elephant up—a dangerous gamble. The extra dose could kill her. Or, if she awoke and rose to her feet quickly, she might charge her would-be helpers out of frustration, fear, and anger; Engel, Jessup, Silverstone, and the whole team might not have a chance to escape. Seeing no alternative, the vet injected the second antidote and the group pushed mightily. Even the assistant cameraman stepped to the other side of the camera to help. It was all hands on deck. Trying to right an animal that weighs so much is no easy task, but for some reason, she responded to the touch of her rescuers.

"The elephant shook her head," says Engel, "struggling to get to her feet. But she couldn't get up. We all had tears in our eyes. We were screaming, begging, praying. Then, miraculously—nearly an hour after being sedated and after she probably should have died—she got to her feet. Everyone ran back to the Land Rovers, afraid that she might still attack." Staggering on all fours, the elephant regained her balance and bearings as the crew cheered her on. She sniffed the air and bellowed, then slowly turned her back on her human friends and walked off into the dusk. Engel adds, "We named her Lazarus because she came back from the dead."

The ability to tell a compelling story—in the way that Engel told me the story about Lazarus the elephant—is crucial to filmmaking. But a good story is just the beginning. Every successful wildlife film also needs the leadership of an impassioned producer; money and staff; scientific expertise; careful scouting; bold, resourceful, and most of all patient cinematographers; some post-production magic; and a marketing and distribution plan that will deliver the masterpiece to an appropriate audience. It's a grand adventure, really, and this chapter outlines its key components and challenges.

Shaping the Story

Choosing a film's subject matter and building a story around it is at the heart of the endeavor, and many factors come into play. These start (one hopes) with the filmmaker's passion but include such considerations as resources, audience tastes, funders' preferences, and much more. Will the film or program focus on one kind of animal, on a special place inhabited by a range of fascinating creatures, on an urgent conservation crisis, or on humans interacting with animals in some way? If just one animal, what kind? Audiences are perennially fascinated by the "charismatic megafauna": bears, wolves, whales, sharks, and elephants. Reptiles such as crocodiles and snakes have become popular subjects for different reasons, in part through the efforts of on-air presenters such as Steve Irwin. Among filmmakers and broadcasters, birds and fish are not generally seen as attracting wide audiences, although shows about these creatures occasionally hit it big.

What finally reaches the screen is driven chiefly by money and ratings, so the more popular animals tend to appear again and again. But another factor determining the choice of subject matter is the background of the producer or cinematographer. Filmmakers who start out as divers naturally gravitate toward featuring marine life in their films. Filmmakers from other backgrounds—whether biologists, photographers, animal welfare advocates, or conservationists—all start with preconceived notions of what their films should focus on.

Whatever the subject matter, it needs to be shaped into a story. A good story can make sense of confusing information. It can change our understanding of the world, giving us new insights into our own lives and the lives of other beings. Telling a story about wildlife can deepen our awareness of nature and the need to protect and conserve it. To do all that, a story often needs a hero.

"Hero stories" feature brave souls who undertake difficult and dangerous tasks. They courageously struggle against the odds despite their fears or failings. The "hero's journey" in simplified form has three phases: (1) seizing an opportunity, (2) facing a challenge, and (3) achieving victory. It's usually a tale of human endeavor, but animals can play leading roles too. When filmmaker David Clark and I made the IMAX film *Whales* (1996), for example, we cast humpbacks as heroes; the opportunity they seize is a perilous three-thousand-mile migration from Hawaii to Alaska.

During the second phase of the journey, facing a challenge, the hero confronts a variety of intimidating, even frightening, obstacles. Defeats and setbacks happen again and again. There might be some supreme ordeal—physical, emotional, spiritual, or psychological—in which the hero's life is in jeopardy. In *Whales,* the migrating humpbacks are threatened by killer whales, fishing boats with drift nets, and big ocean vessels.

In the final phase, achieving victory, the hero succeeds. In *Whales,* that meant that a humpback mother, Misty, and her daughter, Echo, arrived safely at their feeding grounds after swimming thousands of miles. What constitutes "success" in these stories can vary greatly. A human hero may win conventional battles or look inward to overcome personal flaws, conquer self-doubts, or find new opportunities. For an animal hero, victory may mean simply surviving to reproduce, rejoin its kind, or reach the goal of a migration. But in all cases the hero's journey has a beginning, middle, and end. It has compelling characters, rising tension, and conflicts that reach a resolution or denouement of some kind. The story engages its audience on an intellectual and emotional level, making us want to know what happens next at every juncture. This is the essence of a great story—and what a producer searches for when planning a film.

Bill Grant, executive in charge of production for the long-running *Nature* series on PBS, says, "Wildlife filmmaking requires great photography. Everybody knows that. But what is less well known, sadly even to some in the industry, is that a great film comes from a great story. Many are the wildlife films that fail because the pictures are grand but they don't add up to anything. Good stories, well told, are the foundations of all great films of whatever genre." Brian Leith, executive producer in the BBC Natural History Unit, adds, "If you can tell a strong story, then you're already halfway to a strong program. There's a common misconception about movies and television programs that they're all about visually dramatic images, shots, and sequences. To a far greater extent they're about telling a simple, engaging story."

Providing Leadership

The linchpin in the filmmaking process is the producer, who typically handles a variety of roles on a project and possesses a wide range of skills—starting with the ability to spot and develop a great story. The producer's first and ongoing task is to communicate the essential worth and promise of a film project to all who will ultimately be involved with it. So, long before anyone treks off into the wilderness with a camera, producers create a "film treatment," a vision of the final film that colleagues can embrace—and use to pitch the idea to potential funders. An effective treatment explains the purpose and content of the film in detail. It describes who the hero is and what trials that person (or animal) might face. It also includes critical details that make the story come alive.

Ranging in length from one page to more than fifty, a typical treatment begins by describing the "tease," the one or two minutes of a film that precede the titles. One of filmmaker Adam Ravetch's teases showed a mother walrus embracing her infant just as humans do. In highlighting this scene, he wasn't promising viewers that they would see a bunch of hugging walruses if they watched the entire film. He was suggesting that they would learn more amazing things about an animal they knew little about.

"Writing a treatment is a way to envision the program and its structure," explains filmmaker Peter Argentine. "It allows you to share your creative vision with the cinematographer, animator, production manager, editors, and other crew so that they can begin to contribute to that vision. And writing the treatment will force you to think through the elements of production—is a special rig required, a second unit, aerials, or a creative shot to bridge to the next scene?"

Next comes the "pitch," which is essentially a conversation—warm, inviting, and engaging—in which the producer conveys his film concept clearly and concisely to potential funders, who may range from broadcasters to foundation executives to wealthy individuals. The producer must be ready to discuss budgets, talent, logistics, characters, story, and other important issues, but if the pitch doesn't capture a funder's interest within the first couple of minutes, the meeting is over.

If the pitch is successful, some funding or other resources are made available so that the producer can begin to scout locations, find on-camera talent, hire crews, deepen the research, and consult relevant experts. Producers also obtain permits and permissions, make a "shot list" (an inventory of the graphic elements needed to tell the story), and decide whether controversies associated with the topic represent a risk or an opportunity. (Controversy can generate media coverage, but it can also scare away advertisers and sponsors.)

Even after all this preliminary work, a project can get stalled in what's known as "development hell"—sometimes fatally. Studio executives may be afraid to take a risk, or their perception of what will engage an audience may change. But when things go well, the project will at last be formally greenlighted by an executive producer for a network or film studio. Then, when the time is right, producers send cinematographers into the field for principal photography, followed by post-production work and marketing campaigns. More on those phases below.

A producer needs strong nerves in addition to creative and business skills, but above all, producers must believe in the mission of the film. Does the topic addressed by the film justify the faith of the funders and the incredible amount of hard work required to make it? Filmmaker David Clark asserts, "There are many factors that come into play in producing a successful film, but surely one of the most critical is the justification for the film's genesis. You have to ask yourself, is the film's subject truly compelling, novel, or approached in some new and innovative way? The ultimate success all goes back to the power, relevance, and poignancy of your topic."

A producer doesn't necessarily do all the jobs described above. For example, a network such as the National Geographic Channel may do the promotion, outreach, distribution, and financing. There are different kinds of producers, too. Some specialize in field production, post-production, or marketing. But whatever their exact responsibilities, producers typically provide leadership, passion, vision, and resources. They act as the driving force behind the film.

Hiring and Hustling

One of the most important responsibilities of a producer is to raise money. Without money, a film can't get made. Or, if less money is raised than budgeted, the producer and crew might be forced to slash their fees, reduce the number of shooting days, drop one or more shoot locations, or make some other budget cuts. Sources of funding vary; some inexpensive films are funded by the producer or by his or her relatives. More expensive films, perhaps targeted for Discovery or the National Geographic Channel, are funded by a combination of license fees (from a distributor or network), wealthy donors, foundations, or corporate sponsors. We'll talk more about raising money and the role money plays in wildlife filmmaking in the next chapter.

Once the project's coffers are filled, the producer can start hiring writers, cinematographers, sound recordists, editors, and so on. Some of these jobs may be done by the same person; indeed, some producers wear all these hats at once. For example, it isn't uncommon for independent filmmakers such as Larry Engel to act as producer, director, cinematographer, and writer all on the same film. Of course, a film will almost always benefit from different creative minds tackling the same issue, and independent filmmakers often prefer to bring others on board when it is practical to do so.

In many cases, the producer is also responsible for finding the show's Marlin Perkins or David Attenborough or Alicia Silverstone—its "on-camera talent"—to host or narrate the film. This might be someone who is a wildlife expert but unknown to the general public, but often producers seek a celebrity's glamour and cachet. In other cases, especially when a narrator is not used, the producer must find strong human characters around whom to build a story. In today's competitive market, casting is becoming an increasingly important part of the pre-production process.

Working with Scientists

An uneasy partnership exists between scientists and filmmakers. Filmmakers need scientists, especially field biologists who know where and when to find wildlife at particular locations. And scientists need filmmakers to tell the public about their work. (See Jane Goodall's illuminating observations on this subject in her foreword.)

But sometimes filmmakers ask too much of scientists. In 1999 Greg Skomal, a shark biologist with the Massachusetts Division of Marine

Fisheries, worked with a novice field producer on a natural history documentary in the Arctic. The producer wanted to take footage that required Skomal to dive through a hole in the Arctic ice into 29-degree water over and over again. Ice diving, explains Skomal, "is dangerous, cold, and less than fun. After four takes of this one scene, I was so cold that I collapsed on the ice and froze in the fetal position. My scientific colleague slid me into the tent to defrost, and I was useless for the balance of the day." Jeff Carrier, a biology professor at Michigan's Albion College, specializes in shark mating behavior. He remembers once observing the most incredible shark behavior he had ever seen in hundreds of encounters—and then being told by a filmmaker that "the lighting wasn't just right and could we try and position these nine-foot sharks just a bit differently the next time."

Scientists have their own blind spots—often related to not understanding what it takes to produce entertaining and informative footage. But a patient filmmaker can work around those problems. In the 1980s, I commissioned producer and cinematographer Wolfgang Obst to make a film about the California condor, a type of vulture. The largest flying birds in the world, these condors once ranged over a large part of the continent. At the time, though, only six birds remained in the wild. Eleven had been captured in the rugged hills of central California and added to a risky captive breeding program, a last-ditch attempt to keep the species from extinction. The careers of the condor biologists in charge of the program were on the line. And then Obst showed up to tag along and document the outcome. In the eyes of condor biologists, he was an unnecessary nuisance. The last thing they wanted was to see themselves on national television engaged in a multimillion-dollar endangered species recovery program that might end in failure. Obst says it was one of the most difficult films he ever made.

Months passed before the biologists trusted Obst enough to let him have his own blind (a crude shelter designed to conceal the observer). And then the hard work began. By 10:00 A.M., the blind was as hot as an oven. Outside, a dead animal (provided to attract the condors) stank of decayed flesh and attracted throngs of flies. On a successful day, the carcass drew ravens first, signaling to other birds that the feeding site was safe. If Obst arrived late, he scared off the ravens, and nothing else landed on the carcass for the rest of the day. After the ravens, turkey vultures came and quarreled with the ravens, which in turn lured golden eagles to descend for their share of the rotting flesh. Ravens, turkey vultures, and eagles fighting each other set the stage for condors to arrive. Gliding down on their vast wings, they squabbled with the eagles and then fed nervously, ready to take off if something didn't look right.

Obst said that most days "were boredom and suffering to the point of torture. From the hole in my blind, I watched months go by and seasons change. By the time nesting season came around, I had proved to the scientists in the condor recovery team that I could be discreet and stoic in the face of hardship."

As the condor scientists gained confidence in Obst, they allowed him to film biologists taking eggs from a nest on a 300-foot cliff. On the day he was to do that, he had to wait for the mother condor to fly away from the cave where the nest was hidden, and then climb down to it. When he reached the cave, a rock broke underfoot, and he almost plunged to his death. Heart pounding, he somehow managed to scramble into the cave, where he captured good footage of the whole egg-gathering process.

One sign of a good producer is that he or she forms positive, lasting relationships with researchers and is able to approach them with ease during a project as well as after its completion. David Clark and Al Giddings made films for both the giant IMAX screen and Discovery Channel by working closely with whale scientists Mark and Debbie Ferrari in Hawaii and marine mammal biologist Fred Sharpe in Alaska. "It was a mutually rewarding experience," Clark says. "We got great footage, the scientists and their work became an integral part of the films, and compensation for their involvement in the film helped support their research."

When Clark and Giddings produced a big-budget, ninety-minute special for Discovery Channel about the Galápagos Islands, they chartered a 280-foot research boat plus a small submersible and collaborated with several marine biologists. The film enabled the scientists to go to the Galápagos and, for the first time, do research supported by a manned underwater craft. "Here was a situation where the film initiated a research opportunity," Clark says.

Filmmakers Mark Deeble and Vicky Stone have spent years living alongside field biologists in the Serengeti. These scientists are passionate about their work and wary of anything that might interfere with it. Deeble and Stone have found that "most scientists would be happy to work with filmmakers" as long as they believe that the filmmakers respect their work and will publicize it in a measured and fair way.

Scouting

Identifying locations for principal photography is fundamental to any film about animals and their habitats, so this is a critical early phase. Scouting is, in part, a money-saving maneuver, because once a film crew is on location, expenses start escalating fast. It's costly to discover that the noise from a nearby airport makes sound recording impossible, or that the local authorities refuse to grant permission to film at a key location. For this reason the producer or cinematographer must visit potential shooting locations and search for new ones, usually without a video camera, and check things out ahead of time. Money for scouting is not always readily available, so some producers find it well worth the extra time spent doing research on the phone, or they might hire other producers who live near locations of interest.

One summer Hardy Jones and I went to Tahiti to explore the possibility of making a television documentary on spinner dolphins. We dispatched a small plane to scan the surrounding waters for the elusive creatures we hoped to film, while Jones, my sixteen-year-old daughter, Christina, and I waited on a boat with a few friends. But the plane found nothing.

After an hour or so of motoring aimlessly into deeper and deeper water, we heard a barely decipherable voice crackling over the two-way radio. The plane had spotted an oceanic Serengeti—an area teeming with marine life—just a few miles away. We made a beeline for the area and found plenty of dolphins and whales, as well as sharks looking for opportunities to feed. Five of us, excited but wary, put on snorkeling gear and slipped into the water. The sea clamored with moans, clicks, and whistles—a cacophony of aquatic mammals.

Eventually Christina, who kept a worried eye out for sharks, mustered her courage and lowered herself into the water with me on one side and my friend Allen Guisinger on the other. We were trying to protect her, but the truth was that neither of us had the slightest notion how to fend off an attacking shark.

Christina grasped our arms tightly, but after a while, she eased her grip and used her underwater camera to snap photos of the amazing scene beneath us. At this point, I took a deep breath and dove below Christina so she could take a picture of me surrounded by all those magnificent singing creatures. Down I went, holding my breath as long as I could before heading back to the surface with my lungs almost bursting.

That's when I heard the screams of "Shark! Shark!" I looked around for Christina, but she was nowhere in sight. I raced back to the boat. To my great relief, I found her in one piece but badly shaken. Right after I dove down, an oceanic whitetip shark, one of the few shark species with a deserved reputation for being dangerous, sped right up to her and stopped just a few feet away. Choking down panic, Christina had swum back to the safety of the boat as quickly as possible.

Despite the scare—for which my wife still hasn't forgiven me—our scouting mission to Tahiti ended successfully. We met some local people who could handle logistics for our film, and we learned which locations would give us the most dramatic footage. Most important, we gained a better understanding of where to find spinner dolphins, which scientists were best, and which local characters could add color and interest to the story.

The Elements of Principal Photography

When the general public thinks of wildlife filmmaking, the principal photography stage is usually what comes to mind. Thorough preparation is crucial, because principal photography is the most expensive part of making a film, and careless or superficial preparation could result in a financial disaster. Typically, a producer calculates how many days of shooting are required to get all the footage called for in the script—that could be 5 days or 150 days or even more. Then the production team figures out equipment and crew needs, including sound and lighting, and works all this into the budget. Wise producers add a hefty contingency amount, ideally 20 percent, to allow for the inevitable foul-ups and setbacks.

For wildlife films, preparing for principal photography is particularly challenging because no one knows exactly what will happen. Will the animals show up? Will the weather cooperate? Will the cameras function properly in, for example, a humid and hot tropical forest?

Producer Michele Hall says, "We make our wildlife documentaries in remote areas, so planning ahead is vital. By remote I mean that at minimum, we're living aboard a boat at sea. And those boats are often in isolated parts of the world. So when we're on location we must plan on getting by with what we have with us, because there's no camera shop, hardware or electronics store down the street; no FedEx or UPS delivery service; and access to the closest airport may be days away." If she and her crew are to have any hope of a successful filming expedition, they must think through every aspect of the shoot before leaving, including writing a shooting script, planning the budget, hiring the best divers and assistants, contracting with the most appropriate boat, scheduling to be on location during the right time of year, obtaining work visas and permits, and anticipating what they'll be filming so that they have the necessary equipment and supplies.

When filming abroad, a film producer usually has a "fixer." This is a reliable local contact who is familiar with the customs and the key players, and knows how to get what the film crew needs. For example, if a producer or crew member gets stuck in customs because of a missing visa, the fixer is there to contact the appropriate embassy for assistance. The fixer should be able to move the producer to the front of the line in bureaucratic matters, get permission from key officials, and generally solve problems that threaten the viability of the shoot.

Preparations for principal photography may also include clever construction work. In the process of making *Whales*, my colleague David Clark built an underwater framework from which to film dolphins as they swam off the bow of our sailboat. He also built an elaborate boom that swung twenty feet off the side of the boat so the cameraman could film straight down on whales; this allowed the crew to follow whales without disturbing them or running them over. Both rigs captured extraordinary footage. Underwater cameramen such as Al Giddings and Howard Hall constantly create new housings and devices to unobtrusively get their cameras closer to the creatures.

Good preparations are essential, but nature films can't be completely scripted. A producer must always be ready for surprises, which often turn into the most magical moments in a film. While working on *Whales* in Alaska, Clark was motoring in a sailboat with our cinematographer, Andy Kitzanuk. Holding the IMAX camera high up the mast, Kitzanuk was looking for whales arriving from their long migration. "Suddenly," recalls Clark, "a large humpback appeared and starting surfing on the bow wake of our boat, as dolphins often do. But instead of a 300-pound dolphin, it was a 10-ton whale! He stayed with us for hours and we shot the heck out of it." Whale biologist and codirector Roger Payne said he had never seen such behavior in his thirty-plus years of whale research, and it became one of the high points in the film.

When film producer Katie Carpenter was filming in Sri Lanka for *A Year on Earth* (2006), she and her crew had planned to go to a wildlife refuge where their local fixer had said there were plenty of elephants. But, as it turned out, human conflicts with elephants were on the rise and many elephants had been killed or injured. So the crew changed its plans, making the elephants' plight part of their story, and ended up filming in an elephant orphanage instead. As Carpenter notes, "It's best to be nimble and adaptable to changing conditions."

Of course it's easier to be adaptable if you have a big budget and plenty of time. BBC producer Vanessa Berlowitz waited weeks before her crew obtained rare footage of a snow leopard in Nepal. When David Clark made the IMAX film *Galápagos 3D,* he and his crew were almost undone when the water-warming effects of El Niño caused much of the wildlife they wanted to film, such as marine iguanas and hammerhead sharks, to depart the region in search of cooler temperatures. They had to juggle the budget to allow the crew to return to the Galápagos for a second time to obtain the footage they needed.

Early in his career, filmmaker Marty Stouffer decided to focus his lenses on bighorn sheep. After he spent three months working to be "accepted" by the sheep in Glacier National Park, the animals finally let him get close. He even got a ram to lick some salt off his hand and captured what was then unusual footage of two rams fighting. Those few minutes of footage cost him three months, but he had no regrets. He had earned a strong connection to the sheep, their history, and the "natural arc of their lives." Stouffer also tried to get footage of ewes giving birth, but after weeks of trying, he concluded that "maybe some things are not meant to be filmed."

Waiting around is especially difficult for marine wildlife photographers. In many cases, they have to work at depth in cold water, with a finite air supply. But having an understanding of animal behavior can help get them to the right place at the right time.

In 2005, Tom Campbell worked off the dive boat MV *Chertan* in Milne Bay, Papua New Guinea. Toward the end of a dive in about forty feet of water, he saw two scorpionfish facing each other a few inches apart, quivering strangely. Surfacing, he described the behavior to the boat's captain, who explained that such face-offs often end up with the scorpionfish viciously attacking each other in a territorial battle. The fish lock jaws while tumbling over the ocean bottom, hanging on, often for long periods of time. Campbell thought that sounded like a potentially exciting film sequence, so he swam back to the location.

When he discovered the two scorpionfish still facing each other and quivering, Campbell thought, "This could be really great, and my timing is perfect!" The water temperature was a fairly comfortable 75 degrees. But thirty minutes later he was still lying on the sandy bottom, with the shot perfectly framed and in tack-sharp focus, waiting to press the record button. He waited. And he waited. And he waited some more.

He was getting cold and bored, but he was more determined than ever to get the shot.

Nearly two hours passed. He was now freezing and hungry. His camera battery was running out, his whole body was shivering, and he was low on air and facing decompression issues from being down for nearly two hours. He knew he had only moments to go before he would have to abandon his mission.

Suddenly the two fish made a spectacular lunge, grabbing one another by their jaws, biting as hard as they could while somersaulting over the ocean bottom. With his fingers shivering, he tracked them carefully, recording more than a minute of the action before the battery finally died. Although cold and low on air, he was elated to have captured a spectacular sequence with no staging, manipulation, or interference.

Cinematographers who don't have the luxury of time can sometimes get by with discipline—and a little luck. Early in my time at Audubon, I hired Bill VanDerKloot, a seasoned cinematographer and producer, to shoot a segment on grizzly bears. He and his crew knew things were not going to go well the moment they arrived in Bozeman, Montana, on their way to Yellowstone National Park. As they entered the airport terminal, they spotted a headline on a local newspaper: "Woman Eaten by Grizzly." This was unwelcome news at any time, of course, but even more ominous when you're planning to ask park rangers to escort you into the far recesses of Yellowstone. They arrived at the park to find that it was locked down; no one was going to be allowed into the backcountry until the offending bear was killed.

VanDerKloot and his crew were devastated. They would now have to try to film grizzlies from the park's main road, like a bunch of tourists. The tight budget allowed only four days in Yellowstone. There was no money to spare, and VanDerKloot needed to be in Alaska for another shoot by the coming weekend. Something had to be done quickly or the film would fail.

They searched for bears along trails still open to the public. Each morning they crawled out of bed at 4:00 A.M. and drove to key locations before dawn. They moved slowly along the main road, periodically stopping to search across the vast rolling landscape with binoculars. They worked until sunset, without reward. Day one—no bears. Day two—no bears. Day three—no bears.

When day four dawned, thousands of precious dollars had been spent, with nothing to show for it. VanDerKloot wasn't eager to go home empty-handed, and I obviously didn't want to tell Russ Peterson, my boss and the president of Audubon, that the shoot had been an abysmal failure.

Then luck kicked in. As VanDerKloot and his crew rounded a curve in the Lamar Valley, a prime wildlife viewing area, they spotted two large grizzly bears ambling up a small hill. Ahead, a small dirt road veered off in the direction the bears were taking. VanDerKloot had no idea where that road led, but he and his crew decided to take it, hoping that it would wind around the hill and allow them to film the grizzlies up close.

VanDerKloot and his crew followed the road around the hill, and sure enough, the bears were walking straight toward them. "I set up the camera, and my team kept the car engine running with the doors open so we could make a quick getaway," VanDerKloot recalls. "As I watched through the viewfinder, the bears got closer and closer. They must have weighed seven or eight hundred pounds each. The two big grizzlies completely ignored us and continued scratching for whatever food they could find on the ground. At one point they got within twenty yards of the camera. After eating and foraging for another ten minutes or so, they lazily walked away over the hill. I got all the footage we needed."

When a Shoot Goes Wrong

Every crew that's ever shot a nature film has suffered through shy or menacing wildlife, illness, injury, bad weather, and broken equipment—not to mention car accidents, dangerous roads, unstable boats, and marginal helicopters. On one expedition, National Geographic host Brady Barr picked up some parasites that ate into his brain; he needed chemotherapy to get rid of them. A hippo bit entirely through filmmaker Alan Root's calf as he was filming in Kenya. Underwater cinematographer

Al Giddings has suffered embolisms, punctured eardrums, and a damaged lung. Howard Hall once swam up to three blissfully cuddling gray whales, but his visit was unappreciated. One male struck him with his tail fluke, breaking two of Hall's ribs and his left arm.

The catalog of perils is limitless. In 1986, a charging black rhino mother severely gored wildlife expert Terry Mathews while he was filming an ABC television special on African wildlife. He was tossed into the air like a rag doll and badly injured. A bull shark severely bit scientist and presenter Erich Ritter in the calf when he was filming with biologist and on-camera host Nigel Marven. Filmmaker Doug Allan had a scary wildlife encounter in the Canadian Arctic: "I was snorkeling off the ice edge when a walrus grabbed me. It came up from directly below and grabbed my thighs with its flippers. I hit its head with my fists and it let go. It had gone for me exactly the same way they sometimes attack seals, and if it had held on rather than releasing me, well. . . . "

Not finding wildlife can be fatal to a wildlife film, unless the filmmakers can be patient and adaptable. When Howard and Michele Hall set out to make the IMAX film *Island of the Sharks,* they planned to photograph hammerhead sharks at Cocos Island, off the coast of Costa Rica. When they had scouted the island several months before the shoot, they saw hammerhead sharks on virtually every dive. What they didn't anticipate, however, was that they would be filming during one of the worst El Niño events in recorded meteorological history. The warm water from El Niño forced the sharks down to the cooler waters, so the Halls did not see a single hammerhead shark during the first eight months of the shoot. They considered changing the film's name to *Island of the Goatfish*—a creature that was all too plentiful in the area. But sometimes you can make lemonade: when they returned to Cocos for their fourth (of five) filming expeditions, the water had cooled off, the sharks had returned, and they started filming. As an added bonus for their patience, they now had a story enriched by the drama of El Niño.

Weather often figures prominently in these stories. National Park Service filmmaker Charles Dunkerly was once shooting at Mount Rushmore National Memorial in South Dakota. The crew members made it to the top of the famed presidential sculpture, where they set up four cameras and got them rolling. No one noticed the wind picking up. Suddenly one of the cameras was blown off the mountain and cascaded down, ending up totally out of reach. A climbing team had to be brought in to rescue the equipment.

In 1986 I hired Wolfgang Obst to make a film on the Everglades. It was early summer, and every afternoon an intense thunderstorm would break over a colony of wood storks and egrets nesting in trees in a fifty-acre lake. Full-grown birds were blown off their perches, and hatchlings clung desperately to their nests. Some were violently thrown into the water below, where alligators gathered to snap them up.

Obst decided he wanted to feature one of those storms in a segment of his film. He had great shots of a storm approaching—lightning, wind, rain, and branches lashing about—but he wanted more. He decided to position himself on the lake in his small flat-bottomed aluminum boat, which had an unimpressive outboard motor. After securing a tripod with his expensive camera in the middle of the boat and rigging a plastic drop cloth over it, he had a floating tent. He presumed that when the storm hit, the rain would run off the plastic and into the lake. Thus prepared, he drifted through the trees, waiting for the storm to come.

Obst vividly remembers the scene: "I filmed the clouds building up. Tremendous towers of cumulus clouds moved in front of the sun, and it became very dark. There was apprehension in the air, but, under my plastic tent, humming to myself and winding through the trees, I didn't notice it. I was preoccupied with checking my focus and exposure, thinking about composition, and how the footage I was about to get would cut in well with other footage I already had.

"I was not prepared for what happened next. The storm started with a blinding flash of light and a deafening explosion. Then the rain hit like a ton of bricks. My little tent folded instantly, like it was made of paper. The shallow aluminum boat filled with water. The alligators came closer, thinking I was in the same league as the birds that fell from their nests. But what really started to scare me was the fact that I was sitting in an aluminum boat with lightning striking all around me."

The sad remnants of Obst's clever idea slowly began to sink. Sputtering along at the tiny engine's full throttle while bailing water madly, he raced for shore, trailed by hopeful alligators. He made it back safely, but took home only thirty seconds of footage.

Even if a film crew has good weather, there are other things to worry about—equipment failures being high on the list. Filmmaker and author Julia Whitty was one of the first people (along with her then husband Hardy Jones) to swim safely with sperm whales, despite their fearsome reputations. Whitty knew that when a boat sinks, survivors in the water are often pulled down by the ship's wake, and she had often wondered what would happen if a person were directly alongside a whale when it dove into the depths. Would the person be pulled under? In one of her first encounters with sperm whales, a large bull charged Whitty as she snorkeled on the surface.

"For a few moments," Whitty recounts, "I tried backpedaling but quickly realized that this was futile and simply waited to see what would happen. He charged directly up to me, threw his flukes in the air, and I looked up to see this huge canopy of a tail overhead. Here, at last, my question would be answered, with me as the test subject." Whitty watched the whale slip past and could see eddies of water spiraling off his skin as he sank. But his body was so extraordinarily hydrodynamic that it did not exert the slightest pull, and Whitty remained at the surface. It was a great moment—but as with so many great encounters with wildlife, the topside camera that was filming it all had jammed, missing about 90 percent of the action.

Sometimes it's not the animals, the weather, or the equipment that cause problems. It's the human factor—crew members who don't coordinate their actions, local bureaucrats who are unhelpful or inept, or vendors who make promises but then don't fulfill them. "I'm endlessly surprised by the range of things that go wrong," says producer Molly Hermann. "But working with people is usually the biggest hazard."

Bob Drew, renowned for his cinema verité films about President Kennedy, learned that lesson while filming in Panama. As he flew his Drifter ultralight aircraft over Panama City, photographing spectacular

SHOOTING IN THE WILD

formations of migrating hawks a mile or two south of the Panama Canal, a helicopter pulled up beside him. It was a military vehicle, armed with machine guns. One gunner aimed directly at him as the pilot gestured for him to land.

This incident occurred prior to the U.S. invasion of Panama. The secret police of dictator Manuel Noriega had been arresting Americans at random across the city. Drew had felt somewhat protected because Noriega's civil aviation department had approved his film project, but the helicopter moved closer, the pilot gesticulating wildly toward an airfield below.

Obediently, Drew landed on a runway. Toughs in civilian clothes—Noriega's secret police—wrestled him away from his aircraft, shouting angrily in Spanish. They hustled him into an ancient car and drove to a walled compound, the notorious headquarters of the secret police. A family was leaving—a mother, father, and teenage daughter who was fainting and disfigured by bleeding wounds. Drew's heart pounded with fear.

Down a hallway where shouts reverberated, punctuated by screams, the police pushed Drew into a hot, windowless room. A senior commander sat behind a large desk, a heavy leather jacket hanging from the back of his chair. Smoking cigarettes and speaking English, the commander asked Drew what he was doing taking photographs of Noriega's headquarters. A half hour of interrogation ensued, during which Drew produced key documents, including a letter from the National Geographic Society assigning him to produce a program on migrating hawks. Nevertheless, the commander continued to charge Drew with photographing Noriega's headquarters.

Then Drew had an idea. The proof of his innocence, he told his interrogator, would be in the tapes. "Screen our tapes and see for yourself that we were shooting birds." Two guards were assigned this task. Drew sat them down in front of a viewer and played the first of dozens of tapes. They could not know how difficult it is to shoot wild birds from an airplane—Drew was usually glad if a half-hour tape contained one or two usable shots of birds. The rest of the tape contained bouncing stabs

Cameraman Doug Allan filming a burrowing owl in the North Dakota badlands for BBC's *Natural World* series of wildlife documentaries. Photo © Doug Allan.

Sue Flood photographs chinstrap penguins on the Antarctic peninsula during filming for *Planet Earth*. Flood is married to Doug Allan; they have worked together on many films, including the BBC/Discovery series *The Blue Planet* and *Planet Earth*. Photo © Sue Flood.

Joseph Pontecorvo uses a jib arm to film a nesting blue-footed booby in the Galápagos Islands for the film *Equator: Power of an Ocean*. Photo by Alison Balance © NHNZ.

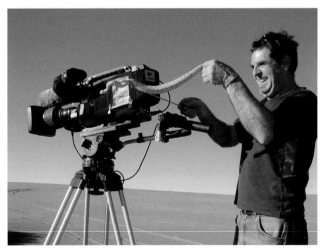

Cameraman Mike Single gets some uninvited assistance from a Mohave Desert sidewinder while filming *Death Valley* in 2004 for Natural History New Zealand (NHZ). Photo by Rachael Wilson © NHNZ.

Brady Barr and his crew filming the unique locomotion of a king cobra in the Western Ghat Mountains, on the west coast of India. Simon Boyce films, while Barr (far left) checks light levels and snake wrangler Gerry Martin manages the cobra. Photo © Brady Barr.

As Graeme Duane films, Brady Barr pulls a crocodile into the boat. This "nuisance croc" had attacked and killed residents of a small village in Sofali Provice of central Mozambique, and would be relocated. Photo © Brady Barr.

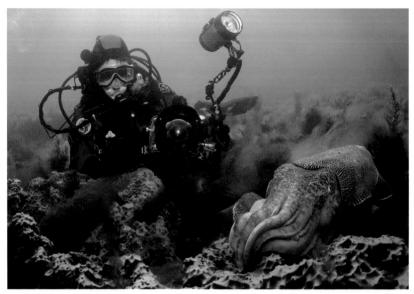

Michele Hall of Howard Hall Productions photographs a giant cuttlefish during production on the IMAX 3D film *Under the Sea 3D* on location at Black Point, Whyalla, South Australia. Photo © 2008 Peter Kragh, used with permission of Warner Bros. Entertainment, Inc.

Tom Campbell, who specializes in marine cinematography, shoots high-definition footage of Caribbean reef sharks as they feed. Photo by Dennis Coffman © SOS Ltd.

Cameraman Doug Allan filming a humpback whale and calf near the Vava'u Islands, Tonga, during production on the "Shallow Seas" episode of *Planet Earth*. Photo © Sue Flood.

Cameraman Doug Allan filming beluga whales that are surfacing to breathe at an ice hole for *The Blue Planet*. Photo © Sue Flood.

Doug Allan waits in his snow hide to film a polar bear at her den at
Hopen Island, Svalbard, Norway. Photo © Doug Allan.

Doug Allan films an arctic fox during production on the
BBC documentary *Polar Bear Special* in the Norwegian
Arctic, near Svalbard. Photo © Doug Allan

Matthew Ferraro, Ocean Futures Society's director of photography,
films details of an iceberg off Baffin Island, Nunavut, in the
Canadian Arctic during an expedition to film *Sea Ghosts*. Photo
© Carrie Vonderhaar, Ocean Futures Society/KQED.

As cinematographer Bob Poole films cheetahs in Ndutu, Tanzania, one hops onto his Land Rover for a better view of the plains. Photo courtesy of Bob Poole.

at panning, zooming, focusing, and searching for birds. Hours later, their eyes bloodshot from watching reel after reel of shaky footage, the guards set Drew free. The final film, *River of Hawks,* conveyed the spectacular natural phenomenon of hawk migration in several locations and was broadcast by National Geographic.

The ultimate consequence of things going wrong on a film shoot can be death, and sadly this has happened numerous times. Philippe Cousteau, son of Jacques Cousteau, died in 1979 when an amphibious plane he was test-piloting crashed. While snorkeling on a shoot, the eight-year-old son of National Geographic underwater photographer Bates Littlehales was sucked into a boat's propeller and died. A husband-and-wife team of volcanologist-filmmakers, Maurice and Katia Krafft, perished when they were overtaken by a sudden rush of hot sulfuric gases at Mount Unzen in Japan. While cinematographer Dieter Plage filmed in Sumatra above a rainforest canopy, his pedal-driven, helium-filled blimp buckled, and he plunged 140 feet to his death. Ultralight pilot Bill Raisner and IMAX cameraman Noel Archambault crashed and died while filming the IMAX production *Galápagos 3D.* Filmmaker John Pearson was accidentally shot dead by a ranger assigned to protect him while filming in the Ngorongoro Crater in Tanzania in 1978. Mistakenly thinking their camp was being raided by Maasai warriors in the night, the inexperienced ranger sent off random shots from inside his tent, one of which hit Pearson in the forehead.

Though it can be a very exciting business, there is no doubt that wildlife cinematography also exposes its practitioners to great risk. Good preparation includes careful and clear assessments of risk, but no amount of preparation can prevent accidents—sometimes deadly ones.

Post-Production

Once principal photography is completed, rough-cut editing begins. All the footage obtained in the field is assembled and edited, and the narration, music, and sound effects are added. If done well, these elements can profoundly affect how the audience reacts emotionally to what it sees on the screen. Sound effects can reinforce and add verisimilitude to the images, and narration can contribute gravitas, energy, passion, or playfulness, depending upon what the producer thinks is needed.

There's a big difference between a narrator who simply turns up at a recording studio for a few hours to read from a script during post-production, and the kind of host who not only narrates the film, but also appears on location and on camera throughout the program. The latter are most often celebrities; Chapter 5 discusses the role of celebrities in wildlife films in more detail. In choosing a narrator, a producer considers cost, availability, and voice quality; the person's appeal to the segment of viewers the film is aimed at; and whether he or she can convey a sense of genuine caring. For most of the films I've worked on, we preferred an on-camera narrator, who can more directly engage the viewer, but for certain projects—where the focus should be solely on the animal—voice-over narration is appropriate.

Of course, not all the shots listed on the pre-production "shot list" are obtained during principal photography. Offsetting those disappointments is the serendipitous footage that could never have been anticipated. It all comes together in post-production, when a filmmaker's dreams meet reality. Until you start editing, there is no way to know whether the available images, juxtaposed with music, sound effects, and narration, are going to cohere into a strong film.

If filmmakers don't have the footage they need to tell their story, they have several options. They can go looking for more money, which might allow them to stay on location or get "pickup" shots that can help the editor fill in the blanks. They can consider the possibility of staging the shots they want, but that may have ethical downsides. They can revise the film treatment so that they no longer need the missing footage. They can buy archival footage, if they can afford it. Or they can use video shot by amateurs. Sending out a call to industry contacts by phone or e-mail, requesting help on listservs, or just trolling the Internet may yield such footage.

When it's time to edit, the producer must keep asking questions: Does the story have a clear beginning, middle, and end? Are the characters, both human and otherwise, compelling? Will the viewers want to know what happens next as they watch? Sometimes a seemingly inconsequential shot or interview clip can turn out to be critical because it makes a crucial segue. The opposite can also happen. As an edit progresses, favored sequences that have been laboriously captured in the camera and polished in post-production can become superfluous and end up on the proverbial cutting-room floor.

Most producers make a rough-cut version and pare it down to an appropriate length. Documentary producer John de Graaf does things differently, however. "I try to provide my editor with a tightly scripted 'paper edit' that is actually a bit shorter than the final length of the program," he says. "The editor is able to assemble this quickly, and then we begin to add fun scenes we captured in the shooting phase that are not essential to the thesis of the film but that add interest for the viewer." Such paper edits are becoming more common, as a way of making the editing process more efficient. But filmmaker Kathy Pasternak wisely observes that this approach dispenses with an important step in the collaborative process of filmmaking. Editors who receive strict guidelines on paper are left without the freedom to "discover the story" and contribute to the production in a meaningfully creative way. She says, "This is a touchy issue. The art of wildlife filmmaking is being whittled away—for budget reasons—to a skeleton of its former self."

Filmmaker Ginger Mauney used to view post-production as one of the worst parts of filmmaking. After spending most of her time in the bush among wild animals, she dreaded the "dark edit suites where there's no escape from cigarette smoke clinging to the air, the computer's incessant humming, and the power plays of office politics." These days, though, the dark rooms and large editing machines are gone. Instead of cutting and splicing film, editors play with pixels, which are much easier and cheaper to manipulate. Producers and editors craft stories on laptops at home, at the office, and even in hotel rooms.

Filmmaker Katie Carpenter considers editing a highlight of the process. "The trepidation that infects your vision in the field, always overthinking what could go wrong—bad weather, missed connections, lost or damaged equipment, a character with cold feet—is removed, and you can view the film for the first time the way viewers at home will see it: framed in a tiny box with your full focus directed at its heart."

Adds Larry Engel, "It is the place and time where everything comes together—all the little and big pieces that until then were separated from one another. In the best of possible worlds, it's as if the filmmaker were the composer, and the editor the conductor, of this wonderfully diverse and multifaceted orchestra of image and sound."

Marketing, Distribution, and Outreach

People think a film is complete when the last bit of editing is done. But actually a film doesn't exist in any meaningful way until it has been seen by its intended audience. The role of marketing, distribution, and outreach is to attract the right audience and give the film its best chance to reach those viewers.

Producers must consider all the possible ways to get the word out. The film might be broadcast, promoted by a nonprofit organization, shown to a particular Senate committee, or marketed on the Web through blogs and social networks. It might be advertised in the *New York Times*, mentioned on a companion Web site, and reviewed in the *Economist*. It might be entered in a festival competition, distributed to schools, packaged as a DVD, or sold internationally through a distribution company. For the enterprising and resourceful producer, the options and opportunities are endless.

All successful films have good marketing and distribution plans, and all successful advocacy films need outreach campaigns as well, to provide viewers with the means to take action on a local, regional, or even global scale. Ideally, the producer spends as much money on outreach as on the film itself. This important part of getting a film and its message before the public is discussed further in Chapter 9.

Producing a wildlife film is like any big project with multiple components. Setbacks happen routinely and can vary from a shortage of money to a difficult colleague, from an injured cameraman to a broadcaster who keeps you hanging for months and then turns you down. Teams of people must work together harmoniously, which is never easy to accomplish. A producer has to be relentlessly optimistic and resourceful, constantly trying new ways of surmounting obstacles. Most experienced filmmakers live by the maxim "prepare for the worst and hope for the best."

The next two chapters take a closer look at two challenges mentioned only briefly here: finding money and working with celebrities. When filmmakers get together over a drink to swap war stories, these issues invariably come up because they are all too often a source of endless frustration and despair.

4

THE MONEY CHASE
Finding Funds without Selling Out

"Hey, Chris, great film, aaahhhmmm," said media magnate Ted Turner, with his characteristic throaty, place-holding roar. "I really loved it, aaahhh, but there's a problem."

My heart started beating faster. There was no money left in the budget. If he wanted changes, we were in big trouble.

"You got one of the ducks wrong," he continued.

Turner was one of my major funders when I worked at the National Audubon Society and the National Wildlife Federation. In 1987 we had just completed a film called *Ducks under Siege,* produced by Pam Hogan, and I had sent it to Turner as a courtesy.

"Ted, what do you mean one of the ducks is wrong?" I asked, baffled. I knew that Hogan had checked and double-checked her facts. Not only did she have a wildlife encyclopedia with pictures of the different duck species in front of her every day as she edited, but she also brought in a biologist to confirm that we had identified everything correctly.

"Aaahhh, you called a canvasback a redhead. I'm pretty sure of it," he added with uncharacteristic diffidence. Turner has loved the outdoors ever since his childhood days on his grandfather's Mississippi farm and has much firsthand knowledge of the natural world. So we checked our birds again and found that he was right. We were able to correct the mistake before the film was broadcast.

When I first met Turner in the early 1980s, he was in his mid-forties, six feet two and slim, with a chiseled jaw, crow's-feet, a dimpled chin, steel-blue eyes, a Clark Gable–esque mustache, and snowy white hair. He spoke his mind, and always with a loud, tongue-dragging, raspy drawl. He survived a punishing childhood, the agonizing death of his younger sister, and a tyrannical, imperious, and hard-drinking father who killed himself when Turner was twenty-four. It has been reported that once, when giving a speech, Turner held up a copy of *Success* magazine with his photo on the cover, stared up at the ceiling, and whispered, "Is this enough? Is this enough for you, Dad?"

Turner's belief in conservation permeates his life. Once when I was talking with him, he took out his wallet and extracted from it a piece of paper with his own ten voluntary initiatives for living a good and honorable life, including, "I promise to minimize my use of toxic chemicals, pesticides, and other poisons and to encourage others to do the same." He has used his wealth philanthropically to support conservation, population control, and curbing the arms race. At CNN and TBS, Turner created many new television programs that promoted conservation and environmental protection.

In short, Turner is the kind of funder every wildlife filmmaker dreams of—a television executive willing to stand for something beyond ratings and profits. I was lucky to find him so early in my filmmaking career. By contrast, when fund-raising for many other projects, getting the ducks right has been the least of my worries.

Where Does the Money Come From?

Wildlife films can vary in cost from a couple of thousand dollars for a YouTube short to $10 million for a 3D IMAX film. I work at both ends of this spectrum. In theory, a producer doesn't need to have all the money in hand before greenlighting a film, but that's a risky situation to be in. If the producer is unsuccessful at raising the rest of the money, donors and investors are left with an unfinished project and nothing to show for their investment or gift. In general, I never give a project the go-ahead without all the funding in hand.

The typical sources of money for wildlife films are broadcast networks, corporations, and foundations, but other sources include individuals, nonprofit organizations, and government agencies. The money can come in the form of loans, investments, gifts, or advertising revenue. And the payback to funders likewise varies: For corporations, it may be enhanced brand recognition or revenue from sales generated by ads aired on the program. For private investors, it's return on investment. For other sources it may be the more subtle reward of prestige by association with a highly regarded film.

Funding influences what kinds of wildlife films get made. Money from broadcasters tends to be for films that will garner ratings—for example, a guy trying to survive in a jungle by catching, killing, and eating small animals. Money from corporations tends to be for films that will reap them public esteem and recognition, sometimes to offset the bad press the company garners by emitting pollution—for example, ExxonMobil sponsoring a film on energy conservation or environmental protection. And money from foundations and wealthy individuals tends to be for films that promote worthy causes, such as protecting the Arctic National Wildlife Refuge; these donors seek to add meaning to their lives and leave a legacy. All these sources of money come with various strings attached—especially, as we shall see, corporate sponsorships.

Independent filmmakers and production companies often seek help from nonprofits in the fund-raising phase. Acting as a fiscal agent for a film, a nonprofit can accept tax-deductible donations, which are easier to find than nondeductible gifts. The nonprofit usually keeps about 5 percent as an administrative fee for overseeing the work and turns the rest over to the film producer. In addition to making funds flow more freely, this kind of partnership can also give a film more impact, credibility, and standing. A nonprofit partner can, for example, organize events around a film to raise money and awareness, and to nurture and encourage grassroots activists.

The Bermuda Audubon Society acted as a fiscal agent for producer Deirdre Brennan's film *Bermuda's Treasure Island*. This film tells the story of one man's incredible journey to save the legendary cahow, a seabird thought to have been extinct for more than three hundred years. The alliance made sense because the local Audubon Society was actively involved in trying to save the bird. Bermuda Audubon president Andrew Dobson, who wrote the definitive book on Bermuda's bird life, tirelessly helped Brennan raise money for the film.

Some filmmakers are reluctant to make those kinds of alliances or to do the other creative work it takes to find money. Derek Bousé, who tried his hand at wildlife filmmaking before becoming a professor, confided to me that "begging for money" was what he disliked most about his former profession. "I found this part degrading and demoralizing. It involved prostrating myself before money men whose core values seemed to have been shaped solely by marketing considerations."

I've made my share of fund-raising mistakes. Sometimes, especially when I was younger, I would be so nervous in a meeting with a donor that I would forget to "make the ask." It's so much easier to promote your cause than to actually say, "Would you consider a gift of $1 million to support our film?" But the biggest mistake I occasionally made was failing to show how impassioned I was about the project. If I didn't care deeply, then why should a donor be inspired to give? Over time, I realized that, by asking for money, I was helping people find meaning and purpose in their own lives. My job was to empower the donor to do great things for a noble cause.

Large-Scale Funding 101

It can take years to raise money for some films. At the National Audubon Society in 1987, we began to look beyond TV documentaries for other ways to influence public opinion and promote conservation. Giant-screen films made for IMAX theaters caught my attention, and it didn't take long to realize that whales would be the perfect topic for this splashy format.

Of the eight years it took to make *Whales*, the first seven were devoted to raising the money. In the end, the film was a good investment. At a cost of less than $5 million, it has so far grossed more than $50 million.

In the early years, however, it often seemed that it would never get made. I remember going home at night and saying to my wife, "This film is hanging by the thinnest of threads and could crash at any moment." We received repeated rejections from potential corporate sponsors.

We started by talking to large consumer-oriented companies such as AT&T about sponsoring the film. We got nowhere, partly because of my inexperience. One thing we learned was that corporations want numbers—vague descriptions of reach and demographics don't cut it. But obtaining reliable audience numbers, demographics, and returns on investment for giant-screen films was (and still is) challenging, because some in the film industry like to keep their numbers secret to avoid helping the competition.

Another thing I learned was that I needed to listen intently to a corporation's concerns. Listening helped me pitch our film in a way that would meet a potential partner's needs. I also learned that I should not ask for too much money. If I requested, say, $4 million, that would immediately reduce my potential target list to just a handful of very big, wealthy corporations.

Between 1987 and 1990 we struggled, getting nowhere. Then in 1990 we had our first breakthrough when the National Science Foundation gave us a grant of just under a million dollars. NSF saw *Whales* and its companion educational materials as a powerful tool to teach people about science and the way scientists go about their work. We promised that key scenes in *Whales* would be great takeoff points for classroom studies in science, mathematics, language arts, and geography. We also agreed to produce a *Whales* education guide on CD-ROM, a teacher guide, and a student guide to help teachers use the film to meet the National Science Education Standards. We even offered to create an interactive game, to be used in the lobbies of theaters where the film was being shown, to promote science and the film.

Despite the foundation's support, however, we failed to attract any further funding. In 1993 we decided to join forces with a competing giant-screen film on whales that was also partly funded. This required us to give up a measure of creative control, but in exchange we preempted a competitor and received substantial funding from Zephyr Productions, our new partner.

At about the same time, we formed a partnership with Destination Cinema in Utah, which put up a million dollars for the rights to distribute the film. So now the film was about halfway funded. We redoubled our efforts to find a corporate sponsor.

Then, in 1994, I was recruited by the National Wildlife Federation to head up its new television and IMAX organization. When I asked the National Audubon Society if I could take *Whales* with me to the National Wildlife Federation, Audubon agreed because it saw the project as having no future. This was a welcome misjudgment on its part.

With *Whales* now at the National Wildlife Federation and half the budget in place, we continued to look for a corporate sponsor. We received a verbal commitment from a high-profile beauty products company for $3 million, which included money for marketing and promotion as well as production. The company was especially attracted to the potentially long life of the film. Educational giant-screen films are usually in theaters for five to ten years, sometimes longer.

A problem arose, however. The CEO of the beauty products company wanted to be prominently featured at the beginning of *Whales*, talking about his commitment to environmental protection. But giant-screen films at that time were shown primarily in museums and science centers, institutions that are understandably resistant to commercial messages. We could not give the CEO what he wanted, so the deal fell through.

By 1995, we were about to shelve the whole project when I decided to approach the National Wildlife Federation Endowment. Independent from the National Wildlife Federation, the endowment had never funded anything as risky as a film before. But our plan convinced its trustees to take a chance on us.

After seven years of struggle, the 250-pound underwater cameras started rolling. We still had no corporate sponsor, but at least the film was under way. At the end of 1996, *Whales* premiered in Boston and has since gone on to more than a hundred IMAX and other large-format theaters worldwide. More than eight million people have seen it so far, with many theaters reporting record-breaking attendance figures. *Whales* was the third-highest-grossing giant-screen film worldwide in 1998. We were able to repay our loan from the endowment, with interest, twenty months ahead of schedule.

Donor Difficulties

Although one of the cardinal rules of fund-raising is to make sure the donor has a good fund-raising experience, being too accommodating can also cause problems. For example, the gold-mining industry paid a well-known science center to produce a giant-screen IMAX film on the topic of gold. Predictably, the film was mute on the subject of the appalling environmental consequences of gold mining. It portrayed gold as a symbol of success, rather than as an unnecessary product that consumes and pollutes vast quantities of precious water.

As discussed in Chapter 2, Marlin Perkins's *Wild Kingdom* heavily promoted its sponsors and even included advertising pitches in the content of the program itself. Author Cynthia Chris writes, "The insurance company Mutual of Omaha gained, through its sponsorship of *Wild Kingdom,* a relatively inexpensive means of keeping its name in the public eye, associating itself with a series believed to contain some educational value, and exploiting the genre's tropes of risk and danger to try to prompt in the viewer a mood receptive to the promotion of insurance products." She quotes host Marlin Perkins as saying on camera and in the body of the show, "Trapping mountain goats takes the skill of an expert. Planning your health insurance needs takes the skill of an expert from Mutual of Omaha." Perkins was giving the insurance giant a "good giving" experience, but he was also prostituting himself.

I have felt similar pressure at times. In 1988, Stroh Brewery Company had just renewed its corporate sponsorship of Audubon Television Specials for another two years, and it also bought ads on the programs. One of the films we made that year was *Greed and Wildlife: Poaching in America,* about illegal trafficking of wild animals, hosted by actor Richard Chamberlain. Our crew came back with dramatic footage of a man being arrested for illegally buying fifty parrots and smuggling them across the Rio Grande. As luck would have it, the man who was arrested just happened to be wearing a Stroh's Lite T-shirt. In an act of cowardice, I decided not to use this footage, in case Stroh would be offended.

On the other hand, while I was working for the National Wildlife Federation, CEO Mark Van Putten and I turned down a $1 million gift from a big auto company to help fund one of our giant-screen films because the company produced gas-guzzling SUVs. That time, we were able to do the right thing, despite the temptation to do otherwise.

My First Battle with Advertisers

While working at the National Audubon Society and the National Wildlife Federation, I produced documentaries for television, mainstream movie houses, and giant-screen theaters. Our goal was to persuade people to join our campaigns for conservation. Innocuous as it may sound, that goal put us at odds with some powerful interests. For example, in 1989, filmmaker Jim Lipscomb and I made *Ancient Forests: Rage over Trees,* hosted by actor Paul Newman, which highlighted a protracted battle over logging on publicly owned forests in the United States. At issue were 3 million acres of ancient, or old-growth, forests in the Northwest that were being clear-cut at a rate of 60,000 acres a year—and the fate of the 30,000 workers who made their living by cutting them.

When advance word got out about the film's content, it led to a logging-industry boycott of our main corporate sponsor (Stroh Brewery Company), as well as all eight corporations (including Ford, Citicorp, and Exxon) that had purchased commercial time slots during the program on TBS. Newman told me he received more hate mail for *Rage over Trees* than for any project he'd ever done.

When Stroh asked me to make the film more sympathetic to the logging industry, I refused because I felt the film was fair. We had tried hard to show the timber industry's viewpoint. But even though Stroh and all the rest of the sponsors pulled their advertisements, Ted Turner broadcast the program during prime time, with public service announcements and promotions for future shows replacing the commercials.

Even in the face of big-industry intimidation, he continued to walk his talk. To him, conservation was more important than making money. Articles about the controversy appeared in major newspapers all across the country, and our opponents triumphantly described the boycott of *Rage over Trees* in a 1993 book called *Trashing the Economy.* Mentioning my refusal to change the film, the authors say, "Maybe Chris Palmer is missing a battery or something."

For all the controversy it stirred up, though, *Rage over Trees* played a pivotal role in convincing the U.S. Forest Service not to log a beautiful Oregon watershed called Opal Creek, full of centuries-old fir, hemlock, and cedar. Audubon and TBS lost a lot of money, but we saved a forest. As author David Seideman, who wrote the 1993 book *Showdown at Opal Creek*, told me later, "*Rage over Trees* really put the ancient forests issue on the map by giving them their first national exposure. Opal Creek and ancient forests went from being a local issue to a national one, which politicians ignored at their own peril. . . . You had to have a heart of stone not to be moved by footage of Opal Creek's big, beautiful trees and Paul Newman's soothing voice. Plus the timber interests really played their hand wrong, insisting the supply of old growth was endless. Once Audubon and Turner got the ball rolling, *Time*, the *New York Times*, and ABC's *20/20* did their own stories." The effort culminated in October 1996 with federal legislation designating Opal Creek as a wilderness area and thus firmly protecting it from logging. Its ancient trees are now enjoyed by fifty thousand visitors every year.

Up Next, a Range War

Corporate sponsors typically dislike controversy. Stroh had been ignominiously chased away from the Audubon Television Specials on TBS and PBS by the *Rage over Trees* boycott, but our programs continued to earn high ratings, get good reviews, and attract other sponsors, underwriters, and advertisers. Then we were hit with another boycott.

In 1991, we made *The New Range Wars,* hosted by Peter Coyote, which dealt with the controversial issue of livestock overgrazing public lands. Aiming for balance, we tried to present the cattlemen's views as well as those of environmentalists. Our aim was to let the viewers decide who was right.

But ranchers strongly objected to the film because it included disturbing (and accurate) images of cattle eroding streams and converting fertile grasslands into barren desert. They pressured all our advertisers to pull their financial support and commercials from the program. Our newest sponsor, GE, was inundated with hundreds of angry calls, letters, and faxes from irate members of the National Cattlemen's Association. Ranchers also boycotted products made by these advertisers and sent letters to every PBS station in the country demanding that they not broadcast *The New Range Wars*. Charles Cushman, director of the National Inholders Association (later renamed the American Land Rights Association), added the voices of thousands of loggers and private-property owners in or near national parks and forests to the uproar.

The harassment and boycott successfully scared our advertisers away. Again, though, that didn't faze Ted Turner. As with the first boycott in 1989, TBS broadcast the show anyway. PBS made the program available to its member stations, but after hearing the complaints from ranchers and their allies, not many of them ran it.

The two boycotts eventually had a significant impact on our film production work. GE abandoned its sponsorship of Audubon programs entirely, although it denied any connection between its decision and the boycott, claiming it was "necessitated by recession-related cutbacks." Like most others, I didn't believe that. Similarly, PBS announced that it was no longer willing to broadcast our shows, after seven seasons in prime time, likely because of the controversies over clear-cutting and overgrazing.

The Turner Effect

Although the boycotts hurt us, the films I worked on with Ted Turner (first at the National Audubon Society and then at the National Wildlife Federation) helped educate the public about environmental issues. Turner's company merged with Time Warner in 1996, and Turner was made a vice chairman of the larger firm. We continued to produce films for TBS until 2001, when Turner lost a power struggle and was forced to stop producing and broadcasting his favorite environmental shows. He finally stepped down as vice chairman of Time Warner in 2006.

Over the twenty years we worked together, my respect for Ted Turner grew, and occasionally we explored the outdoors together. In 1992, he took my family out to see the bison he was raising on his Montana ranch. Early one afternoon, Ted drove my three daughters and me across his vast ranch. Following us in another car were my wife and Ted's oldest daughter, Laura, who was six months pregnant with his first grandchild.

As we drove too fast over mile after mile of rough ground, Ted talked nonstop about Native Americans, wolves, bears, and the history of the American West. At one point he suddenly stopped the car, jumped out, and found some ancient Indian arrowheads on the ground to give to each of my daughters.

At first he couldn't locate the bison, but he wasn't about to give up. After a couple of hours of searching, he finally found the herd and drove right up into the middle of it. Staring warily at us were hundreds of silent, sullen beasts.

"No one get out of the car," ordered Ted. "Bison are unpredictable and dangerous." He was all too aware of how a bison can act docile one minute and belligerent the next; only a few days earlier, he had nearly been killed when one had unexpectedly charged him. We peered around fascinated. After a minute or two of stillness, Ted happened to glance in his rearview mirror.

That's when he started screaming.

"Get back in the car!" he shouted at Laura. "Get back in the car!"

In the mirror, he had seen his pregnant daughter get out of the car to relieve her bladder. He jerked our vehicle forward with the steering wheel hard to the left so he could get closer and try to protect her. Fortunately no bison charged, and, seeing that his progeny were safe, Ted quickly calmed down.

Throughout the time I worked with him, Ted Turner was just as fiercely protective of our films. Threatened with boycotts from industrial polluters and other anticonservation forces, Turner didn't hesitate. He dug in his heels, vigorously defended the films' content and point of view, and moved forcefully ahead to broadcast the shows anyway, despite taking a financial bath when sponsors and advertisers bailed. As *Variety* described our relationship in 1994, "The 10-year marriage of the National Audubon Society and environmental activist/TV mogul Ted Turner has so far produced 40 hours of stinging, no-holds-barred video documentary that has fingered heroes and villains in the on-going battle to stave off planetary self-destruction."

Among the ways in which Turner left his mark on the wildlife film business was by shrewdly recognizing that celebrity hosts would add appeal to the conservation messages in our films. Operating on the assumption that viewers are more interested in famous actors than scientists, our series relied on celebrity hosts from the start, and our association with Turner and his various broadcast networks helped us attract some famous names, including Paul Newman, Jane Fonda, Robert Redford, and Meryl Streep. The next chapter examines the film industry's infatuation with celebrities and how much they really help the conservation cause.

5

CULT OF PERSONALITY
The Celebrity Connection and Presenter-Driven Shows

Before going out into the field, producers study the wildlife they are about to film. They learn all they can about their animal subjects—their daily habits and seasonal patterns, and how they eat, reproduce, and raise their young. They research the issues that threaten these species and their habitats. They talk to biologists, policymakers, and activists on both sides of any controversies, and to the public. By the time they go into the field, they are all geared up, prepared for the extremes of the environment, confident that they can meet the technical challenges, and on top of the story. But here's the great unknown, the thing that really scares them: their celebrity host.

Filmmaker Bill Anderson is intimately familiar with the problem. "Often, we meet our celebrity host for the first time on location," he says. "For all we may learn from their movies, their music, their writing, or from poring over the tabloids, what do we really know about these people? How high maintenance are they? Do they have special diets, allergies, fears, phobias, pets, small children, a sullen spouse, or what? Are they nice? Scary? Mean? Or, God forbid, boring?" Anderson adds, "We have all heard stories of pampered divas who insist that their favorite scent be sprayed wherever they go and brooding actors who feel the need to offend everyone in their path."

I can picture Anderson out on a dirt runway somewhere waiting for his "talent," doing his best to hold a smile from the moment the plane touches down. He alone knows just how substandard their hotel (the only hotel within five hundred miles) is; he alone knows the grueling schedule and how much he is depending on the host's cooperation over the next few days. But he keeps smiling, hoping the shoot, the show, and the careers of all concerned will not come crashing down on account of a host with expectations that may not be met.

This chapter is about the sparks that can fly when the white-hot sizzle of celebrity enters the quiet world of wildlife filmmaking. It includes celebrities who have simply been dropped into a production, as well as those who built their fame around a wildlife show, like crocodile hunter Steve Irwin. Star power sometimes lends a healthy glow to a film, but there can be surprises—for the producer, the film crew, the celebrity, and even the industry as a whole. There's always a risk that someone can get burned.

Working with Stars

Sometimes I worry that people like me cultivate celebrities more for their own ego satisfaction than to promote conservation. I confess to getting a huge kick out of working with famous people. I love to tell stories about camping with Isabella Rossellini on an African safari, about being caught in a blizzard with Jane Fonda in the Montana wilderness, and about being lost in the back passages of a hotel with Robert Redford as his bodyguards tried to keep us out of sight on our way to an event in New York.

But I'm no more starstruck than lots of other Americans. When I worked on Capitol Hill in the early 1970s, Liz Taylor came to visit my boss, Senator Charles H. Percy. As the legendary actor entered the visitors' gallery of the Senate, all work in the chamber abruptly stopped, and the senators on the floor gawked and applauded their unexpected guest. I knew early on that I wanted to tap into that power to make wildlife films stronger and more effective.

When I look back now, I can see that some of the best films I've produced have been aided by a talented, dedicated celebrity host. Good examples are Robert Redford in *Grizzly & Man: Uneasy Truce* (1988), Ted Danson in *Danger at the Beach* (1990), Meryl Streep in *Arctic Refuge* (1990), Michael Douglas in *If Dolphins Could Talk* (1990), Matthew Fox in *Survival of the Yellowstone Wolves* (1996), Daryl Hannah in *Wildlife Wars* (1998), Billy Ray Cyrus in *Return of the Eagle* (1999), Peter Fonda in *Pollinators in Peril* (2000), and Ed Begley Jr. in *Everglades: Troubled Waters* (2000).

Sometimes I hired stars simply to work in the studio as narrators. More often, though, they came along on the shoots and appeared on camera. This made for much greater involvement—and greater commitment, which added life to the program. And, I should be quick to mention, we didn't always hire them. Quite often, the stars felt honored to be asked and were glad to work for free. In all cases, though, celebrity hosts were a well-integrated part of our programs, adding credibility, personal magnetism, and glamour, as well as a conservation message bathed in honey. They also provided promotional hooks for our press department.

Most of the celebrities I've worked with were extremely diligent, setting high standards for their contributions to our films. In 1986 I invited actor Loretta Swit to host a film Ray Paunovich and I made on the highly endangered black-footed ferret. Swit was famous at the time for playing the uptight and self-absorbed nurse Margaret "Hot Lips" Houlihan in the long-running TV series *M*A*S*H*. Having done a good narration for our film, Swit insisted on redoing the whole thing to be sure she had nailed it perfectly.

Luckily for wildlife filmmakers who want to lure celebrity hosts to their productions, promoting conservation and living a green lifestyle are cool in Hollywood these days. Comedian Will Ferrell drives a BMW luxury model modified to run on nonpolluting hydrogen fuel as well as on gasoline. According to *Star Magazine*, he has built a "very eco-friendly house" that includes solar energy. Cameron Diaz and Kirsten Dunst, among other stars, drive hybrid vehicles. Sheryl Crow dresses her son in T-shirts displaying slogans such as "Save some green for me . . . drive a hybrid." Singer Ryan Cabrera converted his Prius into an even more fuel-efficient plug-in car for the TV show *The Rainforest Network*. British actress Elizabeth Hurley stars in a reality show that follows her activities on her organic farm in Gloucestershire. Cate Blanchett is building an eco-friendly theater in Sydney, and her own house runs on solar power. Edward Norton started the "Solar Neighbors" program with BP: whenever a celebrity buys a home photovoltaic system, BP donates the same system to a low-income home in Los Angeles. And the list goes on: Josh Hartnett and Orlando Bloom promote the reduction of carbon emissions; Brad Pitt narrated a TV series that gives advice on building eco-friendly houses.

Some stars go beyond lifestyle changes to more "out-there" activism. In 2006, actor Daryl Hannah staged a twenty-three-day tree-sit in an unsuccessful attempt to preserve an urban community garden in Los Angeles. [5-5] In 2008, Hollywood veteran Harrison Ford made a zany video for Conservation International in which he speaks to the camera about the plight of tropical rainforests, then sits down in a chair to have an attendant wax his chest, and, just after the hairs are ripped out, says, "Every inch of rainforest ripped out there really hurts us here." Pierce Brosnan is a spokesman for environmental groups campaigning to protect whales from blasts of navy sonar—and even has his own Web site on the topic. Leonardo DiCaprio, who also has his own environmental Web site, has worked on three different documentaries concerning ecological issues. The latest of these, *The 11th Hour,* deals with the dangers of global warming. The dean of eco-celebrities is surely Robert Redford, who has served on the board of the Natural Resources Defense Council for more than thirty years. In 2008 his Sundance Channel launched *The Green,* a television show featuring visionary environmental leaders and their cutting-edge ideas.

Of course some stars have jumped on the green bandwagon more out of concern for their careers than for the cause. If an audience senses that lack of authenticity, it can detract from a project's credibility. But most celebrities who get involved are dedicated professionals who are sincere about wishing to help protect the planet.

Afloat with James Taylor

Bill Anderson worked with me in the mid-1990s on several prime-time television shows for the National Audubon Society and the National Wildlife Federation. The first was a profile of the environmentalist and river runner Martin Litton, who, at the age of eighty-seven, was taking his wooden dory through the Grand Canyon again. Litton's passion and leadership helped keep the canyon from being flooded by huge dam projects proposed by the federal government in the 1950s and 1960s.

On the night before their first day of shooting, Anderson was standing on the edge of a runway in Page, Arizona, waiting for singer-songwriter James Taylor, who had agreed to host the show. Anderson knew of Taylor and had been touched by his music, but he was fully aware that he didn't really *know* him. He was in for a pleasant surprise.

Taylor got off the plane and returned Anderson's smile with a wide grin, even after two plane changes and a full day of flying. Once they were in the van and on the way to a motel, the singer's first question was, "Do you think there's a Laundromat open? I've been on the road for a while and I need to do a couple of loads before we head down the river." Anderson told Taylor he would be happy to take care of that for him, but Taylor insisted on doing his own laundry at a facility they found in their hotel. Taylor loaded the washer and went off to meet his son, Ben, who had flown in from New York.

In the morning, James Taylor met Martin Litton. Anderson says it was immediately clear that they were soul brothers. Taylor had read all the research material sent to him and knew of Litton's work—the articles he had written, the wilderness places he had defended. Anderson observed that Taylor was not acting or reading a script; rather, he really cared about this stuff. The crew shot around the infamous Glen Canyon Dam, which drowned a spectacular red-rock canyon under Lake Powell, and the next day headed for the river.

As the boats were loaded, Taylor brought out two guitars, one full size, the other quite small (his "saddle guitar"), and asked the trip leader, Coby Jordan, if there was room for them. Coby smiled and said, "We'll find room." Soon they were on their way, five dories with a boatman at the oars and two or three people in each dory. At first, they whooped and waved to each other, but soon the size of the canyon walls and the beauty of the place became overpowering and they all fell silent.

Their first camp was in Hot Na Na Wash. It was April and the canyon was exploding with beautiful flowers. In the height of the season, mid-June to mid-September, no campfires are allowed in the canyon; but that April night, the voyagers gathered around a driftwood fire, and Taylor asked if anyone would mind if he and Ben played a while. They played for two hours that night and nearly every night for the next four weeks—cowboy songs, jazz and show tunes, hymns, reggae, and folk music. The crew sang along and slept under the stars.

During the day Taylor learned from an environmental legend. He and Litton talked about the defense of wilderness, western water issues, and government and corporate policies that put places like the canyon in jeopardy. Litton's attitude was, "Never compromise. Keep pushing for what you know is right."

For all his years in front of a microphone, Taylor was shy. When he interviewed the boatmen on camera for us, he preferred to have the camera over his shoulder, facing the person he was talking to. He shared in the camp chores. His down-to-earth qualities brought out the best in everyone. A trip down the Colorado through the Grand Canyon is memorable in any circumstance—even under the pressure of making a film—but Taylor's grace and Litton's passion made it perfect.

Mishaps and Calamities

Needless to say, shooting with celebrities doesn't always go so smoothly. Some hosts never show up on time, some behave arrogantly and immaturely, and some carry awkward baggage. The first time I worked with Jane Fonda, for instance, I wasn't prepared for the backlash from viewers who still loathed her because of her opposition to the United States' role in the Vietnam War. If celebrities are used to Hollywood movie sets where makeup artists and hair stylists are all on hand, they may be disappointed with the offerings of wildlife filmmakers, who often sleep in tents with few luxuries.

Or the celebrities may not have packed their bags carefully enough. Actor Alicia Silverstone arrived in Africa with just a small gym bag when my team and I made a film with her about elephants in Zimbabwe in 1998. She knew it would be hot, so all she brought was a sleeveless top with thin shoulder straps and tiny shorts. But we were producing a family show and couldn't have the host wearing skimpy outfits. There was no mall around the corner where we could pick up something appropriate, so my colleague Cathe Neukum asked the associate producer, who was about the same size as Silverstone, to lend the actress some safari-like outfits for the shoot. Moral of the story: always bring clothes for the talent.

Some celebrities take these challenges in stride. Others do not, as veteran BBC producer Tim Martin learned on a ten-day filming trip many years ago. Martin was working on a series about the British countryside that had been commissioned as a vehicle for a well-known British presenter who shall remain nameless. But nothing was easy. Though the presenter wanted to shoot a duck on camera, she complained bitterly about having to walk so far to get to a place where she had a good chance of succeeding. Later she was keen to view some footage on a television to see how it was going, but, to Martin's horror, the framing of the shot looked awful. The top of the presenter's head appeared to have been cut off. What Martin didn't realize at the time was that the television was on the wrong setting and was zoomed in on the image, but the presenter huffed and puffed and demanded that they film the whole scene again "with heads this time!" Another time, due to a misunderstanding between the sound recordist and Martin, they had to do a retake on a ten-minute interview, and she stormed off as soon as they finished filming.

On the last day, Martin had to film her with a fisherman. He had a special all-terrain buggy to transport her and the rest of the crew a couple of miles down the beach. The buggy needed warming up, so while the presenter was putting on makeup in her car, Martin drove the buggy around the parking lot and up a bank, enjoying its incredible traction. When he got to the top, though, the vehicle stalled. He tried to restart it, but it had already begun to slip back down the bank. He tried the hand brake, forgetting that it had broken a couple of days earlier. As he floundered, he felt the buggy rapidly accelerating backward. Looking over his shoulder, he saw in horror that he was hurtling right toward the car in which the presenter was sitting. Martin heard someone shout a warning a split second before the buggy thudded into her car.

The host was not hurt, but the damage to Martin's relationship with her was terminal. He expected her to scream at him, but strangely she stayed absolutely silent, which, he says, was even more frightening. They carried on with the morning's filming pretending that nothing had happened, but, Martin says, "I knew that I had spectacularly overshot the point of no return." He left the series as quickly as he could, before the presenter had a chance to have him fired. After all, as she later wrote in a book, Martin had tried to kill her.

The trials endured by some celebrity hosts have been much more serious. Take, for instance, the tragic story of the former Miss South Africa, Diana Tilden-Davis, who was savagely bitten by an angry hippo in 2003. Tilden-Davis and her then husband, Chris Kruger, owned a safari company in the Botswana Delta. Both a celebrity and a guide, Tilden-Davis was hired by the UK-based television company ORTV to have some close on-camera encounters with wild animals, especially hippos, because ORTV was trying to deliver exciting footage to Animal Planet.

On December 17, 2003, a hippo popped up in front of a dugout canoe that Tilden-Davis was poling through the delta. "The hippo charged, and in doing so jumped into one end of the canoe, tipping it up," she says. "I began to slide down the bottom of the canoe toward him, and I tried to beat him off with the pole and with my fists, as I attempted to get away from his mouth. But the bottom of the boat was too slippery, I couldn't get a grip on it, and eventually he got my left leg in his mouth and mauled me."

Chris Kruger reported that the animal bit the former beauty queen in "the lower leg just above the ankle." The hippo's spearlike teeth chomped down on her leg again and again and basically stripped off all the flesh, as though eating skewers of grilled meat. When she emerged from the water, she was in shock and had lost a lot of blood. Later, she suffered complications due to an infection and had to undergo a series of operations including bone grafts and insertion of a pin in her leg.

Kruger sent me the gruesome photos of her injuries with the warning "Only open these photos if you have a strong stomach." He told me that his former wife will always have a "drop-foot" limp (she'll drag her foot along rather than lift it) because the tendons and nerves in her leg were damaged beyond repair.

Tilden-Davis's life was changed forever. The idea of hosting anymore wildlife shows is out of the question. After four years in rehabilitation, she still could not walk without crutches and spent a lot of time immobilized in great pain. Even so, before Tilden-Davis was airlifted from her camp, she asked that the attacking animal not be shot. She knew—as anyone involved in this kind of filmmaking should—that hippos are likely to attack when they feel threatened.

The Crocodile Hunter

In the tradition of the wildlife filmmaking pioneers discussed in Chapter 2—Martin and Osa Johnson, Frank Buck, Marlin Perkins, and Marty Stouffer—some program hosts have risen to celebrity status through their work. These stars tend to be more knowledgeable about wildlife and the outdoors than the Hollywood types—and seem to have just as much power to broaden audiences and boost ratings. But they can also cause problems. The flashy showmanship that audiences love can lead these hosts to take risks with serious consequences for animals and themselves. Their charisma can also convince their audiences to mimic their folly, compounding the harm.

Take the story of Steve Irwin. Although he had no scientific degree, Irwin grew up studying and caring for animals at his parents' wildlife park, which is now known as the Australia Zoo. At its peak of popularity, his TV show *The Crocodile Hunter* aired in more than two hundred countries. In each program, audiences were thrilled by Irwin's hair-raising encounters with wild animals, which included deadly snakes, spiders, lizards, and, of course, crocodiles.

Even at his most popular, Irwin was no stranger to controversy. He made headlines around the world in 2004 when he was filmed tossing a dead chicken to a thirteen-foot crocodile at the zoo while holding his month-old son under one arm. People were outraged at what they saw as reckless, irresponsible endangerment of a child. Irwin defended himself vigorously, claiming that he knew exactly what he was doing and that his son was perfectly safe. That same year, the Australian government investigated him for getting closer than the law allows to whales, penguins, and leopard seals while filming in the Antarctic. Irwin argued that the whales approached him, not the other way around. In the end, the investigation was dropped, and no charges were filed.

The Crocodile Hunter, which began in the mid-1990s on Animal Planet, ended with terrible finality in September 2006, when Irwin was fatally stabbed in the chest by a bull stingray at the Great Barrier Reef in Australia. Stingrays are typically gentle animals and don't attack unless provoked. This one probably felt threatened by Irwin and his cameraman when they swam too close, a tendency we'll explore in Chapter 7. Yet news anchors repeatedly reported that Irwin was "attacked" by a stingray.

Millions of people around the world mourned his passing with an outpouring of grief. Animal Planet was flooded with e-mail messages, letters, and video testimonials from a public in shock that such a larger-than-life person could be gone so suddenly. One video came from a tearful young woman who wanted the network to know that, because of Irwin, she had become a wildlife biologist and dedicated her life to helping animals. "Irwin wanted to reach a mass audience with his message of conservation and respect for wildlife," says Kevin Mohs, vice president for production at Animal Planet, "and, due to the popularity of his series and specials, millions listened and thousands gave back by volunteering time or donating money to nonprofits or by dedicating their lives to wildlife conservation like the young woman in the video."

Irwin's conservation message shone through vividly in his 1997 autobiography, *The Crocodile Hunter,* and in many of his TV shows. He inspired in millions an increased appreciation for the importance of animals, especially reptiles. Conservationist Jan Cousteau, daughter-in-law of the famed Jacques Cousteau, said, "More than anyone else, he de-villainized the crocs and snakes and spiders that so many people are afraid of by touching and loving them."

But Irwin also inadvertently encouraged people to get too close to the critters he loved, which he provoked into behaviors and actions that may not have otherwise occurred. Filmmaker and environmental journalist David Helvarg says, "It's hard to deny the atavistic pleasure of getting close to (or watching someone else get close to) big things that can kill you with teeth, claws, or venom, which was Steve Irwin's specialty. It's also a pleasure that millions could indulge in guilt-free with Irwin because he often included a conservation message in his shows, mentioning that we should protect and conserve the king cobra, Komodo dragon, or whatever other deadly critter he was handling."

In an essay in Britain's *Guardian* newspaper a few days after Irwin's death, writer Germaine Greer was less charitable:

> What Irwin never seemed to understand was that animals need space. The one lesson any conservationist must labor to drive home is that habitat loss is the principal cause of species loss. There was no habitat, no matter how fragile or finely balanced, that Irwin hesitated to barge into, trumpeting his wonder and amazement to the skies. There was not an animal he was not prepared to manhandle. Every creature he brandished his camera at was in distress. Every snake badgered by Irwin was at a huge disadvantage, with only a single possible reaction to its terrifying situation, which was to strike. Irwin was an entertainer, a twenty-first-century version of a lion-tamer, with crocodiles instead of lions. The animal world has finally taken its revenge.

Blue-chip filmmaker Alan Root calls Irwin and other hands-on, intrusive presenters "narcissistic clowns." He pointed to the "revenge" killing of stingrays after Irwin's death as an indication of the mind-set that he bequeathed his fans. Filmmaker Dereck Joubert, who with his wife, Beverly, has made many award-winning films in Africa, sees increasing numbers of people trying to catch crocodiles, walking up to leopards, and sitting right at the edge of water holes while elephants are trying to drink. "Even in the depths of Botswana, while we as filmmakers are trying desperately to go unnoticed by wildlife, we have seen an increase in tourists behaving badly around us. They defend themselves by saying, 'Hey, if Steve Irwin can do it, so can I.'"

Weighing the Celebrity Factor

We live in a celebrity-obsessed culture. Whatever Hollywood stars do and endorse is noticed and sometimes emulated by millions of fans. Even people not interested in issues such as global warming want to watch documentaries hosted by their favorite celebrities. They also like to watch wildlife experts with big personalities and a flair for drama. But things can get out of hand. A network's interest in celebrities, whether from Hollywood or homegrown, can turn into a compulsion, which really reflects an obsession with ratings. That's when unhealthy pressures start to cascade downward: to attract ratings that will prevent network television executives from losing their jobs, broadcasters pressure filmmakers (and, in turn, celebrity hosts) to take whatever risks they can to capture dramatic and exciting footage. This is the reality of modern television and the fundamental reason Irwin died and Tilden-Davis was so badly injured.

Let's assume, though, that a producer isn't obsessed with ratings—that he or she merely wants to add a little pizzazz to an already promising film. The smartest producers still walk toward the limelight cautiously. Celebrities can help draw an audience (but only if the person is an A-lister), promote the program (as long as they are willing and have time), and bring credibility (unless viewers suspect that the celebrity has no substantive knowledge or experience to share). In short, adding celebrities to a film can be lucrative and fun, but it's no guarantee of success.

In the next chapter, we'll look at another tool the wildlife film industry uses to push for higher ratings: the staging of supposedly "natural" wildlife scenes and other practices that deceive audiences. Celebrities can be seen and assessed by viewers, but you can't see the tricks filmmakers use behind the scenes.

6

AUDIENCE ABUSE
Staging and Other Deceptions

In the summer of 2007, all hell erupted in England's newspapers over an incident involving footage of Queen Elizabeth. The BBC had contracted with independent film company RDF to make a documentary about the monarch. One scene featured a portrait session with the queen and famed photographer Annie Leibovitz, who, thinking the queen was overdressed in full royal regalia, asked her to remove her tiara. The queen firmly rejected the request and, in the trailer for the film, is seen huffily walking out of the photo shoot.

One problem: the queen never walked out in a huff. The footage had been manipulated. What looked like her leaving was actually her eagerly walking *in* to the shoot. Buckingham Palace wasted no time in expressing its outrage to the BBC. A clamor from the public followed, forcing the resignation of the head of the BBC and compulsory ethics training for its staff. The scandal came to be known as Queengate.

Needless to say, Her Majesty is not a wildebeest, but one of the dirty little secrets of wildlife filmmaking is that Queengate-like trickery happens routinely. As television has evolved from three channels to hundreds, the pressure to make more exciting programs and achieve high ratings is intense. In addition, says communications professor and former National Geographic filmmaker Maggie Burnette Stogner, "The budgets have fallen, leading to budget and time pressures that virtually force filmmakers into fakery, deception, staging, and provocation, including baiting and luring wildlife out of hiding, faking scenes and interactions between wildlife, and forcing wildlife behaviors." Stogner maintains that all filmmakers will admit to feeling this pressure—and many admit that they've succumbed to it.

Sometimes the trickery involves manipulation of film or video footage, as with the square-dancing scorpions in Disney's *The Living Desert,* discussed in Chapter 2. Later in this chapter I will discuss the more sophisticated digital tools some filmmakers use to similar ends today. But more often wildlife filmmakers deceive audiences through "staging"— that is, making something "natural" happen artificially for the benefit of the camera. Staging is a shortcut used to film otherwise inaccessible events. One well-known example is David Attenborough's footage of a mother polar bear giving birth in a stellar 1997 documentary for BBC1 *(Wildlife Special: Polar Bear),* which he later admitted was shot in a Belgian zoo.

Staging can also be used to streamline the filmmaking process. Attenborough felt he was justified when he arranged for scorpions to mate in a studio with a painted sunset and Styrofoam clouds: "If you say, 'I wish to explain how scorpions copulate, because it's very interesting,' then you have to do that as clearly as you can. It may involve getting them to do it on glass, so that you can see underneath. It will certainly involve getting an adult male scorpion and an adult female scorpion together. What it does *not* involve is sitting around in the Mojave Desert for nine months, waiting for some scorpions to copulate by your feet."

In addition to making rare natural phenomena accessible and speeding things up, staging can create behaviors and situations that would never happen in the wild. For example, many films on grizzly bears make them seem incessantly ferocious. In truth, these animals spend most of their time in the wild quietly minding their own business and rarely charge people without provocation. The "ferocious" shots are obtained with trained bears conditioned to snarl on command. The audience usually has no idea it is being deceived. In the absence of clear industry standards, filmmakers are left with their own consciences to decide what's ethical and what's not.

This chapter describes some of the ingenious ways that wildlife films can deceive audiences. After pulling back the curtain on those tricks, I suggest some sensible rules for filmmakers and some reasonable expectations for audiences. But, as the saga of filmmaker Marty Stouffer suggests, it's a lot easier to talk about these rules than to figure out who is really breaking them.

Dozens of Ways to Deceive

Concerns over ethics have been with us throughout the history of wildlife filmmaking. But it was a tall, eccentric Englishman, Jeffery Boswall, who began a systematic study of the issue starting in the 1970s. Boswall, born in 1931, spent nearly three decades as a producer for the BBC Natural History Unit and is one of the industry's most probing and illuminating thinkers.

In a 1988 paper on wildlife filmmaking ethics, "The Moral Pivots of Wildlife Filmmaking," Boswall asserted that anything that made an animal behave unnaturally—for example, baiting it or giving it food it does not normally eat—constitutes audience deception. He points out that introducing one animal to another it does not normally interact with—for example, a wolverine and a python—is deceptive. So is having the film crew behave in a way that disturbs an animal's behavior—for example, frightening a bird off its eggs by moving too fast near its nest. Other deceptions include the temptation to exaggerate, to overdramatize, and to sentimentalize. The common sin of anthropomorphism, or attributing human characteristics to animals, Boswall describes as "a kind of lying" because it teaches audiences to misunderstand the real nature of animals.

Boswall's definition of audience deception is sweeping. In his mind, it includes pretending that a recording of a bird's song was made at the same time as the pictures for that scene or recording the flapping of an umbrella and pretending it's the noise made by a bird's wings. Boswall claims that even music can introduce a lie. If you accompany footage of animal behavior with music that suggests that the animal is behaving in a human way (for example, by making it look as though the animal is dancing or feeling romantic), then "you are deceiving the people who are experiencing the film."

Besides deceiving audiences as to what is happening in nature, film producers can, as in the Attenborough example above, lie and mislead audiences about how the film is made, Boswall says. Filmmakers use shots of tame or captive animals, domesticate wild animals themselves, or bring wild animals temporarily into controlled conditions. Then they go to great lengths to present these creatures as if they were wild.

Though these all qualify as deceptions in Boswall's mind, they are not all necessarily bad. Boswall believes it's up to individual filmmakers to decide where to draw the line—but warns that audiences might be surprised to know where filmmakers have been drawing it recently. Even strongly conservation-minded filmmakers sometimes bait sea creatures with chum (an oily mix of fish bait and blood), which can lead to unnatural feeding frenzies, or use bright spotlights to film lions hunting at night, which give lions an unfair advantage. And if you see a bear feeding on a deer carcass in a film, it is almost certainly a tame bear searching for hidden jellybeans in the entrails of the deer's stomach. The candy gives the impression that the proud carnivore is feasting on a fresh kill.

In his book *Snarl for the Camera: Tales of a Wildlife Cameraman*, filmmaker James Gray describes re-creating a snake-mating "bundle" by capturing an assortment of male snakes and one female snake and putting them all in a large oil drum. The next day, he dumped out the barrel and filmed the snakes writhing and slithering in all directions, thus giving his film dramatic, but false, footage of what appeared to be masses of snakes mating. On another occasion, when filming Australia's native mammals, he used a pet cat as a stand-in for a feral cat and then used a dummy mouse filled with dead mouse pieces to get the cat to hunt.

A 1985 article in *Discover* magazine first shattered my illusions about the authenticity of wildlife filmmaking. Author Jamie James described filmmaker Wolfgang Bayer in the Arizona desert introducing a kingsnake and a diamondback rattlesnake "in the hope that the former will oblige by devouring the latter, a natural prey." After choosing a "picturesque gully," Bayer artistically arranged rocks and sticks and then released the two captive snakes. When the king snake ignored the rattlesnake, the filmmaker tried again and again to engage them in combat, with no success. Finally, Bayer's crewmate came up with an idea: he put the rattlesnake into an empty mouse cage for a day so it smelled like a mouse. Problem solved—the king snake soon seized and ate the rattler.

In his book *In the Heart of the Amazon*, filmmaker Nick Gordon describes his own fabrications in the pursuit of exciting storytelling. He built a set (undisclosed to viewers) and was filming a female tarantula in her burrow when a venomous fer-de-lance snake entered the burrow tunnel in search of prey. It's left to readers to speculate on how the snake got there. Gordon doesn't admit to it in his book, but it would be standard procedure for almost all wildlife filmmakers to stage such a confrontation.

As Gordon was watching through his camera, the tarantula immediately detected the snake's vibrations. She spun around to face the place where the tunnel widened out to form her chamber. As Gordon saw the snake's head come into the camera's frame, the tarantula made a lightning dash forward and bit the snake, which died instantly. Gordon continued to film as the spider moved toward the dead snake and picked it up by the head with her fangs to eat it. It took fifteen hours for the spider to devour the two-foot snake, leaving only the skin. As befits a good housekeeper, the tarantula removed the skin from her home, depositing it on the leaf litter outside for the ants to finish off. Unfortunately, she didn't carry the skin out immediately after she had finished eating, and Gordon fell asleep. He woke up horrified to find he had missed this final act. A bit of staging took care of this problem: Gordon found the snakeskin, placed it on the floor of the tarantula's burrow, and waited for the spider to pick it up with her fangs and carry it out again. This time the camera was running.

How does a conscientious filmmaker decide which of these practices are unethical? And how can viewers judge? We'll come back to Boswall and my own thoughts on that later. But first, I'll share some of the experiences and people that have shaped my thinking.

Drawing the Line

My own audience deceptions came soon enough. When I first got into television in the early 1980s, I brought home a film my colleagues and I had just completed to show my wife, Gail. She especially liked a close-up scene of a grizzly bear splashing through a stream and asked me how we were able to record the sound of water dripping off the grizzly's paws. I had to admit that my talented sound guy had filled a basin full of water and recorded the thrashings he made with his hands and elbows. He then matched the video of the bear walking in the stream with the sounds he had recorded.

Gail was shocked and called me "a big fake." She said she wouldn't have been bothered if the film had been a fictional Hollywood movie. But I had made a documentary, which led her to expect authenticity and truth.

Regardless of viewers' expectations, the sound in most wildlife films is not recorded live. Recording sound at the same time as filming, known as "sync-sound," is challenging outdoors, especially in windy conditions. Moreover, getting a camera close enough to a bear or other wild animal to record those sounds is risky. The cameramen I work with use long telephoto lenses to get close to our subjects. Sounds are usually added in post-production from noises created in the studio, sound libraries, or recordings made in the field. Noises fabricated in the studio can be made to sound like the real thing. A person chomping on celery becomes a lion biting into a wildebeest, squeezing a rubber glove full of talcum powder doubles for footsteps in the snow, and flapping an umbrella suggests an eagle taking off.

My crew and I used different kinds of artifice in our giant-screen film *Whales*. The film was based in large part on scientific facts about whales and their migration. In Patagonia we scrupulously filmed from the top of high cliffs so that the leviathans would be unable to sense our presence. But we also fudged a little. We lured southern right whales into a bay by emitting recorded whale sounds into the water so we could film them more easily, and we invented the story of a mother humpback whale we called Misty and her calf, Echo, on a three-thousand-mile migration from Hawaii to Alaska. The film shows the duo surviving predatory killer whales and ships that unintentionally ram them until, finally, Misty and Echo arrive in Alaskan waters—except that the two whales arriving are not the same two whales shown leaving Hawaii, though the audience is led to believe that they are.

Many filmmakers would not consider any of this an ethical breach. After all, the science was accurate, it would have been impossible to film the same mother and calf leaving Hawaii and then arriving in Alaska, and we served the cause of whale conservation by making the film more dramatic. Yet I believe it was wrong to deceive the audience, and I regret it.

In the mid-1990s, when I worked at the National Wildlife Federation's nonprofit film company, we made a giant-screen film on wolves. The goal was to debunk the idea, perpetrated by ranchers, that wolves were "land piranhas" that should never have been reintroduced into Yellowstone National Park because they kill livestock and are generally a menace. We built a national campaign around *Wolves*—including speakers, Web sites, articles, and premieres with activists, donors, stakeholders, and policy-makers—to increase public support for wolf protection.

As the executive producer, I gave many speeches after film screenings. But when people who admired the film asked how we obtained certain shots, I felt awkward and embarrassed. "How did you film the mother wolf in its den?" I was often asked. I didn't want to admit that many of the scenes involved captive wolves, nor was I eager to reveal that the "den" where the mother wolf suckled her newborn pups was a manufactured set. If I exposed such trade secrets, people might feel cheated.

Nevertheless, I came clean, doing my best to explain why we had decided to work with captive wolves in a controlled setting. In the film credits, we disclosed this fact, but most people hadn't noticed the disclosure; each time I gave this speech I could tell the audience felt disappointed.

"Wildlife" from Farms

Game farms are businesses that make some of these deceptions possible. They profit from keeping wolves, bears, bobcats, wolverines, tigers, deer, coyotes, lions, and many other animals in captivity. Their customers range from still photographers who need pictures for hot-selling calendars to filmmakers working for the BBC, National Geographic, and Discovery. Most people watching wildlife films think they are observing natural behavior in the wild. But sometimes a filmmaker is using game-farm animals to deceive them.

How did my crew and I get the captive wolves for the National Wildlife Federation's film? Well, I regret to say they were obtained from a game farm. We made that choice not only because it would have been difficult to get close to wolves in the wild but also because filming wolves in the backcountry could habituate them to humans and thus imperil their survival. That made sense to me then, and it still does now. But I've changed my mind about game farms, for reasons I'll explain below.

Mark Wexler, editorial director of the National Wildlife Federation magazine *National Wildlife,* insists that every photo he publishes of captive or controlled animals is clearly labeled as such. (Sierra Club, the publisher of this book, does the same in its popular desk calendar.) That works well for a magazine but not for a film, where you have to figure out how to be honest about your methods without interrupting the story. In *Wolves,* the credits stated, "Sections of this film were made possible by employing captive wolves. This reduces stress on wild populations that would otherwise be affected by prolonged or intrusive filming requirements. No animals were harmed during the production of this film." That's all well and good, but how many viewers actually read it? Furthermore, now that I know more about game farms, I'm no longer so confident that "no animals were harmed."

Often game farms are merely crude storage facilities for the wildlife media industry. When I inspected one in 2000, I saw lynx, bears, wolves, bobcats, and many other animals penned in cages only slightly bigger than the animals themselves, looking as miserable as you would expect.

While I brooded about the immorality of the animals' living conditions, the owners boasted about the number of high-profile wildlife filmmakers they served.

Wildlife photographer Tom Mangelsen refuses to use game farms to obtain his award-winning images. He argues that game farms disregard the welfare of animals in order to make a profit. He worries about the loss of respect cinematographers and photographers will suffer once the public finds out about game farms' role in the filmmaking business. Not only are the cages where the animals spend most of their lives small and uncomfortable, but many animals are shipped cross-country in tiny tarp-covered cages pulled by trailers. They are forced to "endure the sounds and smells of each other but also the sounds and smells of tires, interstate highways, and big cities," Mangelsen says. "The emotional stress from the noise, the smells, the darkness, and natural predators in cages being stacked together is unimaginable." Animals that don't cooperate are often punished with electric cattle prods or other crude disciplinary devices. For example, when an animal is performing for a client, piano wire might be tied around its neck and then jerked to elicit the desired reaction. Mangelsen argues that to support game farms is "to deny that wild animals feel pain, suffering, joy, and fear."

Wildlife filmmaker Beth Davidow uses game-farm animals occasionally and says the farms vary in quality. At the Triple D game farm in Montana, for example, the owners "care as much for all of their animal charges as you or I would a beloved pet dog or cat. Baby animals, which are purchased from captive breeders and never taken from the wild, are hand raised, often inside the house. When an animal reaches the end of its modeling career, the owners of the Triple D game farm take care of it until the end," she says. But at another game farm, whose name she won't reveal, she watched an animal trainer repeatedly strike a bear with a stick because the bear would not perform. Davidow was sickened, but she believes that this kind of unethical behavior is rare. Besides, she argues, game farms are necessary. They offer a useful service to broadcasters, filmmakers, and photographers and help educate the public about wildlife—all without chasing or otherwise harassing animals in the wild. The benefits Davidow cites are real, but I question her confidence that abusive game farms are rare. From what I've seen for myself and heard from others, most game farms do not have a standard of care that responsible wildlife filmmakers—and their audiences—would want to support.

The wildlife filmmaking heavyweights that still patronize these places could use their clout to raise game-farm standards. As game farms currently exist, the animals are not truly wild, and the clients aren't truly wildlife photographers. These animal gulags are just another form of audience deception.

Unfortunately, few good alternatives exist to sourcing captive animals from game farms. A handful of nonprofit sanctuaries and humanely run zoos allow filmmakers to work with their animals to get close-up shots, always within the confines of those venues. There are private trainers who raise animals, such as bears, for both educational and entertainment purposes; in practice, however, their operations often differ little from game farms. A few filmmakers have gone to great efforts to raise animals specifically for filming, so they can be acclimated to humans and cameras from birth, as did the makers of *Winged Migration*. But that raises a tricky question: What happens to the animals after filming? The only conscientious answer is that they should be donated to well-run sanctuaries committed to their welfare.

One larger issue is the lack of consistent, rigorous regulation concerning wild and exotic animals. The filmmaking community should take part in an ongoing, open debate about ethics and practices in this area and actively seek better solutions in cases where animals cannot or should not be filmed in their natural state. Another important consideration is the kind of animals being filmed. It's one thing to raise or temporarily capture insects, reptiles, or even birds and small mammals for filming (see the description below of the Fosters' work). Dealing with large, powerful creatures such as wolves, wolverines, bears, or leopards is quite another. There are no simple answers here, but the questions need to be faced head-on.

Ethical Staging

Some filmmakers have found creative solutions to working with animal subjects. For the past twenty years, Carol and Richard Foster have made natural history documentaries, mainly about the rainforests of Central America. Their forty-five films have been shown internationally and won many awards, including an Emmy for *Journey through the Underworld* (1994). But they're most famous for the techniques they've developed for filming elusive rainforest creatures, often involving staging. From a remote studio in the forests of Belize, using solar energy to produce their own power, they've filmed a young crocodile making a pool with its body against the river bank to trap prey and then moving its tail to chase victims to its jaws, a baby cantil viper wriggling the green tip of its tail over its head to attract and capture frogs, and a flower mite hitchhiking in the nostrils of a hummingbird. Such footage has opened up worlds previously known only to biologists—or unknown even to them. It has also demonstrated that staging can be honest and open and can minimize harm to animals.

The Fosters' studio and grounds are surrounded by sets that replicate their subjects' natural environments, including jungle settings for jaguars and limestone caves for bats. Their lab is equipped with special water-cooled lights (which don't overheat small subjects) and booms on overhead rails (which can film and follow a creature on the move). They employ "table-top sets," which are microhabitats where animals can exhibit natural behavior in favorable filming conditions—for example, a four-by-four-foot enclosure with a small pool for a cantil viper. Other enclosed sets encompass huge trees. The largest sets encircle a couple of acres of forest with a ten-foot electrified fence, which does the animals no harm but deters them from escaping.

When they start a film, the Fosters try to learn as much as possible from scientists. Next, they try to study their subjects in the rainforest. Small animals such as birds, bats, reptiles, and insects are then caught, as humanely as possible, and transported to the sets. Large animals, such as jaguars, are borrowed from the Belize Zoo. Some creatures settle in quickly, while others stress out and need constant care to nurse them through their first few days in captivity. Getting the food for some of the Fosters' captives requires long hours out in the forest collecting a particular insect or fruit. Finding the appropriate filming technique can take months of experimentation.

One difficult issue is light. To film fishing bats with a high-speed camera, for instance, requires massive amounts of light. A large flight cage has to be constructed, as well as a riverbank and a clear pool of water with a filter system. The set is then stocked with fish, plants, trees, and a suitable hollow trunk for a roost (a dark place where bats sleep during the day). Several fishing bats are then netted from a local river and transported to the set, where they quickly adapt to their new home.

Food rewards are used to condition the bats to voice commands. Initially the bats are fed from a long stick with a small fish stuck on the tip. Later, fish are impaled on flexible pins just below the pool surface and agitated by attached lines. The bats use their innate sonar to sense the ripples, and before long, they are scooping up fish with their clawlike back feet. Now comes the difficult part: Lights with a capacity of 6,000 watts are positioned to shine into the pool. Starting at very low levels, the amount of light is increased a little each night. After several weeks of acclimation, the bats are feeding while the lights are on at full power. Then, during feeding, a specific voice command is used to tell the bats that they can go fish. Eventually the bats will fish on command in bright light. After the filming is complete, they leave their cushy set for the real world back on the river.

Most animals are in captivity for two weeks and then released in good health. (Some bats are held a little longer, about a month.) The Fosters observe them as they fly away into the same habitat in which they were captured.

One time the Fosters wanted to shoot vampire bats drinking human blood. They built an artificial cave to house a small colony of these legendary bats, which emerged every night to dine on the blood of several large and unconcerned pigs sleeping in an enclosed sty nearby. (It's not unusual for bats to feed on domestic pigs in this area; some pigs are exposed to rabies, but actual cases seem to be few.) Beside the pig enclosure the filmmakers constructed a separate set made to look like a jungle hunting camp. A Belizean friend, who had strong nerves and had received a full course of rabies vaccine, volunteered to be the "hunter" and feign sleep in the camp bed. From inside ports in the front of the set, two cameras—a standard infrared and a highly sophisticated thermal one—recorded the scene in multiple colors. Once night fell, the bats wasted little time, scuttling over the man like rats, using their heat-sensitive noses to find the hot spots on his skin where blood was closest to the surface. After a dry bite on the forehead, one bat settled for an elbow, biting out a small divot of skin; anticoagulant in its saliva caused the tiny wound to bleed profusely and thus provide a banquet for all the bats. The "hunter" later said he felt only a tiny nip as from a mosquito bite, but he bled for a long time afterward.

The Fosters recognize that capture and captivity do at times cause stress to the animals. But the couple does an exemplary job of minimizing any suffering, and they believe that the hardships their animals endure are offset by the gains in knowledge and conservation brought about by their films. If they know an animal won't do well in captivity, they don't capture it; they either avoid filming it or do so in the wild.

As to the issue of deception, audiences may or may not hear about the Fosters' methods, because disclosing that information is up to their clients, who include National Geographic, the BBC, and Discovery. But the Fosters do their part: they are completely open about how they obtain their remarkable footage.

Staging after the Fact: Digital Magic in Wildlife Films

Another kind of audience deception doesn't require captive animals or situations staged for the camera; it involves manipulating film after it is shot. The use of computer-generated imagery (CGI) allows film-makers not only to alter existing images drastically but also to create realistic scenes without using any actual footage. In today's films, images that viewers see on screen may be constructed from multiple photographs taken in the real world, they may be a combination of real-world footage and computer-generated images, or they may be complete fabrications—lifelike, three-dimensional representations of our world that have been created by highly skilled digital artists.

CGI and digital visual effects have been seen for some time in Hollywood fantasy blockbusters, and now they are showing up in wildlife films. Audiences don't realize the degree to which some wildlife films contain digitally manipulated images. They assume they're watching authentic and natural images of wildlife behavior, but they may not be. Animals in herds can be multiplied, blood can be added, unsightly roads or people can be erased, and the gap between predator and prey can be reduced. Such manipulations, while deceiving the audience, can increase the market value of the film and help achieve higher ratings. They are relatively easy to do—and very tempting for filmmakers engaged in intense competition for viewers, who have so many entertaining options on other channels.

In June 2009, filmmaker Howard Hall was in a video studio where he watched an editor insert a sea otter into a shot of a shark swimming near the surface of a bay. "Looking at the results," says Hall, "it was essentially impossible to tell that the otter had not actually been there when the shark fin broke the surface." Hall noted that this use of CGI is not necessarily bad (though he would not use it in one of his own films) because—in truth, the otter and the shark had been in close proximity— the cameraman just never got the shot because the two never appeared on the surface at the same time.

Hurricane on the Bayou (2007) was a giant-screen film produced by MacGillivray Freeman Films Educational Foundation (of which I'm the president) and directed by Greg MacGillivray. Initially conceived of as an eye-opening journey into Louisiana's disappearing wetlands and the dire consequences of a hypothetical hurricane, the production was in the process of simulating a catastrophic Category 5 hurricane in New Orleans when the Gulf Coast was struck with the all-too-real Hurricane Katrina, which would become the most devastating and costly natural disaster in U.S. history.

We had extensive footage from before and after Katrina hit, but we still needed a way to capture some of the most intense moments in the middle of the storm, when no cameras were rolling. For these dramatic sequences, we used computer-generated special effects to provide powerful images, including Katrina's approach into New Orleans, the near-instant destruction of the water tower in the town of Buras by 200-mile-per-hour winds, water cresting the New Orleans levees during the storm, and pieces of the roof blowing off the Superdome.

The challenge was to recapture certain moments during Katrina's havoc and to convey a visceral sense of its destructiveness. The CGI effects in *Hurricane on the Bayou* brilliantly demonstrate the sheer brutal power of hurricanes. Without these scenes, the film would not have had the same visual and emotional impact.

In the cases above, graphic manipulations, though somewhat deceptive, helped tell a story more effectively and did not distort physical reality. The danger we face, as technology continues to advance, is in creating apparently realistic film sequences that are complete fabrications. In an article discussing the notable Disney-BBC film *Earth,* Chris Evans writes, "With such advances in CGI technology, it will be hard for nature filmmakers not to be tempted to fake amazing scenes, especially as competition increases." Evans quotes *Earth's* producer Alix Tidmarsh as saying, "It is inevitable that some will be tempted to use CGI, and it makes me cry." Filmmakers on smaller-budget nature documentaries, predicts Evans, will inevitably tinker with special effects to cut back on costs.

Fortunately, we're not there yet. Most of today's wildlife and environmental films avoid the extensive use of CGI. As emerging technologies make it easier and more cost-effective to fabricate visual information, however, filmmakers must consider the ethical concerns associated with such audience trickery. Even when the results of CGI are scientifically accurate, I think audiences have a right to know, through the use of prominent disclaimers, that they are watching manipulated images. With CGI, virtually anything can be faked, which means that nothing can be trusted. Many producers are inclined to conceal filmic manipulations, arguing that their job is to entertain and win over audiences. It's the same argument used to justify any kind of deception, and while digital wizardry doesn't harm any animals, failing to reveal its presence ultimately undercuts the credibility of the whole industry.

What Filmmakers Owe Animals and Audiences

I try to approach these complex issues in both practical and ethical terms. Let's say I'm trying to film an isolated detail of animal behavior such as lobsters spawning. Following a noncaptive lobster around underwater, waiting for the right moment and right light, wouldn't be practical, so I would film lobsters spawning in a tank. With larger animals such as bears, ethical and safety issues become paramount: it's dangerous to get too close and imprudent to habituate wild bears to humans, so it makes sense to use captive, tame bears. It's a paradox, but captive animals make responsible wildlife films possible—so long as certain principles are honored.

As stated earlier in this chapter, I'm determined to avoid using animals from game farms again, but I would consider using captive animals from humanely run businesses. To avoid deception, I would tell my audience how the film was made. Many filmmakers make a virtue out of this, and audiences often find the adventure of the filmmaking process fascinating in and of itself.

At the very least, every wildlife documentary should make some kind of announcement during the opening credits. Ideally it would say, "All animals in this film are completely wild and not captive or controlled in any way. No staging of any kind was used, and no animals were disturbed or harmed." Unfortunately, few natural history films could make such sweeping claims without lying. Honest qualifications of any kind would be welcome. I'd suggest, "Many of the scenes in this film were shot on a set under controlled conditions, but scientific advisers to the film guarantee that all animal behaviors filmed are natural and biologically accurate." Or "No animals were disturbed, injured, or killed during the making of this film." Or "Some of the scenes depicted in this film were shot with tame, captive animals." Or "All the scenes in this film are real and not staged."

Such disclosures are a good way to deal honestly with manipulations that could mislead viewers. But what about artifice that might harm animals? In such cases, merely telling the audience the truth doesn't solve the problem. In fact, it's tough to determine right and wrong in this area. If it's okay to film a lobster in a tank, for instance, is it okay to build a set so viewers can witness the birth of an extremely secretive animal such as the wolverine? Is there an ethical distinction between building a set to rear young animals for filming and building a set to help a predator? Is it ethical for a filmmaker to release a deer and a hungry wolf into an enclosure from which there is no escape in order to record the capture and kill? And if it isn't okay to film a setup deer kill, is it okay to release a drugged fish into shark waters to record aquatic "hunting"?

In the 1970s, Jeffery Boswall gave lectures in which he would ask audiences to vote on a graded series of such moral problems. He invited people to imagine, first, that they were making an important conservation film and needed a shot of a spider eating a fly. How many of them would be willing to artificially introduce a fly to a spider, rather than wait days, maybe even weeks, for it to happen naturally? He explained that every day of the shoot is expensive. Anything that saves time and money would make it more likely that the film would be a financial success. Most audience members typically thought that staging a spider eating a fly was perfectly acceptable.

Then Boswall asked them if they would be willing to introduce a worm to a frog. The number of votes in favor came down a little. Moving on, he asked if they would introduce a snake to a bird, and the votes continued to decline. How about a monkey to a boa constrictor? Boswall explained that monkeys are routine prey for boa constrictors, so there was no problem with scientific integrity, and the film would encourage conservation. But by this time, very few hands, if any, were left in the air. Boswall thus demonstrated the fact that we're programmed by evolution and culture to bond emotionally to our mammal relatives more than to invertebrates and cold-blooded creatures.

The Ethical Trials of Marty Stouffer

Boswall's experiment also showed that reasonable people can have different views of right and wrong—as can filmmakers. There's an ongoing debate in the filmmaking industry on topics such as audience deception, staging, captive animals, and other issues you'll read about in future chapters. No one has been more a more widely publicized figure in these debates than Marty Stouffer, first introduced in Chapter 2.

By 1996, Stouffer was one of the country's leading wildlife filmmakers, and his show, *Wild America,* had been drawing large audiences on PBS for fourteen years. But in March of that year, journalists Mike McPhee and Jim Carrier wrote a three-part series on wildlife filmmaking in the *Denver Post* containing ethical allegations against Stouffer. The articles alleged that he filmed in enclosed spaces, edited scenes in a way that misled audiences, abused animals, and sometimes used animals that were not wild. He had supposedly tied down prey, such as rabbits, with invisible filament, so predators could catch and devour them, allowing dramatic action to be filmed easily. In short, he was accused of behaving in a flagrantly unethical manner.

The series also mentioned a dramatic scene in which a mountain lion attacks a cross-country skier in Stouffer's video *Dangerous Encounters.* Unbeknownst to viewers, the mountain lion was habituated to humans; it belonged to a Boulder, Colorado, veterinarian named Greg Hayes. One of the *Denver Post* articles stated, "After the tame cat runs off, the film's narrator intones: 'This man was lucky.'" Stouffer, who admitted that this scene was a "factual re-creation," clearly misled his audiences (a practice, as we've seen, that's not unusual in this business).

The article also said that three animal suppliers stopped working with Stouffer because he wanted to stage more-violent scenes. However, no names were given to support this statement. Stouffer "flatly denies he ever harmed animals, and admits to only limited staging—taking tame animals for a walk in the woods with camera rolling, for example." The article quoted Stouffer as saying, "The techniques used by me and other wildlife cinematographers are, to me, at times, almost in the Santa Claus/Tooth Fairy/David Copperfield category. They are benign illusions meant to entertain while they educate, not any sort of malicious deception or intentional dishonesty. I make magic as I provide humans with enhanced love for and appreciation of our precious natural world. The 'pictorial essays' which I create are always true and yet they are not always real."

PBS took these and other charges seriously and launched an investigation of all 110 *Wild America* shows. PBS hired Vicki Hughes, a consultant experienced in natural history filmmaking, to take a close look at each episode. Hughes evaluated the professional ethics of the films—including how the animals were treated and whether the audience was misled—and whether the films were scientifically accurate.

Hughes found that "a significant percentage" of the sequences were filmed on a set or in an enclosure. For example, in episode #102, "Wild Dogs," wolves chase and kill a deer. Her report notes that "it is almost certain that the sequence was filmed in an enclosure, and that the deer had little or no chance of escape, a circumstance that is certainly unnatural and to my mind unjustifiable." Stouffer maintains that there was no enclosure of any kind in this scene; rather, "anyone who knows anything about wildlife understands that the prey species will often circle over and over again within their home range when chased by a predator."

In episode #707, a bobcat hunts a snowshoe hare but is ultimately unsuccessful. The PBS report concludes that while the scene may have been filmed in an enclosure, at least it was big enough to encourage a more natural predator-prey relationship. Stouffer denies there was any enclosure at all. The report notes that in later episodes, there appear to be bigger enclosures.

To this day McPhee argues that Stouffer used "numerous fences in his shots, some of which could be seen in the films." He also adds, "There was fishing line tied to the legs of prey." When I mentioned McPhee's remarks to Stouffer, he exploded: "All untrue!" He maintained that the fences were part of the landscape long before he arrived. "We absolutely did not construct fences for the purpose of containing captive filming subjects, and we did not tie fishing line to the legs of prey."

According to Hughes, the most obviously questionable staged sequences "tapered off" after the first four seasons. She concluded that only 15 of the 110 programs "could be improved by a variety of minor revisions," including fact clarification, notification to viewers, and removing or reframing dated material. While the report did find staging in Stouffer's shows, PBS decided that this was not necessarily unethical.

Basically, the investigation exonerated Stouffer. In a memo to member stations, PBS concluded that the program "has great value—as both engaging television and as a trusted source of information about the natural world. PBS is pleased to have distributed the series for over thirteen years and we are satisfied that the series can responsibly continue in distribution through the remainder of the rights period." In a press release in the fall of 1996, Stouffer announced that he was pleased with the "full support" PBS had given him.

Despite this "full support," however, PBS did not renew Stouffer's contract, "courageously eliminating one of its most popular shows," according to McPhee. He argues that PBS's canceling the program confirms the truth of the allegations in his article. Stouffer has a different interpretation, saying that *Wild America* did not air again on PBS because it had been syndicated for use on commercial broadcast networks, where it continues to air today.

Looking back, Stouffer calls the *Denver Post* series "an embarrassment and a time-wasting diversion into a world full of liars and lies that I would not wish on anyone." Still, he sold three times more *Wild America* videos in the year the articles ran than in any year before or since. These days, Stouffer is spending his time and energy on interactive video Web sites, including WildAmerica.com and JohnDenverSpecials.com. He still sells DVD sets by the tens of thousands and has worked with Google, AOL, AT&T, and Comcast to develop new video technologies.

At the 1996 Jackson Hole Film Festival, Stouffer's entrance caused a stir. Some saw him as bringing a bad name to the business, while others believed he had done nothing wrong. Many filmmakers were probably worried that their own practices would come to light. In a *New York Times* article, Stouffer said he was sure his colleagues were relieved that their work hadn't been scrutinized. He added, "I was a lightning rod, and I was crucified for the sins of many."

Mike McPhee was also in Jackson Hole that year; *National Geographic* magazine had invited him in honor of his investigative work. At a dinner he attended with the magazine's staff, McPhee says he was toasted "for exposing the dark side of their industry, which they said irritates them no end."

National Geographic filmmaker Michael Cascio sees Stouffer as a whipping boy. "The stories are legendary about renowned wildlife filmmakers manipulating scenes for the camera," he says. It was standard practice in the old days. A filmmaking colleague who wishes to remain anonymous observed caustically, "Stouffer didn't do anything that everyone else wasn't doing. Those around him deserted him when the going got tough, like a mob guy going down and suddenly all his mob friends don't know him anymore."

At the end of the *Denver Post* series, McPhee and his colleagues published a story about how "true professional wildlife filmmakers" take huge amounts of time, effort, and care to film wildlife behavior exactly as it occurs in nature, without the intrusion of man. Nothing is made up, altered, or coerced. Stouffer thinks it's unfair to suggest that the industry actually has solid, generally agreed-upon standards. "Who is it that's in charge of such matters? Where are these rules and regulations written down and published, and who is it that will enforce them for all of society? Those answers are not at all clear to me, and, therefore, there is no such standard to which I have ascribed. Of course, I am bound by all of the various laws of my town, state, and country. But, as for ethical guidance, I have no compulsion to be controlled by any rules other than my own personal beliefs and philosophies."

It's possible, of course, that McPhee and Stouffer are both right. The following statements are not mutually exclusive:

1. McPhee's reporting was accurate based on what his sources told him.
2. Some of McPhee's sources were out to get Stouffer and may or may not have been truthful.
3. Stouffer used staging and tricks that a lot of filmmakers use.

4. The whole industry has a long way to go before it can honestly say that audiences are not being deceived.

In the next chapter, we'll look at a different ethical issue: cinematographers and presenters who get too close to their wild subjects, endangering animals and themselves. To explore this topic, I'll tell the tales of three larger-than-life filmmakers who stepped over the line for (respectively) money, science, and a misguided love of grizzly bears.

7

TOO CLOSE FOR COMFORT
What Filmmakers Do for the "Money Shot"

While in Kenya in 1991 to make a film on elephant poaching, I came across a group of filmmakers and tourists watching a cheetah pursue a gazelle. The cheetah repeatedly failed to catch its prey, mainly because a dozen or so Land Rovers got in its way as their passengers attempted to photograph every step of the chase. Cheetah populations are in trouble everywhere in the wild—it is Africa's most endangered big cat—so depriving any individual of food can be consequential. In a Land Rover myself, I was part of the problem.

From chasing cheetahs to plunging through dense brush in search of grizzly bears, wildlife filmmakers and presenters often get too close to their subjects. Even the most careful cameramen face an ethical dilemma. They want to obtain memorable and exciting footage, but getting too close disturbs the animals and, ironically, the "natural" behavior the filmmaker is trying to capture.

Even strongly conservation-minded filmmakers sometimes resort to ethically marginal tactics to ensure high ratings for their films. Wildlife scientist Brian Horejsi observed filmmakers engaging in "outright harassment" in National Geographic's *Shooting the Big Cats* TV series. The offenses included rousting two adult female lions from a buffalo carcass, provoking a male lion and a group of elephants until they charged, and coming within fifty yards of the den of a lioness with a newborn cub. They also drove their vehicles right up to an elephant, and stalked a leopard, forcing the animal to change pace and direction repeatedly. All these intrusions, says Horejsi, were accompanied by patently false claims that the film crew was having no impact on the animals' behavior.

British wildlife producer Barry Paine says, "In the bad old days, the animal circus fascinated us. We watched in awe as the lion tamer thrust his head into the lion's jaw. We marveled as the snake charmer worked his spell on the venomous serpent. We wondered at the elephant trainer who lay under the raised foot of his gigantic beast. We learned little about lions, snakes, or elephants, but we watched in fear (or hope) that something might go wrong, that someone might be killed in front of our eyes. Television presenters and hosts who get close to wild animals are reinventing the animal circus."

It's not hard to trace the source of this trend. As professor and filmmaker Tom Veltre points out, "Once presenters like Steve Irwin showed that you could make a show at one-tenth the cost of the old traditional blue-chip natural history shows [and] that pulled in double or triple the audience, it kicked off a 'race to the bottom' for producers of shows featuring inappropriate, demeaning, and sometimes dangerous interactions with creatures that would prefer to be left alone."

Where to draw the ethical line varies among filmmakers, but many strike compromises with their consciences in order to get their films broadcast. This chapter chronicles some of the hair-raising consequences for both animals and people through three stories: Randy Wimberg's harrowing shark encounter, Brady Barr's python entanglement, and Timothy Treadwell's notoriously fatal mauling by a bear. You'll hear from critics of the filmmaking business and get acquainted with the "crittercam," a device that sometimes succeeds—and sometimes fails—in making the filming process safer and less intrusive. And you'll meet filmmakers Wolfgang Obst and Ray Paunovich, who have devised better ways to make engaging films.

Close Encounters with Sharks

Randy Wimberg was with his dive team at Bikini Atoll in the South Pacific, filming shipwrecks and local wildlife. An experienced and capable cameraman, Wimberg was focused on an area known as Shark Pass, which has a large congregation of reef sharks. Crew members built a cage to protect him from danger, but they removed some of the panels to give the camera an unobstructed view. The plan was for Wimberg to be in the cage while someone in the nearby support boat threw chum into the water to attract the sharks.

When he first saw the cage, Wimberg thought the gap in the sides of the cage looked larger than necessary. It measured twenty inches vertically and extended around the whole circumference. But "there wasn't much planning," he admits. "It was our first dive of the job and we were all a little unsure about what to expect."

Wimberg climbed into the cage and was eased out on a tether about fifteen feet from the boat. When a deckhand threw in the chum, reef sharks quickly showed up in large numbers. Some of the chum drifted into the cage.

Wimberg watched helplessly as frantic sharks began crashing into the cage, tearing at chunks of food caught in the wire mesh. "To stop the pounding, I tried to dislodge pieces caught on the wires." But soon more than thirty sharks were competing for food that was either stuck to the cage or drifting through it.

Suddenly a shark shot right through the gap and exited out the other side of the cage, grazing Wimberg as it passed. He tried to remain calm, the camera still rolling. "I was cursing the deckhand in the boat," he says. "He should have kept the chum downstream." Now he was frantically batting away sharks with his camera, but there were too many of them and too much chum. Another shark shot through the gap. To Wimberg's horror, it didn't pass smoothly out the other side. Instead the shark ended up in the bottom of the cage and started thrashing wildly.

Wimberg tried to curl up in the corner of the cage to escape the frightened animal. "I knew that the shark felt very threatened and would use the only defense it had—its jaws. I figured it would start chomping at anything that got in its way and I could get badly hurt."

Wimberg desperately attempted to push the animal up toward the exit with his camera, but that didn't work. He decided his only chance was to get himself out. As he edged toward the opening in the cage, his teammates in the boat saw what was happening and began raising the cage to the surface. And before the shark could get in a position to bite, Wimberg scrambled out of the cage and into the boat. The shark was released unhurt.

This incident raises uncomfortable questions: Why had the deckhand thrown so much chum in the water? Was he acting on instructions from the producer? Was Wimberg's life—and the shark's—needlessly endangered for the sake of getting exciting footage to help push up the show's ratings?

A strong case can be made that this incident was all about the "money shot." After all, a cameraman in a protective chain-mail suit was swimming twenty feet below Wimberg, filming the whole thing. The producer knew that the more dramatic the action, the more successful the film might be. Indeed, Wimberg's brush with disaster became a high point in the film.

If Wimberg was mistreated, so were the film's audiences. They didn't know about the chum, so many viewers must have gone away thinking that such frenzied feeding behavior happens naturally. The cause of conservation was ill served, too. At a time when shark populations are shrinking worldwide, sharks were being unfairly portrayed as ferocious attackers.

Fortunately, Wimberg escaped without injury. Brady Barr and Timothy Treadwell were not so fortunate.

Brady Barr Pursues a Python

Brady Barr hosts the National Geographic Channel's *Dangerous Encounters*, a title that instantly signals his sensational approach. But he blends sensation with science. Aside from being a regular guest on *The Tonight Show,* Barr is a PhD herpetologist—the first person ever to capture and study in the wild all twenty-three species of crocodiles, one-third of which are endangered. What has driven him, he says, is a desire to save these crocs and educate the public. He hopes his films about crocs and other animals will generate widespread support for conservation. But there's little doubt that large, scaly reptiles are among the most shiver-inducing creatures for most people and thus highly attractive targets for filmmakers in search of good ratings.

In late 2007, Barr went looking for reticulated pythons, named for the netlike markings on their bodies. The largest snake on the planet, this species sometimes grows to nearly thirty feet. Little is known about these pythons, which are often slaughtered for their skins. But the truly giant ones are becoming so rare that it's difficult to find one in the wild. Barr's goal was to capture a reticulated python so that he and other scientists could learn enough about its habitat and behavior to save the species from extinction.

On the island of Flores in Indonesia, Barr and python expert Mark Auliya investigated a cave rumored to hold a large number of these elusive creatures. The two scientists planned to take a population survey of the cave, obtain a thermal image of the habitat, and gather data from each snake captured to determine whether pythons were using the cave as a refuge from the searing daytime temperatures outside. They also wanted to know whether the cave was used for breeding, egg laying, and feeding—or was it simply a safe haven from humans and other dangers?

The cave was probably the most miserable place Barr had worked in his ten years at the National Geographic Society. It was filled with scorpions, roaches, maggots, spiders, bats, lizards, and snakes. But it was the unbelievable amount of bat guano that made it unbearable. At times, Barr had to wade chest-deep through liquefied bat excrement.

On day three, about sixty yards inside the cave, Barr spotted a giant reticulated python partly exposed in a crack. He yelled for the film crew to start the camera rolling. As the python started to retreat, Barr waded across the deepest area of fecal sludge to the other side of the cave to grab the last few feet of the snake before it escaped into the wall.

By this time, Auliya had arrived to help him pull the snake out of its hiding place. Barr gave Auliya the snake's tail while he attempted to free more of the body from the crevice. After a brief struggle, the python popped out of the crack in a blur of coils and quickly started to wrap up Barr and Auliya. Amid the waist-deep slurry, the darkness of the cave, and myriad coils, it was difficult to locate the snake's head. With Auliya still holding the tail, the snake wrapped its powerful coils around Auliya's body and around both of Barr's legs. Its head kept popping in and out of the slurry, making it impossible to secure.

Before they could formulate a plan to escape from the quicksand-like soup, the snake bit Barr below his left buttock. Searing pain coursed through every inch of his body. After securing its hold, the snake threw the weight and power of its muscular body into the bite and started ripping downward. Because the bite took place beneath the swampy surface, no one but Barr really knew what was happening. The pain was so intense he couldn't even attempt to remove the snake from his leg—he could only scream. He was terrified that the snake was going to pull him off his feet and drown him.

After what seemed like an eternity, the snake released its jaw-hold but continued to hold Barr with its coils. The team still could not locate the snake's head despite searching frantically, and Barr was worried that if the snake attacked him again, he might lose consciousness. Or, if they didn't secure the head as quickly as possible, the python might well bite Auliya too.

Luckily the snake released some of its coils, and Barr and Auliya spotted its head. Auliya quickly grabbed it and dragged the snake to the shallow side of the cave where Barr threw a capture bag over its eyes.

After they got the snake into the bag, Auliya turned to inspect Barr's wounds, which resembled those from a shark attack. Pythons have dozens of curved, razor-sharp teeth that produce deep, ripping wounds. When team members saw how severe they were, they immediately hauled Barr out of the cave to administer first aid. Infection was their biggest concern. Snake bites are always dangerous because reptiles carry so much bacteria in their mouths, but to receive a bite while submerged in liquefied bat feces has to be the worst of all infectious situations.

Because they were in a very remote area, Barr had to hike out many miles to the expedition truck and then suffer a torturous hour of driving over bumpy dirt roads before arriving at the first village. Its medical facilities were extremely primitive, so Barr refused to let them do anything but clean the wound, a process that was almost as painful as the original bite.

The closest thing to a modern medical clinic was a three-hour drive. Arriving late at night, they found a young Indonesian doctor who cleaned Barr's wounds again and stitched them up, gave him antibiotics, and then directed him to Singapore for further medical attention. Finally, twenty-seven hours after the incident, doctors in Singapore finished his treatment, and he headed home to recuperate. Following data collection, the snake was released unharmed at its capture site.

The entire sequence was filmed and later shown on prime-time television. Barr says, "It is chilling footage to watch, like a train wreck so horrible you don't want to watch, yet you simply cannot remove your eyes. It was an epic snake capture, one to go down in the history books."

Barr fiercely defends his actions in this incident, as well as the rest of his television work. "Many animals are threatened or endangered, and 'hands-on interaction-science' is the only way to answer questions surrounding them. Yes, capture is stressful for the animals, but you have to weigh that suffering against the overall good of the species. For many species, without hands-on science (for example, attaching transmitters, getting blood samples, or obtaining DNA), we as scientists would be doing nothing more than documenting their extinction."

Barr sees a huge difference between presenters with scientific credentials pursuing research on camera and presenters with no scientific credentials pursuing animals purely to create entertainment. "I never put my hands on an animal for TV. There has to be science behind it," he asserts. "I do not put myself in dangerous situations for ratings, but rather a quest for scientific answers." For this reason, he strongly objects to being compared to someone like Steve Irwin or—even worse—our next subject, Timothy Treadwell. But in terms of the risks to the animals and the presenters, there are similarities.

Grizzly Man Timothy Treadwell

He was not a scientist and had no formal training as a filmmaker. But Timothy Treadwell longed for kinship with other species—particularly grizzly bears. In Katmai National Park in Alaska, he deliberately set up his tent on bear trails, feeding grounds, and sleeping areas. He would crawl on all fours toward bears, singing and talking to them in a high-pitched voice. His intention was to become as much like a grizzly as possible to "delve further into the secret ways of bears," he wrote in his book *Among Grizzlies*. "For so long, people have thought of bears as cruel, unfeeling animals. But I know differently." His "first priority was to respect the wishes of all the animals in their wilderness home." His greatest fear, he claimed, was that others might copy his dangerous style of study and be injured or killed.

Even so, he repeatedly infringed on bears' "personal space"—the area around them that, if entered, can cause them to fight or flee. His behavior violated Katmai National Park's safety guidelines, which state that you should never approach a bear or camp in such a way as to interfere with its movements. Rather, you are supposed to view them from a safe distance, eliminate all traces of food from your camp, never hike in the dark, avoid areas frequented by bears, and carry bear-deterrent pepper spray. Treadwell's infractions went even further—he treated the bears like pets.

Treadwell professed to be concerned about the bears' welfare and used his extensive footage to promote their protection. But he was cavalier about the threat to his own life, saying he would be honored to end up as "bear shit." Veteran Alaskan bear biologist Sterling Miller had warned Treadwell to be more prudent—for the sake of the bears, if not for himself. When someone gets mauled by a bear, the animal is usually killed to prevent further incidents and to calm an anxious public.

In October 2003, Treadwell and his girlfriend, Amie Huguenard, were in a remote area of the park inhabited by many enormous grizzlies, or brown bears as they are called in coastal Alaska. This was the thirteenth season Treadwell had visited Katmai, where he would often stay for months at a time, enduring great hardships from being cold, wet, hungry, and tormented by insects. An experienced outdoorsman, Treadwell knew the area well and thought he knew the bears well, too. Their behavior, vocalizations, and postures were familiar to him, and he moved about with a fair amount of comfort.

With winter approaching, the bears were packing on fat before going into their dens. On October 5, Huguenard and Treadwell heard the sound of a bear outside their tent. This had happened scores of time in the past, and Treadwell promptly got out of the tent to make it go away. Perhaps he thought that, if he stayed in the tent, the bear, attracted by the smell of food or just in an irritable mood, might swat the tent down, and then their struggling bodies could trigger a deadly predatory attack.

Treadwell and Huguenard carried no gun or bear-deterrent spray, and Treadwell refused to put an electric fence around his tent, which many bear field biologists do routinely. He knew he was vulnerable, but he also had an unwarranted faith in his ability, honed over thirteen summers, to deal with even aggressive bears.

So Treadwell unzipped the tent and went out to confront the bear. From here on, the details of the story are unclear. The bear may have seen his sudden appearance as a direct threat. It may have made some bluff charges. At first Treadwell wouldn't have been too worried. Sure, adrenaline would be pumping through him, but he seems to have been sufficiently composed to call out to Huguenard to switch on the camera. He was, like any good cameraman, always looking for exciting footage.

Or maybe Huguenard automatically switched the camera on. That was their standard operating procedure whenever bears were close. Either way, for the next six minutes, all the agony that transpired in that remote spot in Alaska was audio recorded. The lens cap was left on the camera, so there are no video images.

Those who listened to the tape pieced together what must have happened next. Within seconds, Treadwell realizes he has failed to scare off the bear. Instead, to his horror, the bear launches an attack, perhaps triggered by his shout to Huguenard to turn the camera on. He has never been attacked by a bear before. The bear probably goes for Treadwell's head with its jaws. Treadwell screams out to Huguenard, "I'm getting killed out here!"

Huguenard shouts back from within the tent, "Play dead!" She assumes that the bear doesn't want to kill and eat Treadwell but simply wants to neutralize the threat that it thinks Treadwell poses. Then the bear breaks off the attack, and Huguenard rushes to Treadwell's rescue. But the bear returns, perhaps because Treadwell moves too soon, and resumes his mauling, biting, and tearing. For reasons we will never know, the bear switches from a defensive to a predatory attack. In other words, the bear goes from attempting to neutralize an invasion of its personal space to wanting to kill and eat Treadwell. It realizes Treadwell could be a meal.

Treadwell sees what's happening and begs Huguenard to get a pan and hit the bear. She screams at him, "Fight back!" On the tape, Treadwell's screams continue. He realizes he's going to die and tells Huguenard to get away. The bear drags Treadwell off screaming into the brush. He is severely injured, facing a slow and certain death.

Huguenard is left alone, screaming hysterically, having witnessed the ghastly attack. She must know she is next. Her cries may have sounded like the shrieks of wounded prey and brought the bear back to kill her. The remains of Huguenard's partially consumed body were found partly buried right by the tent.

There's some debate about which bear killed Treadwell and Huguenard. Although parts of their flesh, bones, and clothes were found inside Bear #141—an old, thousand-pound brown bear tagged in 1989 by Sterling Miller—the fact that Treadwell took so long to die has led some people to speculate that he was actually killed by a smaller brown bear, who was then chased off by Bear #141. The theory is that Bear #141 should have been able to kill Treadwell relatively quickly because it was so big and powerful. We know from the tape, however, that his death took an agonizing five minutes or more. The next day, after a pilot discovered the bodies and alerted authorities, park rangers and state troopers investigated the campsite and killed two bears that seemed to threaten them, including Bear #141.

Treadwell's life and death were profiled in Werner Herzog's 2005 documentary *Grizzly Man*. By using Treadwell's own footage, Herzog shows the young man's foolhardy behavior on camera—how astonishingly close he got to bears that could easily kill him, sometimes even touching them. In the film, Treadwell comes across not as the heroic eco-warrior he aspired to be but as a complex (perhaps psychologically disturbed) man with strengths and weaknesses.

Treadwell's critics say he got what he deserved. He behaved unethically around bears, disturbing and harassing them. He not only got two bears killed but harmed countless others by "habituating" them, conditioning them not to fear humans and making them more vulnerable to hunters and poachers. His actions encouraged his imitators to harass bears, too. He was irresponsible and reckless and an adrenaline junkie. Miller says that Treadwell is a good example of how *not* to behave around bears, with or without a camera, and that his basic message ("bears are not dangerous") is exactly wrong.

Out of fairness, though, let's look at Treadwell through the eyes of those who admire him. Earlier in his life he suffered from serious alcohol and drug problems, which he vanquished by focusing obsessively on bears and bear conservation. Convinced that bears are peaceful and nonthreatening, he aimed to change people's perception of them as dangerous killers. He wanted people to see them as playful, intelligent, and misunderstood. He despised anybody who would harm bears, including poachers, developers, and hunters.

Treadwell became the bears' self-appointed guardian on the Katmai coast. His supporters claim that he stopped poachers from illegally killing bears for fun and profit. They maintain that he was a brave and compassionate person, a "bear whisperer" with a special ability to relate to and communicate with bears. They also claim that he was a warm, charismatic showman, a dedicated animal activist, and a passionate and persuasive advocate for bears. He spoke to thousands of schoolchildren over the years who were thrilled to hear his stories.

But overall, Treadwell did more harm than good, if only because the media glamorized him without conveying the dark side of his behavior. Although he would not have wanted it so, his and his girlfriend's deaths led to the killings of two bears and reinforced the frontier notion that grizzlies are bloodthirsty killing machines.

The Critics of Closeness

Generally the public supports people like Timothy Treadwell. The daring individual is positioned as a brave pioneer, a pathfinder, and a voice of enlightenment. He is invited to appear on talk shows, as Treadwell did with David Letterman; contributions roll in from celebrities. Critics are in the minority, often viewed as party poopers motivated by jealousy and resentment. But I believe that we need to listen to those who criticize Treadwell, Irwin, and other in-the-animal's-face television hosts.

Rupert Pilkington, a wildlife resource management specialist based in Canada, has served as an expert consultant on five films relating to bear conservation. He says that Treadwell and other hands-on, close-up animal enthusiasts—whom he calls "charlatans"—complicate the task of those, like himself, who are committed to a "different, less sensational, less egotistical form of public education." Their messages are more about themselves than the species they are handling, he says. They offer people too much, too easily—the bear "on a plate." The damage done in Treadwell's case, he says, "will take years of hard work to undo, using the sober, staid, non-egotistical approach that I favor."

Chuck Jonkel, president of the Great Bear Foundation in Montana, cofounded the International Wildlife Film Festival in Missoula in 1977 to promote the production of high-quality wildlife films. He argues that too many TV personalities do "foolish, exotic, scary things to jazz up the show (and make wildlife species seem goofy), such as leaping around, crawling up close, holding snakes, wrestling alligators, and jerking animals out of their dens." He believes that such behavior does "a great disservice to wildlife and endlessly spreads wrong concepts about wild animals, and their behavior."

"So the Croc Hunter was done in by a stingray and Treadwell by a brown bear," Jonkel says. "In both cases they earned their own demise, fooling with nature, doing goofy things with large and formidable animals better left alone. Filmmakers should not be allowed to exploit wildlife for money and fame."

Filmmaker Jennifer Shoemaker, who has extensive experience filming wildlife in and around Yellowstone National Park, refuses to get close to animals if that means disturbing them. She sacrifices close-ups to give the animals the room they need to be comfortable. She's had traumatic experiences, being charged by elk, moose, and bear, and now doesn't feel the urge to get the close-up shot. She films animals behaving naturally, as they would if she weren't there.

In footage from other filmmakers, Shoemaker often sees stress behavior in animals, including tails up and ears back. The truth about those classic aerial shots of herds of zebras and wildebeests thundering across the African plains, she says, is often that the terrified herds are being chased by a helicopter or low-flying plane.

Perhaps the most dedicated critic of up-close interactions with wild animals is Chuck Bartlebaugh. Through the Montana-based Center for Wildlife Information, which he founded in 1980, Bartlebaugh has highlighted the toll that irresponsible nature films and TV shows have taken on wildlife and humans. Combing through national park data, Bartlebaugh has found that most of the serious wild animal attacks have been triggered by human carelessness. In many cases, the people deliberately approached the animals that attacked them. When interviewed, these people often said that they had seen other people get close to wildlife on television shows and videos, and so they assumed it was safe.

Bartlebaugh's early passion wasn't bears. For fifteen years, he raced sports cars on some of North America's most difficult road courses. He drove a Group 7 McLaren Can-Am car, a car capable of more than 200 miles per hour. He was on his way to a chance at driving in the Indianapolis 500 when the 1973 oil embargo ended his corporate sponsorships and thus his racing career.

Not long after, Bartlebaugh decided he could get his thrills a different way—by photographing grizzly bears in Yellowstone National Park, one of the few places in the lower forty-eight states where a small population of grizzlies survives. On arriving in Cooke City, Montana, a small town on the outskirts of Yellowstone, he shared his aspirations with a local bartender, who immediately set him straight. "The last thing we need is another idiot with a camera getting himself killed," the bartender told him. He then introduced Bartlebaugh to a local forest ranger, who told Bartlebaugh that almost everything he was doing was wrong. He was getting too close to the bears, causing undue stress and endangering lives. And he wasn't the only one. In 1987 amateur photographer Bill Tesinsky walked right up to a young grizzly, presumably to get tight head shots of the bear. Obviously threatened by Tesinky's proximity, the bear became aggressive. Rangers later found the grizzly feeding on Tesinky's remains. A year later, wildlife photographer Chuck Gibbs followed a retreating sow and met the same fate. The film in Gibbs's camera showed the progression of the bear feeding at a distance at first and then becoming increasingly agitated and threatening as Gibbs got closer.

Today Bartlebaugh still shoots photos, but he works at a safe distance from his subjects, using binoculars and telephoto lenses. The photos show the subjects expressing themselves in a natural way in a natural setting. A key part of his work, however, is teaching filmmakers, scriptwriters, and producers how to do their work safely and respectfully. What those professionals say and show in their work "will influence how the next generation views wildlife," he says.

Enter the Crittercam

In 1986, marine biologist and filmmaker Greg Marshall (now with the National Geographic Society) invented a streamlined video-imaging system that soon became known as a "crittercam." Attached to an animal, this little device (about the size of a TV remote control) enables biologists to gather new information about difficult-to-observe phenomena, such as feeding patterns, mating behavior, and migration routes. The ways of attaching it are almost as ingenious as the device itself: special suction cups for whales, dolphins, and leatherback turtles; an adhesive patch for seals and hard-shelled turtles; backpack-type harnesses for penguins; and fin clamps for sharks.

Despite the criticism that attaching a camera to a wild animal is too intrusive and infringes on the creature's ability to behave normally, the crittercam has been very successful in some ways. During the last twenty years, researchers have attached the device to more than fifty different species, including whales, bears, and eagles. The crittercam has made it possible to gather important data on animal behavior and ecology that have been published in more than thirty research papers. In some cases, the camera has also been a boon to activists. For example, its deployment on Hawaiian monk seals helped identify their habitat and establish a protected area.

This special camera has also produced unprecedented footage for television, but not without some serious problems. In 1992, Marshall decided to launch a crittercam project with sharks, the source of his original inspiration for the concept. The wanton and wasteful destruction of sharks for their fins (to make shark fin soup) was, and still is, causing immense damage to many shark species. By learning more about shark habits and behavior, Marshall and his colleagues hoped to develop ways to help stop the species' decline.

National Geographic hired Nick Caloyianis, a veteran underwater cinematographer specializing in sharks, to go to the east coast of Mexico to shoot underwater scenes of Marshall attaching a crittercam to a shark. A few weeks later, out at sea, local fishermen hooked a bull shark, intending to sell its valuable fins, but they sold it instead to the research team. Bull sharks are famously aggressive. The late Peter Benchley's novel *Jaws* was inspired by a real-life incident with a bull shark, not a great white. These sharks are potentially dangerous even when they are calm and free, but this one was stressed and confined.

While Marshall was attempting to attach the crittercam to the shark, its handlers, mistakenly thinking Marshall was done, released the creature prematurely. A producer asked Caloyianis to get shots of the free-swimming shark, and though Caloyianis knew it was a risky situation, he agreed, resolving to keep his distance. He dove in and began filming. But what Caloyianis didn't know was that shark handlers in another expedition boat had decided to recapture the agitated bull shark and finish attaching the crittercam.

As he was peering through his lens, Caloyianis suddenly noticed a dark shadow in the upper right corner of the viewfinder. He didn't realize that this was the shadow of a shark handler diving in, hooking the bull shark in its mouth (the first step in installing the crittercam), and hightailing it back to the surface.

The shark, now extremely agitated, lashed out at the nearest creature, which happened to be Caloyianis. He turned the camera toward the shark to push it away, and as the animal thrashed and bit at the camera, Caloyianis's hand went into its mouth. Reflexively, he pulled it out, splitting his thumb and forefinger to the bone. He dropped the camera. As he continued to pound and push the shark away with his hands, it lashed out at his legs. He could feel the shark's teeth sinking into his flesh, tearing it open and crushing his anklebone.

Caloyianis somehow got his leg out of the shark's jaws, but the angry animal charged at him again and again as they both headed for the surface. Caloyianis was now badly injured. He and the shark surfaced right next to the shark handlers' small skiff, and Caloyianis was pulled into the boat, his silver wetsuit streaked bright red with blood. Still hooked, the shark swam along next to the boat. Later that day, the handlers decided the shark had to be killed because it "had tasted human blood."

Caloyianis spent weeks in the hospital and months more recuperating. He still has nightmares about the incident and suffers chronic pain from his injuries, but he believes the attack was not the shark's fault. After all, it had been harassed and provoked to an extraordinary degree. At the very least, this episode was another case in which better planning and communication could have averted tragedy. As to the ethics of using crittercams when the attachment process involves some violence toward the animal being filmed, that's another debatable subject.

Close-Ups without Calamity

Beginning with a daring escape from the communist regime in East Germany in 1961, when he was twenty-four, Wolfgang Obst has taken plenty of risks. Those he takes as a filmmaker tend to be offscreen and involve the respectful watching of wildlife in remote places, not touching or wrestling with them. He gets close to wildlife at times, but only when the animals come to him. Needless to say, this approach to making engaging films takes time and patience.

When I started producing environmental documentaries in the early 1980s, I hired Obst to make a film about the threat of oil drilling to the wildlife—especially migrating caribou—in a 100-mile-long stretch of pristine coastline in Alaska's Arctic National Wildlife Refuge. Four months later, Obst and his wife, who was also his filmmaking partner, hopped in a bush plane and flew to the refuge's coastal plain. Within a few days of their arrival, though, they decided their marriage was over. As a plane carried Obst's wife away from the filming location, a dreadful silence descended. Obst knew that being alone would add significantly to his risk. But he had a one-hour television special to make for Audubon, and I was pressuring him to deliver.

With one tent for himself and another for his camera gear, he felt like a minuscule creature out there alone amid thousands of square miles of harsh wilderness. An injury that might be inconsequential back home could prove fatal in the isolated Arctic with no one around to help. He carried a radio so he could call commercial airline pilots to relay messages in case of emergency, but he discovered that it wasn't working. If anything happened, he would just have to wait until his bush pilot returned with supplies once every three weeks.

Walking on the tundra was challenging. Obst watched every step he took and every move he made. Weighed down by a backpack stuffed with his camera, batteries, extra film, a tripod, shotgun, and food, he wobbled from one grassy lump to another, avoiding icy water in between and taking care not to turn an ankle. Finally arriving at his destination, he settled down to wait in the middle of the empty calving grounds of the Porcupine caribou herd, filming little things here and there but nothing of real interest. He knew wolves and grizzlies were nearby. And he knew he was no longer at the top of the food chain.

After three long weeks, the caribou finally arrived, tens of thousands of them, moving rapidly toward him in a broad front. He felt like running, but there was nowhere to go. Besides, however frightening it was to be in the middle of a stream of caribou on the move, this is what he had come to shoot. As the herd got within thirty feet, they parted to go around him and then closed ranks thirty feet farther on.

"In contrast to the previous silence, this was a madhouse swallowing me up," Obst recalls. "Every year the caribou come to the refuge to have their babies. Many of them had little ones already, and some were born around me. Mothers and babies were calling each other. The noise was unbelievable." Taking special care to disturb the herd as little as possible, Obst camped in the middle of this chaos for two weeks, mostly film-ing—and eating, cooking, and sleeping only when he had to.

Wolves came out of hiding to hunt the weaker caribou. At times as close as sixty feet from Obst, they seemed to view him more as entertain-ment than as a potential meal. The grizzly bears that arrived to feed, sometimes taking over carcasses from the wolves, also stayed away from him—perhaps, Obst says jokingly, repelled by his smell since he had not bathed for weeks. "Wolves were feasting on the old and the young caribou, as were bears," Obst relates. "Finally I had something to film.

"Two weeks later, having had their babies, the herd moved on and was replaced by mosquitoes," Obst says. "With the mosquitoes, my film came to an end because they concentrated on anything dark, and one of these dark places was the front of my lens. There was nothing else I could do. It was impossible to continue shooting."

Another filmmaker known for shooting only the most authentic footage possible is Ray Paunovich. He abides by a code of ethics as strict as that of anyone in the profession. Even so, Paunovich sometimes gets pretty close to his wild animal subjects.

While working on *The Great Bears of North America* in the early 1990s, Paunovich and his soundman, Bart Ready, were on horseback in Yellowstone's Hayden Valley looking for grizzlies. They could smell a carcass east of their position. Because grizzlies will feed on carrion, Paunovich and Ready rode in the direction of the smell, keeping their eyes peeled for bears. At the end of the trail, they found a dead bison next to what appeared to be a pile of brush. Closer inspection revealed that the pile of brush was actually another, younger bison that had been dragged from some distance away and covered up. This was obviously the work of a bear who would most likely be back to continue feeding. Paunovich and Ready found an ideal place nearby to set up their camera, where the wind would not carry their scent to nearby bears. They were close but not so close that they would disturb the animals' natural behaviors.

Their observation post was a small gully about 150 yards away that offered cover and a place to hobble their horses. Peeking over the small rise, they could see the bison carcasses and still be safely hidden. Unlike many wildlife filmmakers, Paunovich is an experienced outdoorsman who grew up hunting and fishing and handling weapons, and he knew how to take care of himself in the wild. But even experienced outdoorsmen make mistakes.

About an hour and a half later, a sow with two small cubs emerged from a patch of timber about half a mile away. At first, the bears were just feeding at the edge of the timber, and Paunovich wasn't sure if they knew about the bison. But little by little they fed and played their way toward the carcasses. Then, as if someone had rung a dinner bell, all three grizzlies made a beeline for the bison.

Although the men were not in the direct path of the bears, the grizzlies ended up entering the small gully in which the men were hiding. When they were 250 yards away, the bears suddenly stood on their hind legs, sniffing, and then dropped down and circled around. The sow began to foam at the mouth and snap her jaws, a sure sign of nervousness and aggression.

Then she spotted the filmmakers. The men heard no warning sounds, but instantly the two cubs came together and the mother bear charged, covering half the 250 yards in a matter of seconds. Paunovich and Ready screamed and waved their arms to scare her away. The horses were terrified and, because they were tied, unable to flee.

When the sow got within a hundred yards of the filmmakers, she stopped, jaws still foaming and snapping. She rose on her hind legs several more times and then dropped down for good. She looked back at her cubs, then at the men, and back toward the cubs again. Then, suddenly, she turned again and charged, this time coming within seventy-five yards of Paunovich and Ready. Once again, the filmmakers yelled and waved their arms. Luckily, she stopped, went to get her cubs, and eventually moved on to the dead bison.

"I'm sure it only took seconds for all this to happen, but it seemed like an eternity, and our legs were trembling. Her speed was something I will never forget," Paunovich says. "She could have been on us in a heartbeat had she wanted to. After things settled down, and we gained our composure, we actually shot some good footage of her and the cubs on the carcasses."

Clearly, it's impossible to eliminate all risk when filming large, dangerous predators in their native environments. Even a filmmaker as conscientious as Paunovich has had close calls. But the care he takes to keep what he judges to be a safe distance may have made the difference in his own survival—and that of some of his subjects.

Inside the Comfort Zone

Obst got close to his caribou, as did Paunovich to his grizzlies. So what makes their methods more ethical than those of, say, Treadwell? Key questions to ask include these: Would the action have taken place anyway even if no cameras had been rolling? Was the close encounter accidental or planned? And, if it was an accident, was it one the filmmakers could have avoided? Was this genuine science education or just a bunch of cowboys trying to make their fortunes on the backs of animals that want to be left alone?

According to Michaela Strachan, a British presenter of wildlife programs, filmmakers who step over the ethical line are trying "to be champions over the animals instead of championing the animals." As a result, presenters may be hurt or even killed, and animals are severely stressed and sometimes provoked into attacking in self-defense. Sometimes the animals get used to having humans around, producing unnatural behavior and diminishing their instinctive flight response. And lies are promulgated—the idea that invading an animal's personal space is a bold, acceptable move; that some wild animals (the ones the filmmakers have goaded into violence) are our enemies; and that others are essentially friendly, cuddly pets, an assumption that could endanger the animals' and the viewers' safety in the future.

When challenged about getting too close, filmmakers tend to react rather like a cornered predator. They fight back with words and are quick to invoke phrases such as "artistic freedom." Filmmakers for Conservation, a nonprofit organization I helped found in 2000, is dedicated to promoting conservation messages in films. At the group's conference in 2006, which took place right after Steve Irwin's death, I tried to pass a motion stating that "Filmmakers for Conservation strongly objects to on-air presenters who harass animals in an effort to provide entertainment." Even though the room was full of filmmakers who favor conservation, this motion got shot down. Perhaps they were concerned that it might restrict them in some way, impeding their ability to make films. Or perhaps, as filmmaker Tom Veltre says, "it seemed a bit like spitting on Irwin's grave."

But solving this problem doesn't really require passing motions at film conferences. We just need more admirers of the respectful, patient methods of Obst and Paunovich and some other filmmakers you'll meet later in this book, who make exciting films that minimize disturbance and convey accurate information. In Chapter 8, though, we'll continue our journey through the dark side of filmmaking. Next up: television shows that flaunt sex and violence.

8

NATURE PORN AND FANG TV
The Temptations of Sex and Violence

You may have been lucky enough to miss the video *Animals Gone Crazy*. With its single-minded emphasis on copulation and predation, the film gives viewers the impression that the lions, tigers, frogs, dolphins, fish, giraffes, elephants, sea lions, bats, pigs, and geese it features are perpetually lascivious or violent (or at least menacing), and that all animals do is mate and kill. It is the saddest excuse for wildlife filmmaking ever to make the DVD format.

The sex side of this film is what critics call "nature porn." The predation aspect, with its animal-on-animal violence, is known as "fang television." Mating scenes are shown repeatedly without context, explanation, or any type of narrative device whatsoever. In some scenes, the director slows down the footage at key moments, even freeze-framing at the point of entry during intercourse. Close-ups of male and female genitals alternate in cutaways with mating sequences. In one ridiculously, but strategically, placed shot, a monkey smokes a cigarette after mating—the epitome of anthropomorphic sexual behavior. The music is ugly and screechy, each tune managing to sound worse than the one before. The mood alternates between erotic and mocking. Perhaps the most astute decision the filmmakers made was to leave no trace of credits, not even a production company, except at the very end to claim copyright for "2004 Wild Empire, LLC."

Animals Gone Crazy is perhaps an extreme example, but any nature show that attempts to shock viewers through sex and violence can be seen as part of an unfortunate recent trend toward nature porn and fang television. *Wildboyz* and *Jackass* (discussed in Chapter 1) are off the air, but shows such as the Discovery Channel's *Man vs. Wild* (known in Britain as *Born Survivor: Bear Grylls,* after adventurer Bear Grylls, the "star" of the show) and Animal Planet's *Dark Days in Monkey City* and *River Monsters* are thriving worldwide. Unlike the pioneering wildlife films we discussed in Chapter 2, these productions often make little attempt to conceal their exploitation, demonization, and harassment of animals. They flaunt them as part of the spectacle of blood and guts they are trying to create. In fact, these producers often deliberately *cause* violence to get footage. They "callously taunt and harass wildlife for entertainment," says filmmaker Vanessa Schulz. As she points out, the producers of such shows send a message that greed justifies disrespect for other living beings.

Indeed, these shows perform a gross disservice to the cause of conservation by demonizing wild animals and encouraging viewers to hate and fear them. Another striking example is *Untamed and Uncut,* a popular series on Animal Planet that shows shocking animal attacks (invariably caused by the victim's greed, carelessness, or ignorance): a marlin impaling a boy's face, a lion mauling a zookeeper, a polar bear in a zoo ripping off a woman's leg. Film producer Katie Carpenter says, "If you are a human supremacist, animal abuser, or general despiser of wildlife, this show just feeds the flame. Animal Planet should be ashamed." The problem is that this brand of mayhem and mutilation has a large and eager audience. Indeed, when I've watched *Untamed and Uncut,* I find myself repulsed yet glued to the set, with my heart racing.

More "respectable" versions of nature porn and fang television are shows with high production values that nonetheless emphasize violence and sex. They may not cause the violence you see on the screen, but they do exploit it. Dorothy Patent, a renowned author of books for children, looked at typical offerings on the National Geographic Channel on Saturday and Sunday evenings and found *Hunter and Hunted,* a show about shark attacks on humans; *Cougar Island,* about cougars attacking humans; *Ultimate Cat,* about the ambush tactics of big cats; *Totally Wild,* about killer whales hunting sea lions; *Astonishing Moments,* about shark attacks and dangerous polar bears; and *Most Amazing Close Encounters,* about savage predators attacking and devouring prey. All these titles make an unspoken promise of relentless, supercharged excitement and bloody carnage. Patent says that she has stopped watching wildlife films on television because "so often the emphasis is on violence and on the demonizing of predators."

I've been accused of showcasing violence myself. At the conference in 2001 where I accused filmmaker Ben Stassen of muddying the IMAX brand with violent fictional movies (see Chapter 1), film producer Steve Schklair turned the tables on me. "The real problem, Chris Palmer, is not films like *Haunted Castle,* but the wildlife films you produce for television," Schklair said. "I absolutely cannot let my children watch documentaries about wildlife unless I have prescreened them. The pornographic level of carnage and violence that are present in many of these films would give my children nightmares for years. I have tried to instill in them a compassion for all living things, and watching a lion rip off the head of a graceful gazelle in slow motion is more than they should witness at their young age." I took Schklair's point to heart. There's a big difference between showing the dispassionate cruelty of nature and moving in with the camera to show every graphic, gory detail under the guise of education.

The celebrations of sex and violence on our TV screens come in low-brow and high-brow forms, as we'll see in the examples that follow. Animal Planet's *Feeding Frenzy* was a silly pseudo-science series that was really about setting up scary but fake confrontations with predators. *Predators at War,* on the other hand, was a more pretentious, polished, and perhaps seductive product from National Geographic Television. Then there's advertising and promotion: the magic of marketing can make even the most respectable mainstream shows look like nature porn and fang TV.

Feeding Frenzy

In late fall of 2008, Animal Planet broadcast *Bear Feeding Frenzy, Lion Feeding Frenzy,* and *Crocodile Feeding Frenzy.* This three-part series described "experiments" with bears, lions, and crocodiles conducted by the ruggedly handsome Chris Douglas. A soap opera star and fashion model, Douglas appears to possess no formal training as a naturalist. The film crew built a five-foot cube, which they called a "predator shield," made of see-through Plexiglas with six-inch-wide air holes. For dramatic scenes, Douglas climbed inside while the powerful predators came right up to the shield. Certainly, the show had an entertaining hook. The animals were just inches away from the handsome host, and they seemed powerful enough to break through the cube at any moment.

In the *Feeding Frenzy* shows, Douglas posed questions and then tried to answer them by conducting experiments and observing the behavior of individual animals. To test the taste preferences of grizzly bears, he placed dishes containing different kinds of food—trail mix, muffins, apples, salmon, and hot dogs—right outside the predator shield and waited to observe the bears' choices. The show also tried to see whether Douglas could talk a grizzly bear out of attacking a human mannequin. In the process of these "experiments," Douglas goaded grizzlies into feeding frenzies and violent attacks on lifelike dummies, as well as breaking into cars and tearing into tents. The host accompanied the action with a narration that called the bears "killers" and described them as "cunning," "ferocious," and "monstrous."

Many scientists, including wildlife biologist Sterling Miller, were dismayed at what these shows tried to pass off as research. Scientists already know that bears are omnivores and will eat anything that humans will, along with many things that people are too squeamish to eat. In addition, because these particular bears were penned and fed rations, they could afford to be picky, so observing their choices had little or no scientific value. The mannequin experiment was useless, too, Miller says. Just because an object is shaped like a human, for instance, doesn't mean that bears perceive it as such—or that any reaction to a mannequin can be necessarily used to predict bear behavior toward live humans. Tom

Smith, a wildlife biologist at Brigham Young University, says most of these "experiments" were "hokum and should have been cut."

The production did have what it called scientific advisors, one of whom was Smith. He reviewed some scripts and convinced the producers that it would be illegal and immoral to film the show in the wild (as opposed to working with captive bears). He asked them not to do certain experiments and to give practical advice to viewers about how to behave around bears. A few months later, the producers asked him to watch the filming of a segment for the bears show. While there, they convinced him to discuss on camera what was happening, even though he had not seen how they were going to use the footage. Like a frog in slowly boiling water, Smith did not realize what he was getting into until it was too late. When Smith saw the final product, he realized that the producers had ignored his advice about how bears should be portrayed in the show. Even worse, by appearing in the program, Smith seemed to be sanctioning its content.

Bear Feeding Frenzy had other problems. Viewers had no way of knowing that the show was using captive bears, so in the mannequin sequence, it looked as though Douglas was training wild bears to "attack" a sleeping human. In other scenes, he appeared to be teaching bears to break into cars and to associate food with people. Rebroadcasts included an opening slide that stated, "The bears in this program are not free-ranging bears. They will not have an opportunity to interact with people." Yet on screen Douglas did everything he could to foster the illusion that he was in the wilderness with wild bears. And although the mannequin scene suggested that bears would attack a passive person in the wild, "that's not the way bears behave," asserts bear biologist Larry Van Daele.

"After Timothy Treadwell, I thought it couldn't get worse, and then *Bear Feeding Frenzy* shows up," says wildlife ecologist and filmmaker Rob Whitehair. "This is really sending a horrible message to viewers. I am appalled that Animal Planet would broadcast a show like this. But when your prime goal is to get male viewers eighteen to thirty-five to watch your channel, programs like *Bear Feeding Frenzy* will get broadcast."

Predators at War

Predators at War tells the story of what happens when extreme drought in the South African bush forces increased competition among predators. This ninety-minute program, produced by National Geographic Television in 2005, showed a variety of animals battling one another for survival. Directed in a style broadcasters call "high-octane television," with fast-paced cutting and multiple layers of sound and music, *Predators at War* features Africa's top carnivores—lions, leopards, hyenas, cheetahs, and wild dogs—in unusual, sometimes horrifying circumstances.

Kim Wolhuter, a freelance cinematographer and filmmaker working in South Africa, shot the footage at Mala Mala Wildlife Reserve near Kruger National Park in South Africa. El Niño weather patterns had brought on a widespread drought, causing the predators' territories to expand and overlap, thus increasing friction between individuals and species. In one segment, a lioness climbs a tree to steal a leopard kill, slips, is caught between limbs, and dies of strangulation. The lioness's sisters eventually climb into the tree, release her body, and then eat her.

The program was deemed a massive success by the network, and National Geographic has rebroadcast it numerous times since its premiere. In fact it has become one of the channel's "tent pole" programs, meaning that it's so big a draw that it can enlarge the audience for the rest of an evening's offerings.

The film claimed documentary authenticity, but it was promoted like a work of fiction. The official summary ran, "Fearsome predators battle the environment and one another during a brutal drought. Here's the twist: we cover this deadly competition as a military operation, putting you virtually on the super-predator battlefield." Lions are described as "tanks," leopards as "aerial fighters," hyenas as "special forces," and wild dogs as "roving infantry." The predator's skeleton, muscles, teeth, and claws are machine-like "weaponry." The war metaphors, the frenetic pacing of images, and the dark and intense music further amp up the drama. Wolhuter was included in the story as a "war correspondent," making ominous pronouncements about the "worsening situation" and noting that "Africa's predators were at war with each other."

The program has its strong points: It was well shot and well produced. The photography is spectacular. The animals' "weaponry" is depicted by high-quality computer graphics. But these strengths, when combined with the bellicose language, only serve to make the wildlife situation in South Africa seem much more violent than it actually was.

At the 2006 Wildscreen film festival, trouble brewed over *Predators at War*. Many natural history filmmakers were outraged by the film, saying that they never expected the venerable and respected National Geographic Society to produce such a violent and manipulative program. Walter Koehler, head of the Natural History Unit at the Austrian Broadcasting Corporation, found the film a sickening departure from the goals of wildlife filmmaking. "The mission of the National Geographic Society is to 'inspire people to care about the planet.' How anybody would care more about the planet after watching *Predators at War* is a total mystery to me," he said. "With 3D imaging, the animals were turned into raging tanks and other machines of war, and behaved more like cartoon supervillains than real natural creatures. It almost became a propaganda instrument to legitimize the war on terror."

Keenan Smart, head of National Geographic's Natural History Unit, defended the film as "a product of its time in America," when the United States was at war in Iraq. He felt that, in 2004, Americans were particularly interested in war themes and that the film reflected the prevailing political climate. Smart also argued that *Predators at War* brought a whole new audience to natural history films. He claimed that some of the new audience would "convert" and become regular viewers of other wildlife television shows, including those with a conservation message. Smart also pointed out that critics need to recognize the demands of the marketplace.

Kathryn Pasternak, a fifteen-year veteran of National Geographic Television and senior producer of *Predators at War,* told me that, when surrounded by their peers, she and Wolhuter felt a little embarrassed by the film. But she also sees "some amount of unnecessary angst created around films like this, as though natural history always has to be about conservation and education." When asked if the film harmed the animals of Mala Mala reserve, she says, "I doubt it very much. Is it possible we opened some new eyes to the natural world? I think so."

The hard fact is that, despite National Geographic's traditional education and conservation mission, films produced for broadcast on cable are primarily for entertainment. Their educational value is secondary. Cable channels go off the air if their programs don't achieve the high ratings that pull in advertising revenue. Money is the final arbiter of what National Geographic shows on its network, just as it is for almost all other cable programming. When news of the high ratings for *Predators at War* arrived at National Geographic, the executives involved in the film's production were congratulated for their brilliance.

Selling with Sensation

To my eternal shame, I once approved an ad from TBS's marketing department that featured a close-up of a snarling grizzly bear with the words "Five-inch fangs are no match for a high-caliber rifle." The bear was captive and trained, and I later realized that I was as guilty as anyone else of sensationalizing grizzly bears to attract an audience. When people see animals as dangerous or menacing, they feel justified in killing them.

To promote wildlife films, networks and film distributors often choose to dwell on the exploitative qualities of the films themselves. The same kind of advertising sizzle was added to David Attenborough's series *The Trials of Life*. Distributed jointly by Turner Home Entertainment and Time-Life Video, the series took viewers on a twelve-part photographic exploration of "the challenges faced by animals in their struggle to survive." To promote *The Trials of Life,* Time-Life Video condensed all the predatory and attack scenes into a rapidly cut spot, set to dramatic percussive music and with a hyperbolic voice-over intoning, "See up close how the law of the jungle is kill or be killed. . . . Find out why they call them animals." This spot worked brilliantly as a sales tool. In the five years after its release in 1991, the series earned more than $21 million. But Attenborough was so upset by its sensationalism that he considered taking legal action.

The stumbling block for those of us who would fight sensationalism is that it seems to work—at least in a commercial sense. As television programs go to increasingly dangerous extremes to grasp viewers' attention and win higher ratings, audiences seem to enjoy the supercharged excitement of wild animals mating and violence involving gnashing fangs, spilling blood, and ripping flesh. From the safety of armchairs, they get an adrenaline rush. Filmmaker Tom Veltre asks, "What does it say about us as a society that there continues to be a market for such carnage? We haven't come far since the days of the Roman amphitheater."

Regardless of what these films may reveal about us, though, they produce high ratings, network profits, and executive bonuses. Everyone loves the showmanship and everyone appears to win—except, perhaps, people who are genuinely curious about animals and the animals themselves.

In this and the previous two chapters, we've looked at the dark side of wildlife filmmaking: deceiving the audience, getting too close, and selling sex and violence. In Chapter 9, we'll look at how the industry could make a vital, positive contribution to society by promoting wildlife conservation more wholeheartedly and creatively than it currently does.

9

SINS OF OMISSION
Leaving Conservation Behind

In 1989, I commissioned the film *If Dolphins Could Talk* for the National Audubon Society. Shot by Hardy Jones and narrated by actor Michael Douglas, the film revealed that commercial tuna fishermen were slaughtering millions of dolphins during the setting and hauling of nets for tuna. Since dolphins often swim above tuna, tuna boats would find dolphins, set a net around them, and draw it shut. Tuna and dolphins were indiscriminately captured—and killed—together.

To help the film mobilize the public in that pre-Internet age, we offered a toll-free telephone number that viewers could call for information on how to take action. After the film was broadcast multiple times on TBS and PBS, more than six thousand telegrams from an outraged public arrived on the desk of Tony O'Reilly, chief executive officer of H. J. Heinz. Heinz then owned Starkist, the largest tuna packer in the United States. The telegrams demanded that the company sell only "dolphin-safe tuna"—that is, tuna caught without entrapping dolphins.

Our film contained now-famous footage taken by environmental activist Sam LaBudde, who bravely went undercover as a cook on a Panamanian tuna boat so he could videotape the barbaric behavior of tuna fishermen killing dolphins. Reportedly, O'Reilly's young daughter had watched *If Dolphins Could Talk* and asked, "Daddy, why are we killing dolphins?" A few days later, Starkist announced that it was adopting dolphin-safe fishing practices and pledged not to take tuna caught with dolphins. The company also put a "Dolphin Safe" label on its tuna cans.

Our film, as well as two other prime-time documentaries (by Howard Hall on CBS and Stan Minasian on Discovery) that also used LaBudde's electrifying footage, did not achieve these victories alone. They were part of a much broader campaign led by Earth Island Institute, the Marine Mammal Fund, and other conservation groups that culminated in the passage of a U.S. dolphin-safe tuna law. Still, *If Dolphins Could Talk* helped alert the public to a problem, pointed to a solution, and called people to action. It addressed conservation issues and dealt with policy. In short, it was the sort of wildlife film I admire most: one with a strong conservation message.

Some conservation films can be effective even if they don't talk about conservation directly. *Gorillas,* a 2007 film sponsored by filmmaker Cynthia Moses's International Conservation and Education Fund (INCEF), used the power of images to influence attitudes and behavior in Africa. One of fourteen films in the package "Everyone for Conservation," *Gorillas* consisted entirely of footage depicting the natural behavior of these primates in the wild. In villages of the Northern Republic of Congo, people often eat gorilla meat. But after a village woman saw the film, she said to INCEF educator Eric Kinzonzi, "How are we supposed to know that gorillas carry their babies like we do, embrace each other like we do, that the youngsters play like ours, if someone doesn't tell us? I will not eat gorilla meat again."

This chapter examines what the wildlife filmmaking industry has accomplished for conservation, where it has fallen down, and what it should be doing. *Gorillas* and *If Dolphins Could Talk* are among a small subset of contemporary wildlife films that are clearly linked to changes in public policy and attitudes. They are the exceptions: most wildlife films are not focused on protecting the animals they are filming. In fact some filmmakers are outright hostile to the notion. "For most of the last fifteen years that I've spent in television, the stupidest, most naïve idea for a wildlife film you could suggest was one about environmental and wildlife conservation," says veteran BBC wildlife film producer Tim Martin. "It is the dread 'C' word."

When Conservation Wasn't Cool

Wildlife filmmakers emerge from a wide range of backgrounds, experiences, and viewpoints—one may have been a biologist, another a film student, nature lover, hunter, or citizen-activist. Undoubtedly, the way I approach and evaluate wildlife filmmaking is shaped by the fact that I came to it with the background of someone working in conservation rather than as a professional filmmaker. As an environmental lobbyist on the staff of the National Audubon Society in the early 1980s, I tried to persuade senators and representatives to support conservation measures. I used my expertise as an energy and environmental analyst to testify on Capitol Hill and to lobby those in office. When the opportunity arose, I decided that I might be more effective if I used television to influence politicians' constituents. After all, they were the people who elected the members of Congress.

So, as I've already reported, in the early 1980s I formed a partnership with Ted Turner, producing hard-hitting prime-time wildlife and conservation films for TBS and PBS. By using the mass media to reach a huge audience, I felt sure I was making a difference. I believed unequivocally that such programs promoted conservation and benefited the environment. It never even occurred to me to ask myself how I would prove this claim.

We made scores of films that generated good ratings on all kinds of subjects, including dolphins, bears, global warming, overpopulation, and oil drilling in the Arctic National Wildlife Refuge. This was a period of enormous growth in wildlife films on television. Yet, as Derek Bousé has pointed out, the state of the natural world and its wildlife deteriorated significantly during this expansion (which began in the early 1960s). That doesn't prove that wildlife films are ineffective—the planet's environmental deterioration might have been even worse without wildlife films—but it got me thinking. As author Bill McKibben wrote in *The Age of Missing Information,* "Virtually everyone . . . has seen many hours of gorgeous nature films . . . and yet we're still not willing to do anything very drastic to save that world."

Meanwhile, most of the industry was putting out the usual films in which the conservation message was subliminal rather than overt—if it was there at all. In 2001 the riveting eight-part series *The Blue Planet* (described in Chapter 1) was produced and broadcast by the BBC and Discovery. Narrated by David Attenborough, *The Blue Planet's* celebration of oceans found huge audiences in both the United Kingdom and the United States. It featured remarkable footage of animal behavior, but none of the eight episodes contained any conservation messages. Nothing was said about overfishing, drift nets, marine pollution, or the warming of the oceans.

These issues finally surfaced in a ninth program filmed for the series, "Deep Trouble." Hosted by marine biologist and BBC film producer Martha Holmes, "Deep Trouble" examined the damage humans have inflicted on the oceans, including overfishing, abandoned fishing nets, the loss of coral reefs and mangrove forests, and the harm from deep-sea trawlers (whose fishing tactics Holmes likened to trying to catch a cow by dragging a huge net across a farm from a helicopter). The program concluded that the oceans are in dire trouble and that people are to blame. It argued for the establishment of national marine protected areas, where spawning and feeding grounds, whale migration routes, and mangrove forests can be preserved.

But Discovery refused to buy this episode. "Deep Trouble" was never broadcast in the United States and was shown in England only on the BBC's less-watched channel, BBC2. Why did it meet with such resistance? It was far from feel-good TV, and BBC and Discovery decided that few viewers would want to watch this kind of reality television. They feared it would leave people feeling depressed and powerless. It would be deep trouble, so to speak, for their ratings, their brands, and their bottom lines.

Around that time, I started searching for evidence that wildlife films, including a landmark series such as *The Blue Planet*, could achieve measurable conservation results. I looked hard, seeking reassurance that my years spent producing these films hadn't been wasted. Other wildlife filmmakers told me about their good ratings and about enthusiastic e-mail messages and phone calls they'd received from people saying that their lives had been changed by a film. But those kinds of encomiums often come from people already predisposed to agree with a film's message. And the number of people who watch a program says little about its ability to inspire those people to take action.

As a board member and cofounder of an organization called Filmmakers for Conservation, I decided to see what formal research had to say about the effectiveness of wildlife films. I discovered a distinct absence of such scholarly studies, which is still the case. In 2002 I commissioned a study to measure these films' impact on human behavior and public policy. The researchers worked hard, but they unearthed no rigorous, empirical evidence at all—just more stories. And even when the research seemed to suggest that a film had changed public attitudes or policies, I knew deep down that it was impossible to untangle all the various influences that could have contributed to those changes.

Disappointed by these results, I began to speak out at conferences and film festivals about my growing suspicion that most wildlife films were not doing their job. Our films needed to move beyond the slide-show phase of nature-appreciation television, which depicts wildlife in a bubble, and evolve into films that trigger action. We had a responsibility to raise viewers' awareness of the serious environmental problems facing the world. Otherwise, I believed, there would soon be nothing left to film.

Promoting the beauty of the natural world was not the same as conservation, I argued. Conservation was action with measurable results: a bill passed, money raised, activists recruited. Unless films produced immediate and visible results—such as audience members contacting a member of Congress, contributing money to a conservation group, or joining a grassroots organization—we shouldn't waste time producing them, or at least we shouldn't pretend they were anything but entertainment. In terms of conservation, we'd be better off spending that money on land acquisition, scientific research, or educational programs. I knew just how musician Frank Zappa felt when he joked, "I wrote a song about dental floss, but did anyone's teeth get cleaner?"

As scientist and filmmaker David Suzuki said, "I know the rationale that's been used, especially by the BBC Natural History Unit, that if you get people to appreciate nature, they'll protect it. But I think that's total bullshit. When I look at the Attenborough films, I know that a lot of those animals and plants are going extinct, and yet you don't see anyone speaking out about it, and that's really shocking to me."

At the time, I felt that a feast for the eyes like *The Blue Planet* actually hurt conservation efforts by not telling the truth about the natural world. It encouraged complacency by giving people a false sense of security, a fraudulent promise of endless bounty. Soon after *The Blue Planet* came out, filmmaker Hardy Jones saw evidence of this at a fund-raiser for a marine conservation organization. "I watched *Blue Planet* last week and the oceans seem totally healthy," one of the wealthy guests said to Jones. "Why are we bothering to raise money?" [9-7] As Jones saw it, leaving the bad news out of wildlife films is like making charming films about Germany in the 1930s while ignoring something "enormously sinister happening in plain sight—something that would soon engulf the world in conflagration and cost tens of millions of human lives."

Arguments such as these were not received well by most of our film-making colleagues—even those who made conservation films—who took for granted that their efforts were worthwhile. They believed that promoting nature appreciation was enough, and after that the responsibility passes to others. Filmmaker Howard Hall wrote, "My life has been dramatically influenced by films I've seen on television. No one genre of film caused me to become a wildlife filmmaker and conservationist. The variety of films that helped shape my life is huge, from fantasy to adventure to hardcore environmental. . . . We should applaud our diversity."

Filmmaker Dereck Joubert argued, "I think it would be a dreadful mistake to insist in some impossible way that all wildlife films should be made to be more 'up front' about conservation. We will simply alienate audiences who just want to come home, relax, and be entertained." The majority of wildlife filmmakers were on the side of staying more neutral and avoiding overt conservation messages, and I didn't like that approach one bit.

The *Planet Earth* Phenomenon

Hall's and Joubert's arguments were still swirling around in my mind when *Planet Earth* exploded onto television screens in 2006. An eleven-part BBC-Discovery production narrated by David Attenborough, *Planet Earth* was broadcast in more than a hundred countries, attracting large television audiences in multiple runs. I was poised to criticize the series as yet another blue-chip film that was weak on conservation. But when I watched it at the Wildscreen film festival, in October 2006, I began to change my mind.

At a cost of about $2 million per episode, *Planet Earth* offered stunning views of the earth's landscapes, wildlife, and ecosystems. Its cinematographers captured breathtaking, high-definition footage of Mount Everest and spectacular imagery of the world's deepest and most dangerous caves. It contained sequences never before filmed, such as aerial footage of wolf and wild dog hunts, and amazing shots of a snow leopard chasing a wild goat on a near-vertical mountain face in Pakistan. The crews lived where they filmed, often for months at a time, almost always under harsh conditions.

The main technical innovation was filming in high definition, which nearly doubled the resolution, or sharpness, of the picture. *Planet Earth* producer Alastair Fothergill likened the effect to "having a stocking over your head pulled off." When high-definition cameras were combined with the wobble-eliminating Heligimbal, a gyro-stabilized camera support mounted on a helicopter, the resulting footage was far superior to anything before seen on television.

Planet Earth became news—"breakthrough" or "event" television. People talked about episodes the next day around the water cooler. One-third of Britain's population saw at least one episode. In the United States, more than three million copies of the five-DVD boxed set were sold. Some people watched the whole series straight through; others used its stunning images as a backdrop to rock music in trendy bars and living rooms.

Its popularity was partly a matter of timing. *An Inconvenient Truth* had just raised people's environmental awareness, and people in Europe and the United States in particular were becoming "greener." Advances in DVD and television technology allowed people to have higher-quality viewing experiences in their homes. All these factors—along with the film's unquestionable excellence—helped the series attract an audience that didn't normally watch natural history or wildlife programming. As *New York Times* writer Alex Williams quipped, "This may well be the first time a nature show has become hip."

When Fothergill spoke about *Planet Earth,* he made it sound like just the sort of film I used to criticize. He asserted it was not a conservation film, adding, "With every passing year the world's population has become increasingly urban and out of touch with the natural world. Perhaps the most important job we do as 'blue-chip' wildlife filmmakers is to put people back in touch with that wilderness. By showing them places they may never visit and showing them animals most will never see, we can hopefully inspire them to better care for what remains."

Unlike the films I used to criticize, however, *Planet Earth* didn't ignore conservation. It didn't present animal life in a bubble or give people the feeling that everything was fine. Conservation was mentioned—and in a serious, responsible way—in many of the episodes. In addition, the series was surrounded and supported by books, study guides, Web sites, and many other related projects, some of which contained strong conservation messages.

After watching *Planet Earth,* I had to admit that it was a tour de force. It offered responsibly shot, dramatic, and exciting footage, powerful reminders of Earth's stunning beauty, and a conservation message. The tone was engaging but effective. The film seemed to be reaching new audiences and making them more receptive to weightier environmental messages in the future.

The runaway popularity of the series catalyzed my doubts about my former view—that wildlife films need to produce immediate and measurable results. Suddenly that stance seemed too extreme. Just because a viewer doesn't instantly volunteer to mount the barricades doesn't mean that nothing is happening. Learning takes time, and people have to consider something valuable before they will come to its aid.

David Attenborough's defense of blue-chip films began to make more sense. "Films and photographs are an inspiring and effective means of building environmental awareness, helping to ignite the very first spark of interest in natural history and to stimulate a continuing passion for the wonders of life on Earth," he said. "Most people have never been lucky enough to see a whale in the wild, yet these magnificent animals are icons of the conservation movement because people know what they look like and why they are threatened, thanks primarily to films and photographs."

Three years after *Planet Earth* came out on TV, Disneynature produced *Earth*, a family-oriented documentary feature film that took 60 percent of its footage from the earlier film. Fothergill was involved again, along with another *Planet Earth* veteran, director Mark Linfield. These two experienced and ethical filmmakers used the footage to tell the stories of three wildlife families—polar bears, African elephants, and humpback whales—attempting to survive in the wild today. The film faithfully reflected the duality of nature—the brutal reality of predation, starvation, and drought, along with some of nature's more delightful aspects, including polar bear cubs playing, birds of paradise performing a courtship dance, and mandarin duck chicks flapping adorably to the forest floor from their nest high in a tree cavity.

I was impressed. Fothergill and Linfield took a successful TV documentary series and made it into a scientifically accurate, entertaining feature film. The recycled footage from *Planet Earth* helped reduce stress on animals, but so did careful shooting techniques, with little manipulation or staging. Moreover, the filmmakers managed to incorporate into the story line a message about global warming. In the polar bear sequence, viewers see the father bear eventually perishing because the ice from which it hunts is disappearing. This conservation message wasn't as strong as I (and others) would have liked—for instance, there was no mention of other kinds of habitat loss or pollution. But, taken as a whole, the film seemed sure to ignite viewers' interest in and empathy for the natural world, which is where conservation begins.

When it comes to environmental protection, people's attitudes fall somewhere along the continuum from outright hostility or indifference to passionate support. Different types of films address different audiences. Conservation films speak to the converted (though good journalism can transcend this tendency), groundbreaking landmark series to the curious, and brash Steve Irwin–type shows to the uninitiated. Good wildlife films can move people to a different place on the continuum.

But the first step is getting people's attention; otherwise nothing can happen. Once we have their attention, we can start building awareness, which may lead to active involvement. As filmmaker Vicky Stone says, "There is no best way to deal with conservation issues through film. Sometimes it is appropriate to be hard hitting and direct, and at other times to tackle an issue through entertainment."

Making Better Conservation Films

Although I appreciate productions such as *Planet Earth* and *Earth*, my personal allegiance is still to true conservation films that motivate viewers to take action. In fact, given the state of the planet, I think that good conservation films and programs are needed more urgently than ever. The networks that air nature programming still too often sidestep opportunities to deliver important messages. As David Helvarg points out, Discovery Channel—having made a hit of crab fishing in Alaska with *The Deadliest Catch*—later introduced a show called *Swords,* which profiles long-line fishing for Atlantic swordfish in a similar way—without mentioning how marine life has been decimated globally by long-lining or the toxic mercury loads that top predators such as swordfish carry in their flesh.

I know all too well that conservation films can be boring, one-sided, and lacking in entertainment value. Too many of us in the conservation movement are so convinced of the importance of our issues that we forget our first job: to capture and hold people's attention. We forget the audience. But there are ways to produce films that entertain, inform, and create change.

Every wildlife film has to compete for audience attention with every other film genre as well as other media, including the Internet, video games, and hundreds of television channels. For this reason, entertainment and showbiz must be seen a necessity, not an indulgence. Conservation filmmakers must embrace showmanship because what we do is too important not to be entertaining. And by *entertaining,* I don't necessarily mean enjoyable but rather *engrossing,* even when the subject matter is distressing. It does no good to produce conservation films that no one watches.

Sometimes human interest can be the hook. In 2005, Sierra Club Productions produced *The Sierra Club Chronicles,* a series of seven half-hour programs, with the goal of reaching people who do not think of themselves as environmentalists. The organization's producer, Adrienne Bramhall, teamed up with Robert Greenwald and his production company, Brave New Films. They resolved to reject the traditional doom-and-gloom tone of most wildlife and environmental films by pursuing the stories of local citizens coming together to solve environmental problems—fishermen in Alaska, construction workers in New York City, ranchers in New Mexico. The Sierra Club used these films as building blocks. They didn't inspire people to act all on their own but, rather, to be part of the club's larger conservation campaigns.

One reason that movies appeal to so many people is the universal fascination of watching a character go through significant changes. The protagonist is not the same person at the end of the story that he or she was in the beginning, and it is in our nature to identify with and learn from other people's compelling stories. The heroes in the Sierra Club series were everyday people who looked and sounded like the new audiences the series was trying to reach.

Reaching the largest and most demographically diverse audience today means taking advantage of every possible distribution mechanism. The Sierra Club series was distributed via satellite, digital cable, and Web downloads, and more than five thousand DVDs were sent out for house parties and other outreach events. Posting the series on its own Web site, as well as on Google Video and YouTube, resulted in fifteen thousand page views and downloads. It was shown at fifteen film festivals around the country and was nominated for Best Documentary in the California Independent Film Festival.

When I worked at the National Audubon Society and the National Wildlife Federation, our films were also integrated with our educational programs, Web activities, activist outreach programs, and magazines. We didn't know it at the time, but we were helping to build a model for filmmakers who would change the world. Its components include—in addition to a film—nonprofit organizations, community organizing, special screenings, community-based forums (especially, these days, social-networking sites on the Web), books, articles, public service announcements, Web sites, educational guides, speakers, publicity, and coverage by news organizations. Using this model, conservation films can gain traction as their message reaches an audience several times. In our information-packed world, approaching people through several media is the only way to make a strong connection.

This integrated approach frees up a film to do what it can do best: tell an engaging story about compelling characters. Attending to the film's emotional impact is essential—as a way of bringing facts, logic, and hard environmental realities to life. The next chapter looks at some of the heroes in wildlife filmmaking who have grasped this elemental truth, produced ethical and successful films that lead people to action, and uplifted the reputation of the wildlife filmmaking community.

Finally, I think it's important to gauge the effect of what we do in long-range terms, especially the ways in which wildlife films can motivate conservation impulses among young people. When Katie Carpenter produced *A Year on Earth* for Animal Planet in association with Earthwatch, she and her team sent three high school students around the world on a yearlong environmental research expedition, working with scientists to research endangered species. They hoped that in each location, the students would be able to gather data and raise awareness in some way through community-based projects.

Though their time in each locale was brief, they did find some measure of success, but the more impressive outcome was in the schools that followed their journey on television and online. More than thirty local conservation projects were launched in communities where schools were tracking the *Year on Earth* crew, as a direct result of students communicating with crew members and interacting with their pictures and videos from the field. Some students built bat boxes in the woods, others restored damaged wetlands nearby, still more tracked sea turtles online and raised money to protect them. These small-scale conservation projects, just two degrees of separation from the production, reached hundreds of thousands of people and probably had a more lasting impact than any of the conservation work pictured in the broadcast. Carpenter believes that when we evaluate the impact of wildlife films on conservation, we should also look for the indirect effects—the longer tail, the second reverberation—because that's where we may find conservation gold.

10

DOING IT RIGHT
Profiles in Ethical Entertainment

A n April 2002 article in *Forbes* carried the title "Chick Flick" and the subtitle, "Okay, so they mate in the water. But what else would make you watch a puffin video?" The article began:

> These days in the world of animal documentaries, cute is okay, but sex and violence sell much better. The Fox Network's *When Animals Attack* was a solid Nielsen winner, as is the Discovery Channel's *Shark Week*. As nature writer Bill McKibben once quipped, the most popular documentaries consist of "ungulates and big cats alternatively mating and killing each other." So why did filmmaker Daniel Breton spend four months last year braving blizzards and fighting off frostbite on a barren chunk of rock some 20 miles off the coast of Maine filming a 55-minute documentary on puffins called *Fish out of Water?*

The answer is that Daniel Breton is dedicated to conservation. For four months while filming, he had no running water and no human contact and ate rice every night. Seals were his only company, and they gave him lice. He boiled seawater on his gas stove to create a "foot sauna" so he wouldn't lose his toes to frostbite. Breton used no manipulation of any kind, choosing not to sensationalize his film by provoking his subjects into artificially violent behavior. The result was a film that is fascinatingly authentic, that does not mislead the audience in any way, and that did no harm to animals during its creation. In Breton's hands, the unadorned story of an animal's life makes compelling viewing. As he said in the *Forbes* feature, "Puffins—because they seem so human—are maybe a way to inspire people to learn about something else on earth."

Filmmakers as scrupulous as Breton are a minority, and the standards they observe only makes their work more remarkable. While overcoming incredible hardships during filming, they cope with the ethical challenges described in this book and make exciting, honest, and innovative films that further the cause of conservation. They know how to find and portray compelling characters, engage an audience with riveting narratives, and bring a visual feast to the screen. They treat wildlife with respect, keep their distance, and are honest with their audiences. They construct effective outreach campaigns, work with nonprofits, and distribute their films through many venues and media, finding innovative ways to reach new audiences. They raise money to produce their films without prostituting themselves.

You've met several members of this distinguished group already. In this chapter, you'll read about the adventures of several more.

Larry Engel and the Rhythms of Nature

Larry Engel has withstood hurricanes, been tailed by tornadoes, ventured into dangerous caves, and run from wildfires. From his earliest work with *3-2-1 Contact,* a 1980s PBS science series for kids, he has ably shouldered the filmmaker's responsibilities to audiences and subjects alike. While in Antarctica for *3-2-1 Contact,* he fully complied with the Antarctica Treaty, which demands that humans not interfere with any animal's behavior. Instead of approaching penguins on the ice, Engel sat down and waited. That may have made it more difficult to get good shots, but it didn't lower the quality of the series, and Engel won an Emmy for his cinematography.

Engel has had a chance to learn from scientists and researchers on all seven continents about animals ranging from penguins in Antarctica to elephants in Africa. He uses this knowledge to make sure that he and his team minimize their impact on the environment. Harassing wildlife to capture a "money shot" is simply unacceptable, he says. What he loves most about wildlife filmmaking is not the times of high drama but "the waiting, the quiet, and the moments that can never be repeated."

In 1988, drought had swept through the western United States, contributing to a series of massive fires in Yellowstone National Park and climaxing in a vast firestorm near Old Faithful. The public was furious about park policies that allowed almost 800,000 of the park's 2.2 million acres to go up in flames. But because fires are, in fact, a vital part of the Yellowstone ecosystem—many tree species there would not survive without periodic burning—I commissioned Engel and his colleague Tom Lucas to make a National Audubon Society film that would take a longer-term view.

Engel filmed the scenes I expected, of animals fleeing the spectacular flames and, a few months later, flowers blooming in the charred remains. But he also found a way to tell the story through a quiet moment that none of us could have anticipated. In one of his dead-of-winter shoots, Engel saw a small herd of elk in the distance. He jumped off his snowmobile, strapped on snowshoes, and hiked a few hundred yards. "A young elk, probably a yearling, was struggling to keep up with the rest of the herd," Engel recalls. "I set the camera on the tripod and began to film the slow steps the young elk took. Through the telephoto lens on the camera, it became apparent that this elk was starving to death. Male or female—I do not know—but this elk was nothing more than ribs and skin.

"I filmed its last steps. One foot, then another, went forward. After only a couple of minutes, the elk stopped, out of energy, having given up. She (or he) lay down, and I knew with certainty that the beautiful but emaciated animal would die in this spot before dawn. There was nothing we could do to save it. I had filmed its last steps, its last effort to follow its herd, searching for food."

The young elk succumbed in part because of the rigors of winter (this first postfire winter had scanty forage), but also because many of the lodgepole pines that sheltered the herd had been destroyed by the fire, so it took more calories than usual to keep warm. While Engel felt an urge to help the dying elk, he decided it was his ethical obligation to leave it alone. It seemed an act of hubris to interfere. In the end, Engel made the dying animal part of the story of the region's renewal. Its body would provide food for grizzlies, coyotes, foxes, crows, and other animals, allowing natural cycles to continue.

In 1985, while working on the National Audubon Society film *Panthers and Cheetahs: On the Edge of Extinction*, Engel and Lucas encountered one of the most amazing sights they had ever witnessed. In a Kenyan park called Masai Mara, they came across a dead wildebeest. Vultures had already descended on it, and the filmmakers watched as one vulture attacked one eye while another went after the other. A third and fourth were working up the dead animal's nostrils, and a couple more were fighting for access through its mouth. Another five or six were working inside the abdominal and chest cavities, tearing away at the remaining flesh. There were at least fifty of the birds in all—most pecking, ripping, and pulling, some standing patiently by, waiting for their turn.

"It appeared that every orifice of the wildebeest offered the vultures access to fresh meat," Engel says. "This included the wildebeest's anus. I remember watching in awe as one vulture stuck its head right up there. The overall effect was that this animal, dead for hours, seemed to suddenly come back to life as it pulsed on its side from head to tail. The vultures, tearing tissue from within the body of the beast, helped to create this grotesque but fascinating dance of death. The skin seemed to flow with wave after wave of soft, easy movement, while disappearing piece by piece."

Some observers might have found this sight revolting, but Engel found it fascinating. "I came to respect death and the taking of life in a way that still resonates deep within me more than two decades later," he says. Soon hyenas came and chased the vultures away, and a new dance began. Engel was tempted to push the hyenas off so he could continue filming the vultures. Instead, he let nature be. In the natural order of things, the vultures would once again have to wait their turn.

The Underwater World of Howard and Michele Hall

Howard and Michele Hall are among the best practitioners of the highly ethical do-no-harm approach that sets conservation as its highest goal. Howard started out as a still photographer. He got his first big break in January 1978, when he spotted a California gray whale swimming in a kelp forest off the San Diego coast. In his twenties at the time, he was just starting out in photography. The photos he took of this animal resulted in two double-page spreads in *National Geographic*.

For many years, Howard made a good living selling still photos and natural history stories to magazines and doing assignment cinematography for television series such as *American Sportsman* and *Wild Kingdom*. He did not acquire his skills by going to film school. Rather, he learned by watching films and by studying the works of filmmakers he admired. "If you want a course in making a good film, study a good film," Hall says. "It's as easy as that—at least it was for me. Just turn on your television, select the kind of film you want to make, and study the film for technique."

One day in 1987, while studying an African wildlife documentary by Alan Root, Hall began to wonder why no one was making underwater wildlife films with a focus on animal behavior. As he watched, he repeatedly complained to his wife, Michele, "I could do that underwater." Finally, she suggested he stop talking about it and just do it. Despite the fact that he had never done a film on his own, Howard wrote a letter to *Nature* executive producer David Heely, a man he had never met, proposing an underwater animal behavior film set in the California kelp forest.

Heely wrote back, saying the last thing in the world the Halls expected him to say: "Okay." The couple was thunderstruck. They had somehow gotten around the dilemma facing all new filmmakers. "No one will employ you to produce a film until you have successfully run a budget in a responsible way and produced a good film," Howard explains. "So, how do you make that first film?" Step one, in this case, was for Michele to cut back on her career as a pediatric nurse to devote time to the production; soon afterward, they became a full-time film-making team.

Nature broadcast the Halls' rookie effort, *Seasons in the Sea*, in 1990. Right up until the time it aired, Howard was afraid that the film "would be a dismal failure, the laughable result of an uninspired novice, just a boring watery film about fish behavior." In fact, it was spectacularly successful, winning "Best of Show" at the top two events in wildlife filmmaking, the Wildscreen and Jackson Hole wildlife film festivals. Hall still can't explain why it struck such a resonant chord. "There was no stroke of genius that revealed to me that the television market was ripe for this kind of film," he says. What audiences responded to so strongly was the fruit of Howard's extraordinary patience as a cin-ematographer in capturing comprehensive scenes of animal behaviors underwater—courtship and mating, feeding and foraging patterns, predation, and so on—visuals that previous filmmakers had considered impractical to obtain.

By 1990, the Halls were off again, this time on an adventure in Patagonia, trying to film right whales for a CBS documentary. For ten days Howard braved the freezing waters off the remote coast of the Valdez Peninsula with no sight of whales, and he was feeling frustrated. Right whales are difficult to find, and even when they appear, the wind is often too strong and the water too turbid to successfully film them. On the eleventh day, a gale wind was blowing more than forty miles per hour. Well below the surface, Hall struggled to swim back to his dive boat, his hands numb from the cold, his scuba tank almost empty. At that point he was ready to pack it in.

As he kicked against the current, something suddenly caught his eye over his left shoulder. Startled, he turned and saw a forty-foot-long right whale staring straight at him. She must have weighed fifty tons or more, and her body was marked with protruding white callosities, raised callus-like patches of skin. Howard was shocked to realize that the very animal he had been trying so hard to find and film was now inspecting him!

Like any wild animal, whales can be unpredictable. If provoked or frightened, they can easily kill a diver with a flick of the huge, powerful tail flukes they use to defend themselves and their young. It is unusual for right whales to approach people, but this enormous individual was slowly overtaking Hall. He confessed later, "The adrenaline made my legs tremble."

When the whale came up beside him, though, Hall reached out and dislodged a few whale lice—fingernail-size creatures that feed on dead skin—from the callosity around the whale's right eye. This small gesture was out of character—Hall was normally careful to remain at a safe distance from wild animals so as not to stress or scare them. He was also aware of the dangers of habituation, making wild animals accustomed to people so that the animals lose their instinctive fight-or-flight response. But this whale had approached Hall, and he intuitively and spontaneously reached out to her in a moment of discovery.

As the lice scattered, the lumbering giant leaned into Hall's touch, as if encouraging him to scratch harder. As he scratched the whale again, Hall was overwhelmed with a single thought: "This can't be happening." In the end, he and his colleagues captured some amazing images for their one-hour documentary, *Dolphins, Whales, and Us.* "I had looked closely into a great whale's eye," Hall says, "and the whale had looked back." That extraordinary encounter remains imprinted in his mind, helping to sustain and drive his lifelong dedication to saving whales.

In 2003 Howard Hall put his life in danger again to make the IMAX film *Coral Reef Adventure* (2003), which I helped produce. He got in trouble by taking an IMAX camera the size of a large microwave oven—and weighing 250 pounds at the surface—370 feet down in the open ocean. At that depth the pressure is a staggering twelve times greater than on the surface. No one had ever dived so deep with this kind of camera before, and it's possible that the distraction of the heavy equipment contributed to an error in judgment: he suffered a life-threatening case of decompression sickness—what divers call "the bends." Within a month of that episode, though, the relentless Hall was back diving to the same hazardous depths to get more IMAX shots.

The Halls work as a highly functioning team, with Howard doing most of the cinematography and Michele handling production and logistical functions—everything that enables Howard to get in the water safely with his camera—as well as some photography. Over the years, they have produced and directed numerous films for television, including several episodes of the PBS series *Nature,* a National Geographic special, and the five-part PBS series *Secrets of the Ocean Realm.* They have also made several IMAX films, including *Into the Deep, Island of the Sharks, Deep Sea 3D,* and *Under the Sea 3D.* Their films have won six Emmys and three film festival awards.

If you ask Howard Hall to reflect on this distinguished record, he'll say that they have been lucky, which is true. But their luck stemmed from boldness, toughness, hard work, solid ethics, and being prepared to take advantage of unexpected opportunities.

Dereck and Beverly Joubert and the Big Cats

The husband-and-wife team of Dereck and Beverly Joubert is another example of wildlife filmmaking gone right. (In case you're wondering why so many filmmaking teams consist of married couples, the reasons are obvious: filmmakers want to work with people they trust, feel bonded with, and get emotional support from. Furthermore, spending weeks or even months in the field can be painfully lonely: What better strategy to fight isolation than to have your spouse with you?) These filmmakers, writers, and conservationists are National Geographic explorers-in-residence, a coveted designation that recognizes them as among the world's greatest filmmakers and conservationists. Dereck directs, films, and writes the scripts; Beverly produces, shoots still photographs, and records sound.

Based in Botswana, the Jouberts have been filming, researching, and exploring in Africa for more than twenty-five years. Their coverage of predator behavior has led to twenty films, six books, and many articles for *National Geographic* magazine. The Jouberts have recently turned their attention to the dire plight of lions, cheetahs, and leopards. Lions number fewer than twenty thousand and may cease to exist in the wild beyond 2050. Cheetahs are in even worse shape, with only about ten thousand remaining in the wild.

To create the 2006 documentary film and book *Relentless Enemies: Lions and Buffalo*, the Jouberts lived for two intense years among a pride of lions and a large buffalo herd in the Duba region of Botswana's Okavango Delta. The film includes dramatic first-ever footage of lions hunting in water, demonstrating to biologists worldwide the surprisingly adaptive nature of these animals. The Jouberts' award-winning film *Eye of the Leopard* (mentioned in Chapter 1) also aired in 2006 on the National Geographic Channel and documents a young leopard's life in wild Africa over a period of three years, demonstrating the species' advanced intelligence as well as its hunting prowess.

Dereck Joubert goes to extraordinary lengths to remain unobtrusive, so that he can film natural, unaffected animal behavior. He cringes if a leopard even looks up at the camera. "If an animal even takes a cinematographer into its awareness, by a look or reaction, we have failed in our job," he says. "If it charges us, or runs away, we have failed twice."

The Jouberts use their films to promote conservation and encourage others in the business to do the same. "If we have to be subversive about getting our conservation message across by sneaking it into scripts, now is the time to do it," Dereck asserts. "This is a global state of emergency in which we can all be playing an active and positive role."

Going beyond filmmaking, the Jouberts helped create an African initiative called Great Plains to help stem the downward spiral of the environment through low-volume, low-impact ecotourism. The revenues go to conservation projects, including the creation of large, linked areas of protected wildlife habitat. They are also targeting for conservation the tropical rainforests and mountain gorillas of Rwanda, as well as the fisheries of the Seychelles, an island nation northeast of Madagascar.

By crafting in-depth portrayals of the lives of Africa's wild creatures, the Jouberts have exemplified thoughtful and constructive wildlife filmmaking, and they continue to inspire other conservationists and wildlife filmmakers.

Kathy Milani Calls Us to Action

Kathy Milani used to work in broadcast television, but her passion for animals led her to the animal protection movement. Today she is vice president of investigations and video at the Humane Society of the United States. HSUS uses low-budget, high-impact short films to document animal abuse in creatures ranging from horses to baby seals. These films are by far the most activist-oriented of those described in this chapter.

Two of Milani's most famous works are *Bearing Witness* and *On Thin Ice,* both of which document the savagery of the Canadian seal hunt. Following animal protectionist Rebecca Aldworth (director, Humane Society International Canada), *Bearing Witness* exposes the cruel commercial slaughter of young harp seals for their skins. The film has won multiple awards, including the top award at Wildscreen in 2006. *On Thin Ice* features HSUS personnel as well as Paul McCartney and his then wife, Heather Mills, on the ice floes trying to stop the slaughter.

Milani is determined to convey the reality of the situation. With more than a million seals killed between 2007 and 2009, Canada's commercial seal hunt is the world's largest mass killing of marine mammals. Veterinary experts who have studied the hunt have concluded that it causes unacceptable suffering. Biologists argue that it poses a threat to seal populations, particularly in light of the potentially devastating impacts of climate change on these ice-dependent animals. The film contains shocking images of the killings, but Milani periodically breaks away from the violence. She believes this gives viewers time to absorb the message, which can't happen if they shut their eyes or turn away.

To tell the story, Milani and her colleagues faced miles of exhausting travel, unstable ice floes, and extreme weather. They have also been threatened and even assaulted by sealers with clubs, knives, and (while in helicopters) even gunfire. The Canadian government, outraged that a U.S. organization is trying to tell it how to behave, accuses HSUS of "eco-imperialism" and has increased restrictions on filming to protect its sealing industry. HSUS observers cannot come within ten meters of a sealer or sealing vessel without breaking the law and risking arrest.

Marine cinematographer Tom Campbell filming an inquisitive giant manta ray at San Benedicto, Mexico, for the award-winning feature *Giant Mantas of San Benedicto*. Tom, on closed circuit rebreather, is using a Sony F900 HD camera in an Amphibico housing. Photo © Andrea Marshall.

Howard Hall and Peter Kragh film Australian sea lions in IMAX 3D at a remote location off Hopkins Island in southern Australia during production on *Under the Sea 3D*. Photo © Michele Hall/howardhall.com.

Matthew Ferraro of Ocean Futures Society gets tips from Junior, a capuchin monkey, in the use of a Sony HDW-F900/3 high-definition camera at an animal orphanage in Iquitos, Peru. Junior was a favorite with the team filming the society's *Return to the Amazon*. Photo © Carrie Vonderhaar, Ocean Futures Society/KQED

Marty Stouffer with his Arriflex HSR camera and a remarkably tame mountain goat near Mount Evans, Colorado, not far from Idaho Springs. Photo by John King, courtesy of Marty Stouffer Productions, Ltd.

Mark Deeble films the emergence of fig wasps for *The Queen of Trees* from a treetop platform on the banks of the Ewaso Nyiro River in the Rift Valley, Kenya. This phenomenon happens over about one minute close to sunset on a single evening in the wasp's two-month life cycle. Photo by Victoria Stone.

Mark Deeble filming an enormous Nile crocodile on the Grumeti River, Serengeti National Park, Tanzania, for *The Tides of Kirawira*. The Deeble and Stone team got to know this 17-foot male croc well during almost a decade of filming him on the river. Photo by Victoria Stone.

Adam Ravetch filming thousands of Pacific walrus hauled out on shore during a snowstorm in Russia. Photo by Maxim Kuznetsov.

Adam Ravetch uses a crane-cam to shoot Pacific walrus in Russia. Photo by Anatoly Kochnev.

Three sealing vessels wait for the opening day of Canada's commercial seal hunt—the largest slaughter of marine mammals in the world—in the Gulf of St. Lawrence, 2005. This harp seal was most likely clubbed for his skin during the hunt. Photo © Kathy Milani/The Humane Society of the U.S.

Filmmaker Cynthia Moses's International Conservation and Education Fund (INCEF), uses the power of images to influence attitudes and advance conservation in Africa. Here, at an afternoon screening in the Cuvette Ouest region of the Republic of Congo, the audience watches a film on preserving great apes. Photo © INCEF.

Kim Wolhuter filming hyenas at a Cape buffalo kill for the National Geographic TV special *Predators at War,* Mala Mala Game Reserve, South Africa. He's able to get so close without peril because the hyenas do not see him either as a threat or as prey. Photo © Barend Van Der Watt.

Dereck and Beverly Joubert, award-winning filmmakers and National Geographic explorers-in-residence, filming lions at a buffalo kill, Duba Plains in the Okavango Delta, Botswana. Photo © Wildlife Films.

This young leopard was photographed in the Serengeti, Tanzania, during filming on the 1991 production *Sunlight and Shadow: The Dappled Cats* for Survival Anglia, which was broadcast in the United States by National Geographic. Photo by Mark Deeble and Victoria Stone.

Marine cinematographer Tom Campbell shooting high-definition footage of a 15-foot
great white shark off South Africa, 2001. Photo by Dennis Coffman © SOS Ltd.

Doug Allan films a humpback whale mother and calf in the Vava'u Islands, Tonga,
during the making of *Planet Earth*. Photo © Sue Flood.

Using Milani's films, however, HSUS has raised hundreds of thousands of dollars from private donors and is leading a boycott against Canadian seafood to pressure the government to halt the slaughter. In May 2009, the European Union banned trade in seal products, cutting off a primary market for the global sealing industry. It was a major victory for HSUS.

Most of Milani's films are short—two to ten minutes. Although bits of the footage are used in major-media news programs, the films themselves are not designed for traditional broadcast. Indeed, for the most part, they're too graphic for mainstream outlets. Their primary goal is to educate and reenergize already-dedicated activists, but today's communications tools extend the films' reach. Through the HSUS Web site, e-mail blasts, and social-networking sites, these films also can also bring new people to the cause.

Milani has proven the effectiveness of short-format films and small budgets. She captures viewers' attention, increases their awareness, and leads them toward involvement. By asking her audience to travel with her to dark places, she enables them to witness cruelty and injustice and work for change.

Cynthia Moses and the Quest for Local Buy-In

Cynthia Moses began her remarkable journey more than thirty years ago as a Peace Corps volunteer in Africa. One day when she was out in the rain on her first expedition into the lush African rainforest, she looked around and told herself that this was exactly where she wanted to live and work for the rest of her life.

After her Peace Corps tour, Moses studied media and television at Columbia and Stanford, where she discovered a passion for documentary filmmaking. After stints at PBS, ABC, and the National Geographic Society, she went on to earn a number of awards as an independent filmmaker. Her work has aired on the National Geographic Channel, PBS, Discovery, A&E, and NBC, as well as internationally. Her film *New Chimpanzees* (1995) is still considered the definitive film on chimpanzee cultural traditions. Her other films include *Odzala: Islands in the Forest*

(1995), which helped expand that park, and *Living with Gorillas* (2000), which documented the behavior of western lowland gorillas.

Moses's work all over the globe, especially in Africa, inspired her to become actively involved in conservation issues. Instead of making films for developed countries, she decided to try to reach the people most in need of her conservation message—those living in and around the rainforests she was filming, who had rarely seen their own wildlife in the wild. They are the ones who have to be responsible for protecting the ecosystem on a day-to-day basis.

So Moses began to help Africans make films about their own environment. To fulfill this mission, she founded the International Conservation and Education Fund (INCEF), which produces videos on such issues as sustainable hunting, the costs of poaching, conservation laws, and the value of national parks. The filmmaking process begins with teams of Africans traveling to local communities to discuss what the important issues are, what is the most vital information to convey, and how the eventual film can best be used. Once the videos have been made, teams of educators use them to spark discussion in the communities where the process began. By helping indigenous people make wildlife films for local audiences, Moses is pioneering an entirely new type of wildlife film.

Follow-up studies have shown that these films change attitudes: as noted in Chapter 9, many viewers of her *Gorilla* film said they would no longer eat gorilla meat after learning about the creatures' humanlike family structure. Local buy-in is very important. A film with a message that local populations can relate to, that is told in a language they understand, and that recounts real-life stories of those who have engaged in, for example, poaching and destruction of habitats, has a very different impact than a DVD narrated in English by David Attenborough—which Africans can't afford to buy anyway.

Eric Kinzonzi, one of INCEF's education coordinators, says, "The films use local languages, local people, to speak about local issues—that is why INCEF is successful. We reach the entire community, and the methodology invites discussion by the audience, thus giving them a voice, not only within the screening sessions, but for many days to follow. The only way to solve issues is for people to relate to the issues and to talk about them and find their own solutions." One cannot change behavior without knowing what motivates the behavior and also what resonates with audiences. Both, INCEF feels, are necessary. The organization found that, after watching its films, 94 percent of the population said they would not eat great apes. When asked why, more than 52 percent replied, "Because they are like humans." They were less interested in the fact that great apes are endangered, that they help perpetuate the forest by dispersing seeds, or that it is illegal to hunt them. They cared that the gorilla families resembled their own. One local resident said, "If my husband brings home gorilla meat for dinner, I will refuse to cook it," and another declared, "If we eat great apes, we are no better than cannibals." INCEF uses that type of guidance and feedback when making its films.

This chapter has looked at just a few of the heroes who use wildlife filmmaking to advance conservation. Their chosen settings range from the highest peaks to the ocean floor; their audiences, from insiders to the masses; their voices, from gentle and descriptive to provocative and evangelical. What they all share, though, is a profound conviction that animals' needs should be put ahead of the exigencies of filmmaking—an idea that inevitably leads to films born of patience and courage, not aggression and intrusion. Each of these filmmakers, in his or her own way, provides a superlative example of how to make ethical films that serve honorable ends. The next and final chapter focuses on the future: what wildlife filmmakers, broadcasters, and audiences can do to help the industry survive and thrive.

11

THE WAY FORWARD
How Wildlife Films Can Make a Difference

Wildlife filmmakers possess powerful tools for shaping public opinion, even if their impact is difficult to quantify. In an ideal world, they would use those tools to create a huge variety of appealing films for television, movie screens, and other media. For all their fascinating differences, these films would have certain qualities in common: They would be engaging and have memorable visuals. They would be built around captivating stories and characters. They would faithfully reflect what nature is really about—whether the brutal realities of predation and starvation or gentler scenes that amaze, intrigue, and inspire. During their production, these films would cause little or no stress on the animals being photographed and involve little or no staging or other manipulation. The films would not mislead or deceive the audience; any fabrication or fakery would be disclosed by the filmmaker. Finally, filmmakers would find artful ways to embrace and advance the cause of conservation. At a minimum, they'd strengthen people's ties to the natural world. Most would also help audiences work to protect that world.

In earlier chapters, I've addressed the challenges that even the best filmmakers face in trying to achieve these goals. There are the usual looming deadlines, bad weather, budget shortfalls, equipment failures, contract disputes, and logistical crises. Then there are the even tougher challenges of finding funding, deciding whether and how to use celebrities, reining in out-of-control cinematographers or hosts, and challenging the conventional "claws and jaws" wisdom in an industry driven by ratings and profits.

In previous pages, you've read about several filmmakers who have successfully met all these challenges. How can we learn from their experience and also from the filmmakers and broadcasters who have failed this challenge in various ways?

Ratings and profits still drive the industry's engine to a perilous extent, but there are glimmers of hope. As I mentioned in Chapters 1 and 9, some serious, responsibly made documentaries have drawn big audiences lately—everything from *An Inconvenient Truth* to *Planet Earth*. And conservation filmmakers such as those profiled in Chapter 10 are producing more interesting, engaging films than ever, which new media are helping deliver to larger audiences.

To build on these successes, I've outlined an eight-point plan for wildlife filmmaking reform. This plan was developed in consultation with many colleagues, from my decades of work in the field, along with my more recent investigations of the industry and its ethical responsibilities. It aims, first and foremost, to influence wildlife filmmakers and broadcasters. If the industry is to prosper and play a positive role in society, we'll need to consider every one of these ideas seriously. If we don't, our audiences will dwindle, and the places and animals we find so photogenic may be irreparably damaged—or destroyed.

The plan is also important for our audiences. The more they know about the work we do, the more vigilant they'll become. If they are privy to the tricks of the trade, they'll be able to tell when a producer is trying to get away with deceiving the audience or abusing wildlife. Discerning audiences can choose to stop watching films that are manipulative, misleading, or destructive—and encourage others to do the same. They can cheer on and support the most skillful, responsible filmmakers. In short, they can become more powerful than the filmmakers they admire and create a demand for ethically produced entertainment. Such heightened audience awareness and response may make some in the business uneasy—some might even claim that their artistic freedom is being curtailed—but such growing pains will be worthwhile in the end. The time for greater transparency is now.

Eight Steps to Wildlife Filmmaking Reform

What should wildlife filmmakers and broadcasters do to survive, thrive, and make a difference? Consider the following recommendations:

1. Start with a statement of intent.
2. Work closely with reputable scientists.
3. Make conservation films that entertain.
4. Use new media effectively.
5. Disclose how the film was made and establish an ethics ranking system.
6. Practice green filmmaking.
7. Diversify the wildlife filmmaking community.
8. Improve ethics training and guidelines.

Let's look more closely at each of these.

1. Start with a statement of intent. Guidelines issued by the National Academy of Sciences state that, before conducting experiments with animals, scientists should write a report stating their intentions and describing the methods they'll use. They are required to research current best practices and outline the most humane way to achieve their desired results. Filmmaker JP Eason believes that wildlife filmmakers should do something similar. A wildlife filmmaker's statement of intent would describe plans to ensure that a film would be honest and ethically made and not harm animals or habitat.

Questionable decisions are often made in haste, when producers and cinematographers come under budget and time pressures and have no well-thought-out contingency plan to fall back on. If filmmakers were required to formulate statements of intent before going into production, they might be able to minimize their use of last-minute staging and manipulation.

To promote this idea, major broadcasters should begin requiring such statements up front. Universities and other research-based institutions (a major source of story ideas for wildlife filmmakers) could decide to cooperate with filmmakers only after full disclosure of their filming methods. U.S agencies such as the National Park Service and similar agencies in foreign governments could make their cooperation contingent on filmmakers' signing full-disclosure contracts prior to filming on their lands.

2. Work closely with reputable scientists. The 1996 IMAX film *Whales,* which my colleagues and I made from 1987 to 1995, would not have been possible without the help of highly qualified scientists. They told us where the whales were, when they were likely to breach, sing, tail-slap, and perform many other intriguing behaviors. They taught us how to interact with the whales to ensure mutual safety and minimal disturbance. The scientists' permits allowed us to enter the water in close proximity to whales in Hawaii, Alaska, and other key areas. Scientists' discoveries about wild animals—how they breed, survive, and feed—are often what make wildlife films so fascinating. Scientists need filmmakers as well. If a film tells a scientist's story well, it's easier for that researcher to find funding for further study and to cultivate a scientifically literate public.

But while a good scientist-filmmaker relationship can be mutually beneficial, it's important to choose partners carefully. Before they begin, the parties need to agree on both the goals of the project and the most ethical way to accomplish them.

Wildlife filmmakers often assume that if something is done by a scientist, it must be acceptable. But not all scientists are equally credible or ethical. Filmmaker Howard Hall once sent me photos of hot-branded seals, disfigured by hideous burn marks across the width of their bodies. The practice is supposed to help with identification during field studies, but it is inhumane and cruel. Likewise, researchers who tag otters in their rear feet are causing them excruciating pain, as are those who embed instruments in animals' body cavities or attach heavy transmitters around their necks, restricting their natural movements.

The bottom line is that scientists and filmmakers should work closely together. But both sides need a basic grounding in—and a healthy skepticism about—each other's methods and techniques.

3. Make conservation films that entertain. If conservation films were more entertaining (not necessarily in the sense of being fun to watch but in the sense of being captivating, even when the subject is grim) and told more compelling stories, broadcasters would be more willing to air them. They would get better ratings, audiences' connections to nature would be strengthened, and the Earth would enlist more defenders. Here are a few thoughts on how filmmakers could move toward that goal—and how some already have.

THROUGH DRAMA. Adding drama to any film is usually a matter of finding good characters who face interesting challenges. A 2008 Animal Planet program called *Whale Wars* provides one interesting example. Instead of hand-wringing about the plight of whales or lecturing about what viewers should do to help protect whales, Animal Planet vice president Jason Carey decided to focus on one controversial whale advocate, Paul Watson. "This activist's story has everything you need for great television," Carey says: danger, action scenes, good versus evil, underdogs who prevail, compelling characters, visceral emotion, outlaw pirates, and the renegade behavior of "bad boys trying to do good."

Here's how the story goes: In 1977, Paul Watson was expelled from the leadership of Greenpeace by a vote of eleven to one—Watson himself casting the sole dissenting vote—after serving as one of the conservation organization's cofounders. (Watson now accuses the organization of timidity and ineffectiveness.) Following his ouster, Watson founded the Sea Shepherd Conservation Society, an organization designed to "end the destruction of habitat and the slaughter of wildlife in the world's oceans in order to conserve and protect ecosystems and species."

Today, Watson captains a vessel based out of southern Australia, the MS *Steve Irwin* (named after the deceased TV host). Nearly every winter, Sea Shepherd members try to find and stop Japanese whaling ships. Their tactics include ramming ships, boarding whaling vessels and fighting with their crews, and disrupting operations that process whale carcasses. On occasion, Watson's crew has attempted to bolt cover plates onto whaling vessels' drainage outlets and has thrown butyric acid, a mildly caustic chemical, onto the vessel in an effort to interfere with the ship's operations. Whereas much of the worldwide mass media cast Sea Shepherd members as environmental heroes, the Japanese government and media portray their work as illegal acts of piracy.

Much of the film is built around Watson. His actions have been so extreme that one television crew feared for their lives and asked to leave the boat when Watson threatened a Japanese whaler. Watson maintains that every member of his own crew has signed a waiver affirming that they are willing to die for the whales. In scene after scene, Watson does not come across as a hero but rather as a complex character with strengths and weaknesses.

Whale Wars is different from other programming on Animal Planet, Carey says. It isn't just about animals; it's also about an environmental controversy. He suggests that the network is inventing a new type of storytelling in an effort to increase ratings, though in a sense its approach is similar to the people-focused tales in the Sierra Club Chronicles (see Chapter 9). Kevin Mohs, vice president of Animal Planet, says that the goal of *Whale Wars* is not to make a judgment but to bring the conversation to the surface. He calls it "great television with a purpose." It also shows just how dramatic conservation stories can be.

But you don't necessarily need a law-breaking group such as the Sea Shepherds, or even a controversial character such as Watson, to make a dramatic film. Many highly rated conservation films deal with more conventional people, such as scientists, park rangers, citizen activists, and whistle-blowers. Placed in extraordinary circumstances, these people rise to the occasion and bring about changes in society that benefit wildlife and people. *A Life among Whales* (2006), for example, examines the fascinating life and admirable work of whale biologist and activist Roger Payne. Like Paul Watson in *Whale Wars,* Payne forces audiences to reassess their relationship with our fellow inhabitants of planet Earth. Unlike Watson, though, Payne is a thoroughly law-abiding citizen.

THROUGH HUMOR. Making viewers laugh is a powerful way to grab their attention and hold it long enough to deliver an important conservation message. This is true in most areas of communication: about a quarter of the prime-time television advertising in the United States is intended to be humorous. Mark Levit, a professor of marketing at New York University, asserts that many of the most memorable ad campaigns are funny because "people will pay more attention to a humorous commercial than a factual or serious one, opening themselves up to be influenced." So why haven't conservationists discovered this same tool?

Of course, there have been some attempts. One ad for the green mutual fund Altshuler Shaham shows a suave man in alligator-skin shoes entering a hair-removal clinic (to a hip techno beat). As he relaxes on the bed for what he thinks is a routine waxing, suddenly the music changes to over-the-top psycho music, and a creepy lumberjack enters with a tweezers. The screen then displays "Now imagine how the earth feels. . . . Stop deforestation."

The United Kingdom's Friends of the Earth put out a short animated film that discusses global warming from the point of view of talking polar bears. The bears blame global warming on everything from the way one bear is sitting to the type of hat another one wears. They dismiss the idea that humans could be causing it, asking, "Do you think, for one moment, that they would allow that to happen to us?"

Why aren't filmmakers doing more to incorporate humor into conservation messages? One reason is that it's hard! As someone who has dabbled in stand-up comedy, I assure you that it's easy to fall flat on your face. Second, we conservationists tend to take ourselves too seriously. Because the issues we face are so daunting, we sometimes forget about the power of humor. Third, humor doesn't move across borders and cultures reliably, so using humor effectively in programs that are distributed internationally is particularly challenging. Finally, humor has the potential to offend. It can cross lines that are controversial.

Besides, getting people's attention is not our only goal. We also want people to understand the conservation information behind the film and learn what they can do to help. According to research, funny advertising increases brand recognition but does not necessarily increase product recall, message credibility, or purchases. So the trick is to combine humor with strong conservation messages. How does one go beyond laughter to tangible results—for example, getting people to vote a certain way, volunteer for grassroots environmental groups, or make a donation to a conservation cause? Humorous videos must lead an audience to other forms of media (environmental Web sites, for instance) where they can find more substantive information about the issues and become more involved.

What is humor's role in crafting effective messages that produce real results? What is the relationship between humor and learning? Why does laughing open people up to new ideas that they might otherwise reject? Universities need to do more research on the connection between humor and persuasion, and film schools should offer more classes in humor as a communication tool.

THROUGH INSPIRATION. Another way to make conservation films entertaining is to make them encouraging and inspiring. People come away from such films knowing what they are for, not just what they are against. Solutions as well as problems are discussed, so rather than feeling depressed at the end of such films, people feel motivated to get something done.

Remember "Deep Trouble," the poor, orphaned ninth episode of *The Blue Planet,* discussed in Chapter 9? Perhaps one of the reasons this program was never broadcast in the United States was that it had none of the inspirational elements so richly offered in the other eight *Blue Planet* episodes. Just as no film should be all cuteness and fluff, no film should be all threats and exhortations.

Jean-Michel Cousteau, son of the legendary Jacques Cousteau, seems to have mastered these principles in making what he likes to call "outcome-based documentaries." The first two episodes of his 2008 PBS series, *Jean-Michel Cousteau: Ocean Adventures,* focused on the beauty and looming degradation of the Northwestern Hawaiian Islands, a 1,200-mile archipelago stretching out from the main Hawaiian Islands. These pristine habitats have been sullied by cities thousands of miles away, resulting in filthy, debris-strewn beaches.

Cousteau was asked to preview the episodes at the White House, for then president George W. Bush and key federal and state decision makers. Apparently the president, not known for his pro-environmental leanings, was impressed by the gorgeous scenery and inspiring stories and instructed his staff to "get it done." A few weeks later, Cousteau was invited back for a White House ceremony declaring the Northwestern Hawaiian Islands a national monument—the largest protected marine habitat in the world.

Of course, other factors besides Cousteau's film were in play, including years of scientific research and activist support from organizations such as the National Oceanic and Atmospheric Administration and the Environmental Defense Fund. Films—even inspiring ones—can't change the world all by themselves. But they can help us reach the outcomes we seek.

4. Use new media effectively. Every wildlife film should have a Web-based action plan, using tools that engage viewers in their online communities, including social-networking Web sites such as Facebook and Twitter. Anyone who's been moved by the film can then continue the journey online: find out more about the subject, perhaps support a non-profit's campaign and get directly involved, and pass the word to friends and colleagues in his or her social networks. The action plan can also include celebrities, policymakers, scientists, and other issue experts. It can involve sharing ideas, recruiting new members, taking action, signing petitions, donating money, making lifestyle changes, buying books, reading in-depth articles, and forming discussion groups. BBC film producer

Tim Martin says, "Our live British wildlife series, *Springwatch*, has become a leader in this field, and has established whole online communities who debate and respond to the television content, and get involved in local action like putting up nest boxes and bird feeders."

Similarly, the National Geographic Society encourages audience involvement beyond television viewing. Its Web site features not only supplemental articles, photos, videos, and games, but also content that allows users to become working conservationists. Included on the site are a "green guide" that offers advice about making lifestyle changes that benefit the environment and banner ads targeting environmentally minded visitors to the site. One such ad by the World Society for the Protection of Animals asks users to donate money to help stop the practice of bear-baiting, a gruesome manufactured conflict between captive, often abused bears and dogs. By including content that encourages direct action, the National Geographic Society has greatly increased its effectiveness as a conservation organization.

Using this Web-based strategy, television producers don't have to weigh down the ends of their films with lots of depressing information. The key, says Martin, is to give people enough information in the television program to make them care about a subject, then direct them to the Web, where they can find out more.

The Web is also a revolutionary distribution tool. More computers, faster Internet connections, and simplified technologies such as YouTube have allowed viewers to post and view digital video clips in mere seconds. This, in turn, has allowed wildlife programming to reach more viewers. Examples include clips of wildlife films from PBS and other networks, nature videos on science Web sites for children, and advocacy messages from conservation groups. YouTube and similar sites (such as the Web channels Joost and Hulu) allow these clips to be seen by hundreds of millions of people.

Conservation-oriented filmmakers have been using the Web for years to distribute films and messages. Hardy Jones's films at BlueVoice. org (which he cofounded with actor Ted Danson) involve Web-based campaigns that allow viewers to sign up for membership in wildlife conservation organizations. Jones produces live Webcasts from the field that can be made into multipart series that attract large, responsive audiences, already self-selected for advocacy. Jones has at times reached audiences of more than three hundred thousand with his films on the Web.

British cinematographer Rebecca Hosking made good use of the Web in distributing a film about pollution in Hawaii. The film documents how tons of plastic materials are washing up on the islands every year—killing turtles, albatrosses, monk seals, and other animals that try to ingest them or become fatally entangled in them. Hosking made the film and these facts part of a Web-based anti-plastic campaign. Her savvy combination of film, facts, and activism convinced the shopkeepers in her local town of Modbury, Devon, to stop using plastic bags in 2007. Other communities—even major cities such as San Francisco—have followed suit by banning plastic grocery bags as well. Overnight, Hosking has become an eco-hero. Her success demonstrates what's so exciting about this new era. If you've got something important to say, you don't need a broadcaster's permission to say it.

One Web-based media nonprofit has gone a step farther. The Environmental Media Fund (EMF), founded by Bob Silvestri in San Francisco, finances and produces films. Each project that receives the organization's support is required to post Web pages with information about the issues raised by the film, along with tools for taking action that can be shared with visitors' friends. EMF also encourages filmmakers to create materials for teachers and to team up with nonprofits and grassroots organizations to create more potent action campaigns. (Full disclosure: I serve on EMF's board.)

The rise of the Internet has already broadened the ranks of the wildlife filmmaking industry by allowing amateur videographers to post home videos online. Conservation groups have a new platform for their advocacy, and viewers can play a major role in the publicity and promotion of wildlife programming as they e-mail friends and family links to video clips, add video clips to their MySpace and Facebook pages, and submit podcasts to the audio distribution site iTunes.

The people creating these clips may well need further training in the fine art of responsible filmmaking. Currently, much of their work would never be shown on network or cable television because of its controversial nature, its brevity, or its amateur production quality. But by 2010, more than a billion people worldwide are predicted to have video capture features in their mobile phones, and the quality of that video will eventually reach high definition, a technological leap that could give amateur filmmaking a new look.

5. Disclose how the film was made and establish an ethics ranking system. In 1998, Jeffery Boswall published an article in *Image Technology* magazine arguing that wildlife filmmakers should make better use of "disclaimers." By that he meant that they should tell viewers if trained or captive animals or staging was used. Such disclosures would give viewers information about the tricks of the trade used to make the film.

In the past, many wildlife films carried disclaimers such as "All scenes in this film, whether actual or re-created, represent authenticated facts." This suggests that the producers did their best to get the science right. But it leaves viewers scratching their heads. Were animals harassed? Did the cinematographers get too close? Were computer-generated images used? Was there any staging or manipulation? We have no idea. Another old-style disclaimer might admit that captive bears were used in a film but stop short of mentioning that wild bears and captive bears are likely to behave differently.

Many filmmakers are inclined to hide this information, fearing that the truth could turn audiences away. That may be true in some cases, but conscientious filmmakers have much to gain from disclosure. If audiences know the details concerning the use of staging, tame animals, special effects, and digital image manipulation, wildlife filmmakers will then be inoculated against accusations of deceit and dishonesty. Better to have disclaimers than disillusioned viewers who feel hoodwinked. Besides, audiences often find this information fascinating—just look at the popularity of the "extra features" about the filmmaking process that now accompany most Hollywood films on DVD.

The ideal disclaimer would describe in a nutshell how the film was made. It would let audiences know if, say, footage of birds flying was taken using hand-raised and trained birds or if a wild-looking leopard was really from a game farm and filmed on a set. To publicize this information, the Web site for every film—especially for scenes that use some manipulation—should include a "how the film was made" page, billed as a behind-the-scenes peek into the industry. Viewers would be directed to the site by a URL appearing prominently in the credits. Such details could also be revealed in a short documentary feature at the end of every wildlife film. Typically such "making of" features are little more than self-serving plugs from the producer, and the only tricks of the trade revealed are those that make the producer look tough, brave, patient, or smart. Wildlife film producers should be encouraged to widen the focus of these features; to tell the audience that one scene was created using computer graphics, another was shot in a zoo, and a third involved dropping a snake out of a tall tree. If they are reluctant to do so, it probably means that they need to examine their filmmaking practices.

To get around the problem of self-serving disclosures, the filmmaking community should come up with a kind of ethics ratings system. Just as there is an international Leadership in Energy and Environmental Design (LEED) standard for green buildings, which rates buildings as "certified," "silver," "gold," or "platinum," there could be ratings for films. Conferred by an independent organization, the ratings could range from the lowest level of ethical acceptability to the highest: from the lax "No animals were harmed in the making of this film" to the strict "No staging or manipulation was used in the making of this film" to the very strict "The footage in this film contains only wild, free-ranging animals that were not disturbed by the filming." As viewers learned about these ratings, they could pressure producers to strive for the highest levels by voting with their remotes—and their wallets.

6. Practice green filmmaking. Films with a focus on conservation can certainly be considered green in content, but what about the production of the film itself and its contribution to climate change, pollution, and environmental degradation? The Code of Best Practices in Sustainable Filmmaking was created by American University in Washington, DC, and Filmmakers for Conservation in the United Kingdom to provide a well-founded set of principles to help documentary filmmakers reduce the impact of their productions on the environment. (Disclosure: I teach at American University.) Authors Larry Engel and Andrew Buchanan include practical advice on ways filmmakers can reduce, reuse, and recycle and find the most reputable carbon-offset providers to make up for greenhouse gas emissions that they can't avoid. The initial goal is to reach carbon neutrality (that is, add no new carbon to the atmosphere), but the ultimate goal is to calculate and reduce each film's ecological footprint, a broader measure of how filmmaking activities use and affect the planet's environment and its resources.

Buchanan knows what he's talking about. He made a film for the National Geographic Society called *Earth Report 2006,* which was carbon neutral. Al Gore did the same with *An Inconvenient Truth.* Of course, some emissions *were* created by the production of both films, even after following the "reduce, reuse, and recycle" rule. But those unavoidable emissions were tracked, and the films' production budgets paid the money needed to buy carbon offsets. In both cases, the money went to build wind turbines on a Native American reservation.

Syriana, a movie from Participant Productions about the geopolitics of oil, was produced carbon neutral: 100 percent of its carbon dioxide emissions during production were offset through investments in renewable energy. It wasn't the first Hollywood movie to do this, however. *The Day after Tomorrow,* a natural-disaster movie in which climate change precipitates global environmental catastrophe, was the first big-budget film to attempt climate neutrality, although it did so through tree planting rather than renewable energy. And, of course, it is always better to reduce emissions in the first place rather than try to offset them later.

7. Diversify the wildlife filmmaking community. When I give presentations, I sometimes prod the audience by saying, "Some of you may be new to the conservation movement. We are a very diverse community. We have white people from every state in the country." It's a small joke, but I tell it because it reveals a sad truth about not only the environmental movement, but also about the worldwide community of wildlife filmmakers. We are seriously deficient when it comes to diversity. At wildlife filmmaking festivals and conferences, few nonwhite faces can be seen.

In 1995, when I worked for the National Wildlife Federation, an African American man named Jerome Ringo joined the board and later became chairman. For many years he was the only African American at the board meetings. National environmental organizations such as the National Wildlife Federation and the Sierra Club have traditionally drawn their support mostly from the white and affluent. The need for racial diversity in their ranks is widely recognized by their leaders as a top priority, and the wildlife filmmaking community must make the same commitment.

Local participation and emphasis, on an international scale, is another facet of diversity. As noted in Chapter 10, Cynthia Moses is training people in Africa to make wildlife films that reflect the interests of their own communities. Another innovator is Richard Brock, who produced some of the BBC's landmark television series (including *Life on Earth* and *The Living Planet*), but later became disillusioned with the state of wildlife programming on television—including the kind of shows he had helped produce. "Wildlife television continues to decline and be reduced to limited derivative types ranging from predictable predation shows, snake or croc-wrangling, to epic expensive series such as *Planet Earth*," he says. He sees most of this programming as a waste of money and resources and believes that wildlife TV shows produced for the international market are lying to audiences about the state of the planet. In 2005 he struck out in another direction, launching the Brock Initiative, which uses both donated archival footage and inexpensively shot new footage to create programs not for a general television audience but for "those who are really connected to the situation in hand: local communities, decision makers, even that one fisherman who uses dynamite fishing over that one coral reef—often people who have never seen TV. It's about reaching those who have a direct impact—those who can make the difference." Brock's production company, Living Planet

Films, uses local people to shoot footage, contribute music and graphics, and distribute the films.

If other experienced filmmakers took up this challenge, our entire industry would benefit. We need the insight and vitality that can come from having people of many different backgrounds producing wildlife films. Moreover, our films will not win the world over to conservation if they are being created solely by the world's most advantaged ethnic group.

8. Improve ethics training and guidelines. In 2003, Filmmakers for Conservation (FFC) published "Guiding Principles for Documentary Filmmakers," a two-page document that described standards of conduct defining the essentials of ethical behavior. The principles included these:

- Always place the welfare of the subject above all else.
- Be aware that habituation, baiting, and feeding may place your subjects at risk and may be lethal.
- It is unacceptable to restrict or restrain an animal by any means to attract a predator or to give an audience abnormal, false, or misleading information about a subject or its behavior.
- Be aware that filming at a den or nest site could attract predators.
- The use of tame or captive animals should be acknowledged.

Do such guiding principles help? Some of my colleagues say that they are impossible to enforce in the field, which is true in some remote places. But they could be enforced by rangers in U.S. national parks and on other public lands and on international reserves. And even where enforcement is impossible, such principles serve an important purpose. They publicly set a higher standard for our profession, establish grounds for debate, and begin to set limits on the conduct of film broadcasters, producers, cinematographers, and presenters. Moreover, if broadly disseminated on the Web or promoted via mentions in popular films, these guiding principles could even influence the new wave of amateur filmmaking described in Chapter 1 and earlier in this chapter.

This is not to say that standards alone can resolve all controversies. FFC's "Guiding Principles" mention the topic of habituation, for example, but don't get into the finer points. A habituated creature has become used to a specific set of circumstances (such as vehicles containing film crews and tourists in African parks) but is not necessarily tame. Conscientious wildlife filmmakers need to ask some hard questions: How much should wildlife filmmakers habituate an animal in order to film it? How much interference is too much and would outweigh the good a film might do? Presenter Simon King has concluded that offering animals food goes too far, but there's no consensus among filmmakers about this. The FFC principles offer no guidance on this issue.

Neither do these principles help on the issue, say, of spotlighting predators and prey at night. There's a big difference between using a well-managed soft light and a bright spotlight. In more than seventeen years of using soft lights with lions in Botswana, Dereck and Beverly Joubert (profiled in Chapter 10) have managed to film only twenty-five or so kills, a sign of how sensitively they operated their lights. At the same location, filmmakers with a less ethical outlook have blasted away with powerful and disruptive spotlights and managed to film more than twenty-five kills in two weeks. The reason for this great discrepancy is that lights can help predators find their prey, giving them an unnatural advantage. If the Jouberts suspect this is happening, even with the soft lights they use, they shut down their operation for the night or switch to image intensifiers, which allow them to see in the moonlight. The FFC "Guiding Principles" state only that "night shooting with artificial lights can require precautions to avoid making the subject vulnerable to predation."

Inevitably, promoting ethical behavior in wildlife filmmaking requires more than just a set of standards. It involves the exercise of judgment, discretion, and common sense. Nobody wants to create an all-knowing "ethics police." Even the highly conscientious filmmaker Howard Hall (also profiled in Chapter 10) says, "I think each of us must act independently following our own morality when making a film and when evaluating the techniques of others. If filmmakers violate common morality in making their films, let broadcasters ban their work. Let critics expose their abuses. That puts pressure on all of us to do a better job. But let no one dictate ethical standards to me. Filmmakers should follow their conscience instead of interpreting other people's rules."

Nonetheless, I believe that ethics training and guidelines have valuable roles to play. Just as medical students have mandatory classes on medical ethics, so should film students have mandatory classes on filmmaking ethics. In them, veteran and novice filmmakers would discuss questions such as whether it is acceptable to insert radio tags inside animals (as happens routinely) so the animals can be tracked, thereby reducing field time and saving money. Few institutions currently offer such classes.

Clear guidelines and lively discussions—not only in classrooms but at film festivals, at conferences, and on the Web—would establish a better sense of the profession's ethical boundaries. For example, at wildlife film festivals, which occur throughout the year, workshops should be offered for educators, filmmakers, and broadcasters on why ethics is important, how to teach it, and how to raise filmmakers' and students' awareness of their ethical responsibilities.

Greenlighting Reform

Good wildlife films feed the public's strong curiosity about the natural world. What I've learned over the years is that audiences want the portrayals to be authentic, and they want to see wildlife and wilderness in their natural state, free of human influence or degradation. They don't want filmmakers to harm animals or their environments. When viewers discover that something in a wildlife film causes unnecessary suffering, or is packaged, inauthentic, or contrived, they feel cheated and misled. But the line between authenticity and artifice is thin and easily crossed. Filmmakers disagree on exactly where the line falls and where unethical behavior begins.

My hope is that this book can bring that debate to a wider audience. Perhaps it can also help encourage filmmakers to produce dramatic, inspiring, and even humorous new work that delights audiences, elevates our profession, and leads to greater protection for wild animals and their habitats. Audiences have a key role to play, too. Once they have learned about the tricks of the wildlife filmmaking trade, perhaps viewers will no longer settle for deceptive films that hurt wildlife and habitats. Perhaps they'll blog about the problems, write letters to elected officials and broadcasters, or even protest films at film festivals. I'll be cheering every time I hear that audiences have sent a message to our industry saying that ethics, accuracy, and conservation matter.

When I was growing up in England after World War II, we still had rationing. Butter was in very short supply, though there was plenty of milk. My father used to make me stand in the yard and shake a heavy bottle of creamy milk. My arms would start to ache painfully, but as I watched the milk sloshing around, a miraculous thing happened. Butter would suddenly appear, seemingly out of nowhere. Every shake of the bottle got me closer to the butter, just as every ethically made wildlife film brings us closer to treating the world the way it should be treated. It won't be easy, but even the best endeavors need shaking up from time to time.

I've worked in wildlife and environmental filmmaking for an incredibly fulfilling thirty years. I've met fascinating people, made many close friends, and seen amazing sights in faraway places. But, most important, I've become part of a growing community of filmmakers who want to make wildlife films with a conscience. Together with them—and the well-informed audiences that can hold us all accountable—we can build a wildlife filmmaking industry that is vibrant, profitable, and principled, and make our own unique contribution to sustaining the integrity of life on this planet.

ACKNOWLEDGMENTS

Many friends in the wildlife filmmaking industry have also been my teachers, generously sharing the stories and insights I now share with readers of this book. Those colleagues are, in a very real sense, also its authors, and I am deeply indebted to them. Scores of other friends, colleagues, and students offered invaluable advice and guidance during the writing; if not for their unwavering assistance, the manuscript would never have been completed. I particularly thank Derek Bousé, David Clark, Mark Deeble and Vicky Stone, Roger DiSilvestro, Howard and Michele Hall, Dereck and Beverly Joubert, Diane MacEachern, Joan Murray, Jenny Palmer, Kathy Pasternak, and Elizabeth Ruml.

I also thank Chris Albert, Peter Argentine, Martin Atkins, Brady Barr, Chuck Bartlebaugh, Dan Basta, Ben Beach, Eric Bendick, John Biffar, Jeffery Boswall, Jeremy Bradshaw, Adrienne Bramhall, Dan Breton, Karen Buckley, John Burgess, Bill Campbell, Tom Campbell, Sandy Cannon-Brown, Jason Carey, Katie Carpenter, Purcell Carson, Michael Cascio, Haroldo Castro, Raymond Chavez, Jacqueline Christy, Jan Cousteau, Jean-Michel Cousteau, Philippe Cousteau, Beth Davidow, John de Graaf, Chris Dickinson, Bob Drew, Charles Dunkerly, Larry Engel, Alex Fischer, Carol Fleisher, Smokey Forester, Carol and Richard Foster, Robin Gerber, Bill Grant, Fred Grossberg, Lisa Grossman, Carl Hall, Judy Hallet, Neil Harraway, Dave Helvarg, Jenny Hile, Brian Horejsi, Sarah Humphries, James Hyder, Ansu John, Hardy Jones, Chuck Jonkel, Steve King, Jo Knight, Walter Koehler, Chris Kruger, Sheila Laffey, Brian Leith, Maureen Lemire, Jim Lipscomb, Cara Blessley Lowe, Julia Mair, Tom Mangelsen, Greg Marshall, Tim Martin, Dan Mathews, Ginger Mauney, Kieth Merrill, Kathy Milani, Lance Milbrand, Sterling Miller, Kevin Mohs, Jenn Molay,

Cynthia Moses, Cathe Neukum, Julianne Niemaszyk, Neil Nightingale, Liam O'Brien, Wolfgang Obst, Brad Ohlund, Barry Paine, Dorothy Patent, Ray Paunovich, Kathleen Pearce, Rupert Pilkington, Adam Ravetch, Lori Rick, Rose Ann Robertson, Alan Root, Rob SanGeorge, Justine Schmidt, Vanessa Hiemenz Serrao, Jen Shoemaker, Bob Silvestri, Delores Simmons, Liz Smith, Susannah Smith, Holly Stadtler, Maggie Burnette Stogner, Marty Stouffer, Ronald Tobias, Rhett Turner, Alexis Van Dyke, David Vassar, Tom Veltre, Piers Warren, Bruce Weide, David Weiner, Rob Whitehair, Julia Whitty, and Randy Wimberg.

I am grateful to those who helped me source photographs for reproduction here, including Gracie and Paul Atkins, Tim Barksdale, Brady Barr, Dan Breton, Tom Campbell, Katie Carpenter, Jean-Michel Cousteau, Beth Davidow, Mark Deeble, Jim and Jamie Dutcher, Nick Easton, Howard and Michele Hall, Neil Harraway, Renee Jackman, Dereck and Beverly Joubert, Kathy Milani, Cynthia Moses, Neil Nightingale, Bob Poole, Adam Ravetch, Neil Rettig, Lori Rick, Marty Stouffer, Dyanna Taylor, Carrie Vonderhaar, and Randy Wimberg.

I want to single out for praise four of the world's best wildlife film festivals, which have supported my efforts in a thousand ways and given me a platform from which to argue some of the ideas in this book: the International Wildlife Film Festival in Missoula, Montana, led by Janet Rose; the Jackson Hole Wildlife Film Festival in Jackson Hole, Wyoming, led by Lisa Samford; the Wildscreen Festival in Bristol, United Kingdom, led by Harriet Nimmo and Sarah Mitchell; and the Environmental Film Festival in the Nation's Capital, led by Flo Stone, Peter O'Brien, and Chris Head.

My thanks to all my faculty colleagues at the School of Communication at American University, especially Dean Larry Kirkman, who helped me create the Center for Environmental Filmmaking and who has been such an extraordinary supporter of my work. My students have also been wonderfully generous with their feedback and comments. I thank Brad Allgood, Andrea Bloom, Joe Bohannon, Nate Brigham, Heather Danskin, Claire Darby, Lauren Demko, Kelly Donnellan, Jonathan "JP" Eason, Kai Fang, Sarah Farhat, Joe Grimme, Julian Guerrero, Dustin Harrison-Atlas,

Sarah Katz, Paul Kim, Peter Kimball, Danny Ledonne, Alex Morrison, Jeremy Polk, Ted Roach, James Sanborn, Mike Shubbuck, Adam Sincell, Shanon Sparks, Arya Surowidjojo, Suzanne Taylor, Marco Theophil, Ellen Tripler, Larke Williams, Michelle Williams, and many other students.

My thanks to Sierra Club Books publisher Helen Sweetland and senior editor Diana Landau for their faith in the book. Diana and my wonderful collaborating editor, Joan Hamilton, turned my scribbles into prose, and I am very grateful to them for their superb work. Karen Wise copyedited the manuscript with exemplary thoroughness and sensitivity. I also thank my terrific agent, Bob Murray, and his wife, Suzanne, for seeing the potential in this book and working hard and creatively to sell it.

I thank all my colleagues at the MacGillivray Freeman Films Educational Foundation and at MacGillivray Freeman Films, including Kathy Almon, Chip Bartlett, Alice Casbara-Leek, Patty Collins, Mary Jane Dodge, Janna Emmel, Nadine Ferdousi, Bob Harmon, Jeff Horst, Steve Judson, Jennifer Leininger, Mike Lutz, Greg and Barbara MacGillivray, Shaun MacGillivray, Pat McBurney, Matthew Muller, Brad Ohlund, Cindy Olson, Lori Rick, Harrison Smith, Lenka Spejchalova, Tori Stokes, Rob Walker, and Susan Wilson. I also thank my colleagues at VideoTakes, Incorporated, especially Allison Barnett, Andrea Bloom, Sandy Cannon-Brown, Miranda Gale, Dan Gallagher, Matt Nagy, and Olivia Yeo.

Above all, I thank my wonderful wife, Gail; our three extraordinary daughters, Kimberly, Christina, and Jenny; and our son-in-law, Sujay Davé, for their loving support and affection and for keeping me grounded. They are my anchors and I love them more than I can say. This book exists because of them.

NOTES

INTRODUCTION

Page 3   Weide hunting anecdote: Adapted with permission from Bruce Weide, "A Wolf in the Crosshairs," Wild Sentry, www.wildsentry.org/Wolf_In_Crosshairs.html.

Page 5   Hours American children spend watching TV: Robert Kubey, "How Media Education Promotes Critical Thinking, Democracy, Health, and Aesthetic Appreciation," Center for Media Literacy, www.medialit.org/reading_room/article547.html (previously published in *Cable in the Classroom*, November 2002).

Page 5   Size of Sierra Club membership: Sierra Club, www.sierraclub.org/history/timeline.asp.

Page 5   Box-office revenue for *An Inconvenient Truth*: Box Office Mojo, boxofficemojo.com/movies/?id=inconvenienttruth.htm.

Page 5   Size of audience for National Geographic Channel programming: Chris Albert (executive director, communications, National Geographic Channel), e-mail message to author, October 17, 2008.

Page 5   Households reached by Animal Planet: Kevin Mohs (vice president, Animal Planet), e-mail message to author, October 18, 2008.

Page 6   *March of the Penguins* revenues: Brooks Barnes, "Disney Looks to Nature, and Creates a Film Division to Capture It," *New York Times*, April 22, 2008, www.nytimes.com/2008/04/22/business/media/22disney.html.

Page 6   IMAX revenues: Lori Rick (director of promotion and publicity, MacGillivray Freeman Films), e-mail message to author, October 16, 2008.

Page 6   Disneynature plans: Barnes, "Disney Looks to Nature."

Page 6   "a strict code of ethics": Howard Poskin, "If the Bear Won't Come Out, Do You Lure It into Camera Range?" *TV Guide*, December 3, 1988.

CHAPTER 1

Page 12 Jones sperm whale anecdote: Hardy Jones, personal communications to author, 1989–2009.

Page 14 Characteristics of blue-chip films: Derek Bousé, *Wildlife Films* (Philadelphia: University of Pennsylvania Press, 2000).

Page 17 Lieberman blamed *Jackass*: Office of Senator Joe Lieberman, "Lieberman Calls on MTV to Clean Up 'Jackass' Program, Prevent Future Copycat Injuries" (press release), February 7, 2001.

Page 18 *Wildboyz* quotation: TV.com episode guide to *Wildboyz*, www.tv.com/wildboyz/russia-ii/episode/650375/summary.html.

Page 19 Highest-grossing animal films: Wikipedia, "List of Animal Films," en.wikipedia.org/wiki/List_of_animal_films.

Page 20 *Arctic Tale* as cross between documentary and fiction: Adam Ravetch, personal communication to author, July 22, 2008.

Page 20 "*Arctic Tale* is really a metaphor for humans": Adam Ravetch, e-mail message to author, July 24, 2008.

Page 21 *Finding Nemo* leading to death of clownfish: "I Can't Find Nemo! Pet Trade Threatens Clownfish," Times Online, June 26, 2008, www.timesonline.co.uk/tol/news/environment/article4220496.ece.

Page 23 "the sharpest, clearest, richest, most colorful, and near lifelike images": Brad Ohlund, e-mail message to author, July 12, 2009.

Page 24 "the most impractical motion picture format": Howard Hall, e-mail message to author, August 2, 2009.

Page 25 Giant-screen film facts: MacGillivray Freeman Films Web site, www.macfreefilms.com/; IMAX Web site, www.imax.com/.

Page 26 "candor excitingly superseded civility": Bayley Silleck, e-mail message to author, April 22, 2003.

Page 27 "passive 'viewers' are replaced by active 'users'": Eric Bendick, e-mail message to author, July 24, 2009.

Page 27 Facts about TERRA: Eric Bendick, personal communication to author, October 20, 2008.

Page 28 Views of *Battle at Kruger* video: YouTube, www.youtube.com/watch?v=LU8DDYz68kM, October 24, 2008.

Page 28 Audience of Obama's nomination acceptance speech: Breitbart, www.breitbart.com/article.php?id=D92S3HOG1&show_article=1.

Page 29 Views of *Beyoncé on the Spot* video: YouTube, www.youtube.com/watch?v=qlgsHBOYfIw, October 24, 2009.

Page 29   Facts about *An Inconvenient Truth*: Box Office Mojo, boxofficemojo.com/
movies/?id=inconvenienttruth.htm; "An Inconvenient Truth," Wikipedia,
en.wikipedia.org/wiki/Inconvenient_Truth.

Page 29   Survey on environmental concerns: Juliet Eilperin, "Despite Big Honor for
Gore, Climate Not Top Issue in U.S.," *Washington Post*, October 13, 2007.

Page 29   "Al Gore jolted the world": George Schaller, e-mail message to author,
April 25, 2009.

Page 29   Environmental topics no longer "eat your vegetables" television: Michael
Cascio, e-mail message to author, July 19, 2009.

Page 30   Corney would rather have "exploding snakes": Alicia Androich, "Five's
Wildlife Needs," *Realscreen*, October 30, 2008.

CHAPTER 2

Page 34   For readers who wish to learn more about the history of wildlife films
and filmmaking, an excellent resource is WildFilmHistory (www.
wildfilmhistory.org), an online guide celebrating more than a century of
wildlife filmmaking, pioneers in the field, and landmark films. The site
features hundreds of free film clips of all the films mentioned in this book
and many more, more than fifty filmed interviews, as well as biographies,
behind-the-scenes still photos, and further information and links.

Page 34   Description of the Johnsons with the cannibals: Patricia Eliot Tobias,
"Adventure on Film," *Written By*, August 2003.

Page 35   The Johnsons "brought more popular acceptance to wildlife films than
anyone prior to Disney": Bousé, *Wildlife Films*, 53.

Page 36   Facts on Buck's life: Frank Buck, *All in a Lifetime: An Autobiography* (New
York: McBride, 1941).

Page 36   "enclosures somewhat less glorious than the Coliseum": Bousé, *Wildlife
Films*, 54.

Page 37   "real animals are often funnier and more surprising": Walt Disney,
press release for *True-Life Adventures* DVDs, www.ultimatedisney.com/
truelifeadventures-pressrelease.html.

Page 37   Disney championing middle-class morals: Cynthia Chris, *Watching
Wildlife* (Minneapolis: University of Minnesota Press, 2006); Ronald
Tobias, "Film and the Moral Vision of Nature" (unpublished manuscript,
2009).

Page 39   Roy Disney on being "ahead of the ecology movement": Roger Moore, "A
Different Animal," *Orlando Sentinel*, December 2, 2006.

Page 40   Perkins's early career: Museum of Broadcast Communications, www.
museum.tv/archives/etv/W/htmlW/wildkingdom/wildkingdom.htm.

Page 40 *Wild Kingdom* audience statistics: Marlin Perkins, *My Wild Kingdom: An Autobiography* (New York: Dutton, 1982), 186.

Page 40 Perkins working his sponsor's name into content: Chris, *Watching Wildlife*, 59.

Page 40 Awards won by *Wild Kingdom*: Gregg Mitman, *Reel Nature* (Cambridge, MA: Harvard University Press, 1999), 150.

Page 40 *Wild Kingdom's* influence on audience's views: Perkins, *My Wild Kingdom*, 186.

Page 41 Naïve review of *Wild Kingdom*: Mitman, *Reel Nature*, 151.

Page 42 *Cruel Camera* withdrawn from second showing: John Corry, "Where the Driver Ants and the Drill Baboon Dwell," TV View, *New York Times*, April 27, 1986.

Page 43 "the imbalance of habitats caused by man": Perkins, *My Wild Kingdom*, 44.

Page 44 Cousteau's formula became the industry norm: Chris, *Watching Wildlife*, 57.

Page 44 Cousteau "placed the underwater world at the door of an audience as extensive as the oceans themselves": Al Gore, review of *The Human, the Orchid, and the Octopus,* by Jacques Cousteau and Susan Schiefelbein, Cousteau Web site, www.cousteau.org/media/books.

Page 44 Stories of Cousteau killing sharks: Richard Munson, e-mail message to author, February 26, 2009.

Page 44 Philippe Cousteau's defense of his grandfather: Philippe Cousteau, e-mail message to author, April 27, 2009.

Page 45 Description of laboratory work: Andrew Langley, *The Making of the Living Planet* (Boston: Little Brown, 1985), 16.

Page 46 BBC's expertise in nature films: ibid., 55.

Page 46 Goodall raised Americans' consciousness about plight of wild chimpanzees: Tom Veltre, personal communication to author, June 6, 2008.

Page 47 "sometimes shocking reality of life in the wild": Marty Stouffer, *Marty Stouffer's Wild America* (New York: Times Books, 1988), 189.

Page 47 Praise from *TV Guide* and the *Los Angeles Times*: quoted in Marty Stouffer, e-mail message to author, August 16, 2009.

Page 48 "never making it back": Stouffer, *Marty Stouffer's Wild America,* 26.

Page 49 "I returned to America to film life": ibid., 58.

Page 49 "She sure got an eyeful of me": Marty Stouffer, e-mail message to author, August 25, 2009.

Page 50 Filming wild hogs in Georgia: Stouffer, *Marty Stouffer's Wild America*, 220.

Page 50 "It's not Walt Disney": Marty Stouffer, e-mail message to author, August 25, 2009.

CHAPTER 3

Page 52 All quotations in Chapter 3 come from personal conversations or e-mail messages between the author and the filmmakers quoted.

CHAPTER 4

Page 84 Perkins quotation about mountain goats and Mutual of Omaha: Cynthia Chris, *Watching Wildlife* (Minneapolis: University of Minnesota Press, 2006), 59.

Page 86 "Maybe Chris Palmer is missing a battery or something": Ron Arnold and Alan Gottlieb, *Trashing the Economy: How Runaway Environmentalism Is Wrecking America* (Bellevue, WA: Free Enterprise Press, 1993), 240.

Page 86 "Audubon and Turner got the ball rolling": David Seideman, e-mail messages to author, January 29, 2008, and December 29, 2008.

Page 86 Designation of Opal Creek as a wilderness area: Opal Creek Web site, www.opalcreek.org.

Page 87 GE denied that its withdrawal of sponsorship was connected to the boycott: Jane Hall, "Audubon Specials: An Endangered Species," *Los Angeles Times*, December 17, 1991.

Page 90 "40 hours of stinging, no-holds-barred video documentary that has fingered heroes and villains": Alan Rich, "TBS 'Audubon' Retro Is Best of the Best," *Variety*, November 17, 1994.

CHAPTER 5

Page 92 Ferrell's eco-friendly house: Suzy Byrne, "Celebrity Planet: Will Ferrell's Love of the Environment Is No Laughing Matter," Gaiam Life: Your Guide to Better Living, life.gaiam.com/gaiam/p/Celebrity-Planet-Will-Ferrells-Love-of-the-Environment-is-No-Laughing-Matter-and-More.html.

Page 92 Diaz and Dunst drive hybrid cars: Jill Serjeant. "Some Celebrities Who Made Green Issues Cool," Planet Ark, ww.planetark.org/dailynewsstory.cfm/newsid/40523/story.htm.

Page 93 Hurley's organic farm: Byrne, "Celebrity Planet."

Page 93   Pitt narrated a TV series on eco-friendly houses: Mike Hirn, "Climate Change: Celebrities Weigh In on Global Warming," E-Zine Articles, ezinearticles.com/?Climate-Change---Celebrities-Weigh-In-On-Global-Warming&id=1041536.

Page 93   Hannah's sit-in: Serjeant, "Some Celebrities Who Made Green Issues Cool."

Page 93   Ford video about tropical rainforests: Hirn, "Climate Change."

Page 93   DiCaprio's documentaries about ecological issues: Serjeant, "Some Celebrities Who Made Green Issues Cool."

Page 97   Tilden-Davis's account of hippo attack: Witness statement of Diana Tilden-Davis.

Page 97   Kruger's account of hippo attack: Witness statement of Chris Kruger.

Page 97   Tilden-Davis's hippo bite: "Former Miss SA Recovers after Hippo Attack," Independent Online, www.iol.co.za/index.php?click_id=125&art_id=qw1072335966674B243&set_id=1, December 25, 2003.

Page 98   Tilden-Davis's recovery: "South African Beauty Queen Still Recovering from Hippo Attack," Duke Marine Lab Local Web Server, moray.ml.duke.edu/projects/hippos/Newsletter/news146.html, October 9, 2005.

Page 99   People volunteered time or donated money to nonprofits after Irwin's death: Kevin Mohs, e-mail message to author, June 20, 2009.

Page 100   Irwin "de-villainized" crocodiles: Jan Cousteau, e-mail message to author, June 29, 2009.

Page 100   "getting close to big things that can kill you": David Helvarg, "The 'Crocodile Saver,'" *Los Angeles Times*, September 6, 2006.

Page 100   "The animal world has finally taken its revenge": Germaine Greer, "That Sort of Self-Delusion Is What It Takes to Be a Real Aussie Larrikin," *Guardian*, September 5, 2006, www.guardian.co.uk/world/2006/sep/05/australia.

Page 100   "narcissistic clowns": Alan Root, e-mail message to author, December 2, 2008.

Page 101   "If Steve Irwin can do it, so can I": Dereck Joubert, e-mail message to author, September 22, 2008.

CHAPTER 6

Page 102   I am grateful to film director and broadcaster Barry Paine for bringing the Queengate scandal to my attention: Barry Paine, e-mail message to author, July 23, 2007.

Page 102 Compulsory ethics training for BBC staff: Broadcast, www.broadcastnow. co.uk.

Page 103 Budget and time pressures that force filmmakers into fakery: Maggie Burnette Stogner, e-mail message to author, June 29, 2009.

Page 103 Polar bear anecdote: Janine Gibson and Stephen Armstrong, "Box of Tricks," *Guardian*, July 17, 2007.

Page 103 Attenborough on staging to streamline the filmmaking process: Jamie James, "Art and Artifice in Wildlife Films," *Discover*, September 1985.

Page 104 Boswall on wildlife filming ethics: Jeffery Boswall, "The Moral Pivot of Wildlife Filmmaking," *Diffusion* (Summer 1997), www.ism-info.de/ism-info.html?qdb=ism&a=13f65bb6a3583a12.

Page 105 Faked footage of snakes mating: James Gray, *Snarl for the Camera: Tales of a Wildlife Cameraman* (London: Piatkus, 2002), 38.

Page 106 Faked footage of king snake eating rattlesnake: James, "Art and Artifice in Wildlife Films."

Page 106 Faked footage of tarantula: Nick Gordon, *In the Heart of the Amazon* (London: Metro Books, 2002), 70–72.

Page 110 "game farms disregard the welfare of animals": Thomas Mangelsen, "Point of View: Game Farm Photography," NatureScapes, January 19, 2009, www.naturescapes.net.

Page 111 "game farms offer a useful service": Beth Davidow, e-mail message to author, January 29, 2009.

Page 113 Fosters' care of bats: Carol Foster, e-mail message to author, February 6, 2009.

Page 115 CGI video anecdote: Howard Hall, e-mail message to author, June 3, 2009.

Page 116 Tidmarsh quotation: Chris Evans, "Nature Filmmaking: Ready for Their Close-up," *Independent*, November 7, 2007, www.independent.co.uk/news/science/nature-filmmaking-ready-for-their-closeup-399342.html.

Page 119 The story about Marty Stouffer is based on a study of all of Stouffer's private papers on the matter, conversations and e-mail messages between the author and both Stouffer and journalist Mike McPhee, and the following sources: Jon Burstein, "Denver PBS Dumps Marty," *Aspen Daily News*, February 15, 1996; Jon Burstein, "PBS Clears Stouffer," *Aspen Daily News*, October 10, 1996; Jim Carrier and Mike McPhee, "Marty Stouffer Broke Filming Vow," *Denver Post*, March 10, 1996; Louise McElvogue, "Jaws, Claws, and Cash: Show Biz Jungle of Wildlife," *New York Times*, October 29, 1997; PBS, "Statement to Stations" on Marty Stouffer; PBS, "Wild America: Overall Assessment"; Marty Stouffer, memo to Jim Carrier, March 8, 1996.

Page 119 Stouffer's claim of "factual re-creation": Ira Robbins, "Dangerous Encounters," *Entertainment Weekly*, August 9, 1999, www.ew.com/ew/article/0,293654,00.html.

Page 120 Allegations of fishing line tied to legs of prey: Mike McPhee, e-mail message to author, October 30, 2008.

Page 121 Stouffer felt he "was a lightning rod": Louise McElvogue, "Jaws, Claws, and Cash."

Page 122 "I have no compulsion to be controlled by any rules other than my own personal beliefs and philosophies": Marty Stouffer, e-mail message to author, October 12, 2008.

CHAPTER 7

Page 125 Filmmakers engaging in "outright harassment": Brian Horejsi, e-mail message to author, May 4, 2009.

Page 125 "reinventing the animal circus": Barry Paine, e-mail message to author, July 17, 2008.

Page 125 "inappropriate, demeaning, and sometimes dangerous interactions with creatures": Tom Veltre, e-mail message to author, October 11, 2008.

Page 128 Barr python story: adapted with permission from Brady Barr, personal communication to author, July 23, 2007.

Page 130 "I do not put myself in dangerous situations for ratings, but rather a quest for scientific answers": Brady Barr, e-mail message to author, August 2, 2007.

Page 131 Treadwell quotations: Timothy Treadwell, *Among Grizzlies* (New York: Ballantine Books, 1997), 55, 67, 152.

Page 131 Treadwell would be honored to end up as "bear shit": Sterling Miller, e-mail message to author, July 11, 2008.

Page 131 Many newspaper accounts, magazine articles, blogs, and television documentaries, as well as many of my friends and colleagues in the bear conservation community, have discussed Timothy Treadwell's life and death. My account of Treadwell's death is based on these sources. I am particularly grateful to two excellent and well-researched books on Treadwell: Nick Jans, *The Grizzly Maze* (New York: Plume Books, 2005); and Mike Lapinski, *Death in the Grizzly Maze* (Guilford, CT: Falcon Press, 2005). Also helpful was *In the Land of the Grizzlies*, the 1992 documentary we made about grizzlies and Treadwell when I was at the National Audubon Society.

Page 133 Bear #141 had human flesh in its stomach: Sterling Miller, e-mail message to author, July 11, 2008.

Page 135 Damage done by Treadwell: Rupert Pilkington, e-mail message to author, November 11, 2008.

Page 135 "spreads wrong concepts about wild animals and their behaviors": Charles Jonkel, "President's Letter," *Bear News* 15, no. 4 (2000).

Page 135 "Filmmakers should not be allowed to exploit wildlife for money and fame": Charles Jonkel, "Save a Grizzly, Visit a Library," *Counterpunch*, September 25, 2006, www.counterpunch.org.

Page 136 Background on Jennifer Shoemaker: personal interviews with author, July 2007.

Page 136 Bartlebaugh on animal attacks triggered by human carelessness: Scott Sandsberry, "Mixed Messages," *Yakima Herald-Republic*, May 3, 2007.

Page 137 Gibbs bear anecdote: Lapinski, *Death in the Grizzly Maze*, 164.

Page 137 Today's filmmakers influence the next generation: Chuck Bartlebaugh, e-mail message to author, August 29, 2009.

Page 143 Being "champions over the animals instead of championing the animals": Michaela Strachan, *Wild Film News,* May 2006, www.wildfilmnews.org/displayNewsArticle.php?block_id=290.

Page 144 "a bit like spitting on Irwin's grave": Tom Veltre, e-mail message to author, May 21, 2009.

CHAPTER 8

Page 146 "callously taunt and harass wildlife for entertainment": Vanessa Schulz, e-mail message to author, March 16, 2008.

Page 146 "Animal Planet should be ashamed": Katie Carpenter, e-mail message to author, August 25, 2009.

Page 147 "so often the emphasis is on violence and on the demonizing of predators": Dorothy Patent, e-mail message to author, May 15, 2009, and personal communications with author on other occasions.

Page 149 experiments were "hokum": Tom Smith, e-mail message to author, February 3, 2009.

Page 149 Van Daele quotation about the mannequin scene: Craig Medred, "Grizzly TV Show Horrifies Experts," *Anchorage Daily News*, January 2, 2009.

Page 149 "I thought it couldn't get worse, and then *Bear Feeding Frenzy* shows up": Rob Whitehair, e-mail message to author, January 6, 2009.

Page 149 "programs like *Bear Feeding Frenzy* will get broadcast": Rob Whitehair, e-mail message to author, February 2, 2009.

Page 151 "a propaganda instrument to legitimize the war on terror": Walter Koehler, e-mail message to author, September 5, 2007.

Page 152 "Is it possible we opened some new eyes to the natural world?": Kathryn Pasternak, e-mail message to author, June 6, 2007.

Page 152 Blurbs about *The Trials of Life*: Mitman, *Reel Nature*, 205–6.

Page 152 Attenborough considered legal action: Bousé, *Wildlife Films*, 1–2; Mitman, *Reel Nature*, 205–6.

Page 153 "We haven't come far since the days of the Roman amphitheater": Tom Veltre, e-mail message to author, May 24, 2009.

CHAPTER 9

Page 155 "I will not eat gorilla meat again": 2008 Republic of Congo Performance Report on the Great Ape Conservation and Ebola Prevention Program.

Page 156 "the dread 'C' word": Tim Martin, e-mail message to author, June 2, 2008.

Page 156 The state of the natural world and its wildlife deteriorated: Bousé, *Wildlife Films*, xiv.

Page 157 "we're still not willing to do anything very drastic": Bill McKibben, *The Age of Missing Information* (New York: Random House, 1992), 73–74.

Page 158 Researchers unearthed no empirical evidence: Amanda Webber, "Are Wildlife Programs Broadcast on Television Effective at Producing Conservation?" (report prepared for Filmmakers for Conservation and sponsored by the National Wildlife Federation, October 2002).

Page 159 "a lot of these animals and plants are going extinct": David Suzuki, interview by Brendan Christie, *Realscreen*, August 2006, 28.

Page 159 "Why are we bothering to raise money?": Hardy Jones, e-mail message to author, May 28, 2009.

Page 159 "something that would soon engulf the world in conflagration": Piers Warren, *Careers in Wildlife Filmmaking* (Norfolk, UK: Wildeye, 2002), 172–73.

Page 159 "We should applaud our diversity": Howard Hall, *Do Natural History Films Make a Difference? A Comment on the Question Raised by Chris Palmer* (essay distributed to members of Filmmakers for Conservation, June 10, 2002).

Page 159 "alienate audiences who just want to come home, relax, and be entertained": Dereck Joubert, *The Debate Continues* (essay distributed to members of Filmmakers for Conservation), transmitted via e-mail by Piers Warren to author, June 19, 2002.

Page 160 "having a stocking over your head pulled off": David Nicholson-Lord, *Planet Earth: The Making of an Epic Series* (London: BBC Books, 2006), 8.

Page 161 *Planet Earth* copies sold, trendy bars, and quotation: Alex Williams, "'Planet Earth' Rocks (or Even Waltzes). You Pick," *New York Times*, April 17, 2009, www.nytimes.com/2009/04/19/fashion//19planet.html.

Page 161 "inspire them to better care for what remains": Alastair Fothergill, e-mail message to author, October 11, 2008.

Page 162 Attenborough's defense of blue-chip films: Raymond Chavez, e-mail message to author, October 16, 2008.

Page 163 Dealing with conservation issues through film: Vicky Stone, e-mail message to author, March 16, 2008.

Page 163 Discovery Channel show *Swords*: David Helvarg, "The Blue Beat," *Blue Notes,* September 18, 2009, www.bluefront.org/bluenotes/bluenotes.php?recordID=65.

Page 164 Everyday people who looked and sounded like the new audiences the series was trying to reach: Karen Hirsch, "Documentaries on a Mission: How Nonprofits Are Making Movies for Public Engagement," Center for Social Media, School of Communication, American University, March 2007, www.centerforsocialmedia.org/resources/publications/docsonamission/.

Page 164 Sierra Club series nominated for Best Documentary in the California Independent Film Festival: Adrienne Bramhall, e-mail message to author, May 26, 2009.

Page 166 More than thirty local conservation projects were launched: Katie Carpenter, e-mail message to author, July 5, 2009.

CHAPTER 10

Page 168 Article on Daniel Breton: Monte Burke, "Chick Flick," *Forbes*, April 15, 2002, www.forbes.com/forbes/2002/0415/284.html.

Page 168 Except as noted, all quotations in Chapter 10 comes from personal conversations or e-mail messages between the author and the filmmakers quoted.

Page 169 1988 Yellowstone fires: "Yellowstone Fires," Yellowstone National Park Web site, www.yellowstoneparknet.com/history/fires.php.

Page 175 Lions may cease to exist in the wild beyond 2050: National Geographic Speakers Bureau Web site, events.nationalgeographic.com/events/speakers-bureau/speaker/beverly-dereck-joubert/.

Page 175 Only ten thousand cheetahs remain in the wild: "Cheetah Facts," Cheetah Conservation Fund Web site, www.cheetah.org/?nd=cheetah_facts.

Page 175 "a global state of emergency": Dereck Joubert, WildFilmNews, 2007, www.wildfilmnews.org/displayNewsArticle.php?block_id=901.

Page 178 Results of work of INCEF in the Republic of Congo: 2008 Republic of Congo Performance Report on the Great Ape Conservation and Ebola Prevention Program.

Page 179 Eric Kinzonzi quotation about using local people to speak about local issues: Cynthia Moses, e-mail message to author, July 8, 2009.

CHAPTER 11

Page 184 "This activist's story has everything you need for great television": Jason Carey, presentation at event sponsored by the Center for Environmental Filmmaking and Filmmakers for Conservation, School of Communication, American University, Washington, DC, March 3, 2009.

Page 184 Watson accuses Greenpeace of timidity and ineffectiveness: Greenpeace, "Paul Watson, Sea Shepherd, and Greenpeace: Some Facts," March 20, 2009, www.greenpeace.org/international/about/history/paul-watson.

Page 184 Sea Shepherd's mission: "The Sea Shepherd Conservation Society Describes Its History," Animal Planet, animal.discovery.com/tv/whale-wars/sea-shepherd/.

Page 185 "efforts to interfere with whaling operations": "Whalers Aid in Antarctic Rescue of Environmentalists," Times Online, February 9, 2007, www.timesonline.co.uk/tol/news/world/asia/article1358479.ece.

Page 185 The Japanese government and media portray Sea Shepherd's work as illegal acts: "The Sea Shepherd Conservation Society Describes Its History."

Page 185 Animal Planet is inventing a new type of storytelling: Jason Carey, presentation at American University.

Page 185 "great television with a purpose": Kevin Mohs, e-mail message to author, April 2, 2009.

Page 186 A quarter of prime-time television advertising is humorous: Marc Weinberger and Charles Gulas, "The Impact of Humor in Advertising: A Review," *Journal of Advertising*, December 1992.

Page 186 "People will pay more attention to a humorous commercial than a factual or serious one": Mark Levit, "Humor in Advertising," Concept Marketing Group, 2005, www.marketingsource.com/index.php?v=article_view&cat=2190.

Page 186 "Stop deforestation" video: Altshuler Shaham, "Hairy Situation," www.youtube.com/watch?v=4BdMHOJe-wI.

Page 186 Talking polar bears video: Friends of the Earth, "Polars Bears," www.youtube.com/watch?v=EDIP71Lviys.

Page 187 Research on funny advertising: Levit, "Humor in Advertising."

Page 188 "outcome-based documentaries": Jean-Michel Cousteau, "Great Expectations," *Realscreen*, August 1, 2006, www.realscreen.com/articles/magazine/20060801/page30.html.

Page 189 *Springwatch* causing people to get involved in local action: Tim Martin, e-mail message to author, June 10, 2009.

Page 191 Predictions for video capture features in mobile phones: Alexis Gerard and Bob Goldstein, *Going Visual* (New York: John Wiley, 2005); Alexis Gerard, personal e-mail message to author, May 18, 2009.

Page 191 Wildlife filmmakers should make better use of disclaimers: Jeffery Boswall, "Wildlife Film Ethics: Time for Screen Disclaimers," *Image Technology*, October 1998.

Page 193 The Code of Best Practices in Sustainable Filmmaking (www.sustainablefilmmaking.org) was produced by American University's Center for Social Media and Center for Environmental Filmmaking and the United Kingdom's Filmmakers for Conservation. It was backed by the Ford Foundation in the United States and supported by WWF in the United Kingdom.

Page 194 The Brock Initiative: "The Making of the Brock Initiative," www.brockinitiative.org/about2.htm.

Page 196 Offering food to animals goes too far: Simon King, "Touched by Your Presence," *BBC Wildlife Magazine*, November 2002.

Page 197 "Filmmakers following their conscience": Howard Hall, e-mail message to author, June 14, 2009.

INDEX

ABOUT THE AUTHOR

Chris Palmer has produced more than 300 hours of original programming for prime-time television and theatrical release in the past twenty-five years. His films have been shown on the Disney Channel, TBS Superstation, Animal Planet, PBS, and in the global system of IMAX theaters, and have won many awards, including two Emmys and an Oscar nomination. In the course of his work as a producer, he has swum with dolphins and whales, confronted sharks, come face to face with Kodiak bears, camped with wolf packs, and waded hip-deep through an Everglades swamp. In 2009, Palmer was named recipient of the Lifetime Achievement Award for Media at the International Wildlife Film Festival, and in 1994 he received the Frank G. Wells Award from the Environmental Media Association for his contributions to environmental protection.

In the early 1980s, Palmer left his career as an energy policy expert to devote his life to producing environmental and wildlife films that promote conservation, serving for many years as president and CEO of the film and large-format arms of the National Audubon Society and the National Wildlife Federation. Palmer currently directs the Center for Environmental Filmmaking at American University's School of Communication, where he is Distinguished Film Producer in Residence. He is also president of the MacGillivray Freeman Films Educational Foundation, which produces and funds giant-screen films shown in IMAX theaters, and he is CEO of VideoTakes, Inc., a company that produces films, video, and new media. He serves on the boards of numerous nonprofit organizations in the fields of conservation and media and is a frequent speaker at film festivals and conferences.